INFINITY LOST

INFINITY LOST

THE INFINITY TRILOGY

S. HARRISON

SKYSCAPE

SKYSCAPE

Published by Skyscape, New York

www.apub.com

Amazon, the Amazon logo, and Skyscape are trademarks of Amazon.com, Inc., or its affiliates.

ISBN-13: 9781503945074
ISBN-10: 1503945073

Cover design by M. S. Corley

Printed in the United States of America

For Lucy

SUNNY DAYS UNDER A BLACKSTONE SKY?

BY PRESTON HARROW, POSTED THREE DAYS AGO

Today the World Financial Authority officially recognized Blackstone Technologies as the most influential company in human history. The mega-corporation has been estimated to be worth more than the next four largest companies combined, and it's easy to see why. From that Jett 10 holographic phone in your pocket to the custom-made sports heart beating in your chest, Blackstone Technologies' amazing advancements have, in less than two decades, drastically and fundamentally changed almost every facet of human society.

Even the most fervent anti-Blackstone campaigners are powerless to escape its influence. Despite their passionate complaining, this sunny weekend that we voted for is shining down on the protesters, too, all thanks to Blackstone Technologies' Global Weather Management Array.

Blackstone is everywhere. It's an integral part of our lives. And yet what do we actually know about its founder, Dr. Richard Blackstone? His face is certainly a familiar one; he's the wealthiest and most famous man on the planet, but Dr. Blackstone has never been photographed or televised outside the highly secured walls of his luxurious office at Blackstone Technologies.

He's known to be kind and affable, he's widely respected, and his generosity is unparalleled, but his private life is shrouded in mystery. Call it a reporter's intuition, but my gut tells me that some of the stories I've read concerning his past are far too carefully crafted to be genuine. Is he hiding something? If so, what?

A recent Blackstone press release explained that Dr. Blackstone is a deeply shy man with a few harmless eccentricities, but a weak excuse like that won't stop skeptics from diving headfirst into the realms of conspiracy. Some even claim that he's nothing more than a computer-generated figurehead, a modern-day Wizard of Oz conjured out of thin air with the best smoke and mirrors that money can buy.

Conjecture aside, Blackstone Technologies has become the technological cornerstone of the modern world, so it comes as no surprise that many suggest the company has grown too big and powerful. Some equate it to a drug, and assert that we the consumers have become mindless technology junkies, glassy-eyed and salivating at the mere thought of the latest Blackstone innovation. Has the company that we've trusted for so many years become one that we're all far too dependent on?

Blackstone feeds, clothes, employs us, and entertains us, it's true, but perhaps the juggernaut is so completely entwined with our lives that many are reluctant to question the possibility of deeper—perhaps darker—motives. If the conspiracy nuts' suspicions were justified and we asked the right questions, would we get any answers?

If Dr. Blackstone were forced to tell the truth, my question to him would be this: Is Blackstone Technologies really a cure for the woes of the world, or are we being gently brought to our knees by an iron hand wrapped soft in poisonous promises of a glorious future?

As I upload this blog and take in the balmy climate-controlled morning outside my window, part of me can't help but think: Would a lifetime of man-made sunny days at the feet of Dr. Blackstone really be that bad? Another part of me worries: Do we have any other choice?

·Level·Ten Classified Net Surveillance File·

Subversive blog detected.

Blogger identified as influential award·winning journalist Mr. Preston Harrow.

Mr. Harrow's public opinion level graded as: HIGH. Potential future threat level: EXTREMELY HIGH.

Threat Management Protocol 4 initiated.

Blog intercepted and altered to reflect a sympa·thetic and complimentary opinion.

Mr. Harrow's Navi·Car computer successfully re·programmed.

Mr. Harrow delivered to the nearest Blackstone facility for behavior modification. Modification was successful. Threat neutralized.

Have a nice day. ☺

CHAPTER ONE

Absolute silence.

So quiet I can feel it in my bones.

There's no air, no gravity, no hot or cold, nothing but this oily darkness spanning out in every direction, coiled around my body like an invisible snake, pressed tight against my naked skin.

Even though there isn't a speck of light, I can see my limbs as clearly as if they were lit by the midday sun, suspended like a marionette in an ocean of shadows that exists only for me. I slowly carve my hand through the blackness and a jittering fan of kaleidoscope colors trails behind my long pale fingers. It shimmers, fleetingly frozen in place, before gently merging back into the void.

I know I'm not really here. This place doesn't exist. It's all in my mind; I realize that.

I know that I'm actually fast asleep in my dorm room at school right now, but knowing that doesn't help to explain why every time I fall asleep, I wind up right back here again, vacuum-packed in this limbo of darkness, nervously waiting for another unwanted dream to crawl out from the corners of my mind and invade my every thought. The first time it happened was on the night of my seventeenth birthday, only four short weeks ago. Before then, I'd never had a dream before. Not one dream in my entire life. But since then, everything has changed. Four weeks ago, the floodgates of my subconscious were smashed wide open.

I was always curious about dreams, maybe even a little envious that everyone except me had them, but I never imagined that they would be anything like this. I thought they were supposed to be random creations of the imagination, fanciful visions of a sleeping mind, but if that's true, why are mine so . . . different? While other people dream of flying through the clouds, or walking into math class naked, or having a tea party with talking monkeys in the Grand Canyon, all I ever dream about are days that I've *already lived.*

Every night, the dreams pour down and engulf me. An hour, or a day, or even a whole week from my past spills out from the dark, wrapping up my mind in a cocoon of old sensations I thought I'd left behind. Like there's a time machine in my head, I'll be catapulted backward, uncomfortably squeezed into my younger skins like shoes that I've outgrown. The person that I am slowly becomes the girl I used to be, until eventually I surrender, saturated in my days gone by, feeling every moment for the first time . . . all over again. I've told myself that there's nothing to be afraid of, that they're only memories, but I know now that I've been lying to myself. They're more than just dreams of days that I remember. They feel tainted and strange somehow, almost as if when I'm there, watching my life, my life is watching me back.

My skin crawls as a cold shiver prickles up and down my spine. They're coming. I can feel them, moving quickly, storming toward me in a rolling wave, crashing and boiling through the valleys of my mind, so fast that there's only an instant between feeling them and hearing them. A writhing avalanche of tangled voices barrels though the void, getting closer and closer and louder and louder with every passing second until—in a heartbeat between breaths—they're here.

They've found me.

I screw my eyes shut, bury my face in my hands, and pull my knees to my chest as the voices rear up into a wall of sound high above me, a frothing apex of garbled whispers. Peeking out between my fingers, I see it: an undulating mass, distorting the darkness. It curls over, slowly leaning, lingering as if it has thoughts of its own.

Suddenly the thing topples too far and it drops. Pounding heavily onto my head like a breaking wave, it rushes fast around me, blowing my hair straight back, rippling my skin. Flashes of color spark behind my eyes, and flickering faces pulse in and out like strobing specters; echoing whirlpools of familiar voices swirl in my ears as ribbons of nostalgic aromas spiral up through my nose and down into my mouth, dancing across my tongue like a thousand scented raindrops. I can feel myself shrinking down as the years are stripped from my body, peeling away in chunks, shucking off and falling into the darkness like layers of caked earth. I slowly spin, drifting in the current as the river of old flows through me. It slows, waning quickly; then, as suddenly as it came, the torrent is gone. The voices in my head become whispers that fade into nowhere. The colors and flavors pale and dissolve as an over-whelmingly peaceful feeling of sleepy contentment bubbles up from my toes. It spreads up my legs, through my stomach, chest, arms, and face, filling me completely as I drift down through the dark, gently coming to rest on a thick, downy blanket, soft and safe and warm.

I rub my weary eyes and peer down at my chubby little fingers, poking out from the baggy sleeves of my pink bunny-print pajamas. Beyond the towering bay windows in the corner, I can see bundles of stars twinkling in the night sky. My bed seems huge. In fact, everything in my bedroom is gigantic. I yawn wide and long as I snuggle down deeper in my bed, comfy and happy. The lamp on my bedside table casts a cozy glow across the walls and down over the thick meadow of gray carpet, gently bathing the mountain of plush toys beside my doll-house with a comforting orange light. Prince Horsey the unicorn sits at the peak, drowsily guarding the slumbering stuffed animals below. I was told he used to be my father's favorite when he was a boy, and now he's mine. The king of the toys and the ruler of Toyland.

I'm three years old again.

I listen to the creaks of this big old house as the bricks and boards settle in the cool of the night. Sometimes I like to close my eyes and hitch my imagination to those comforting sounds, riding along with them out my bedroom door and down the narrow hall, passing by the many rooms on the entire floor that I've claimed as my personal playground. Down the tall main stairs my drowsy thoughts drift, weaving through the speckled marble pillars at the bottom and on through the huge, high-ceilinged sitting rooms, studies, dining rooms, ballrooms, and kitchens.

I once heard one of our servants describe this house as a "sprawling mansion." And that is undoubtedly what it is. My home. Blackstone Manor.

During the day when I'm not being tutored by my teacher Raychel, one of my favorite games is "count the rooms." I always come up with a different number. Sometimes it's eighty, sometimes ninety. I know I must miscount sometimes, but there seem to be magical rooms that disappear and reappear depending on whether or not they feel like being discovered that day.

It's getting late, and all the servants have either gone home or retired to their quarters. The shadow goblins rule the house at night. I know now that they were just figments of an eager imagination, but I'm three years old again and, at the thought of them lurking, I pull the covers closer to my nose, my eyes wide as I stare into the darkness beyond the door, dreading the possibility of a goblin's head leering around the edge of the frame at any moment. Just when I think one will, the floorboards in the hall creak beneath the weight of heavy footsteps. They stop just outside my door and I know that for at least one more night, I'm safe from the little monsters in the dark. I'm safe because I know who those heavy footsteps that are trying their best to be quiet belong to: our head of security and my protector. Everyone in the house calls him Major Brogan.

I call him Jonah.

Even the biggest, meanest shadow goblin in the whole house would cower in fear at the feet of the mighty Jonah. I look to the spot in the doorway where I know his kind round face will appear and, suddenly, there it is. Right at the top in the corner, his big brown eyes and his caterpillar eyebrows, the crown of his large bald head hidden by the top of the frame.

"Are you awake, Finn?"

My given name is Infinity—Infinity Blackstone—but Jonah calls me Finn. Jonah always asks exactly the same question at bedtime, and tonight is no exception. Surely he knows by now that I fight off the sleepiness until he has read me a story. I like to hear one chapter of a different book every night, and for almost a year now, Jonah has tasked himself with the job. In my little world where everything seems so big, Jonah is truly a giant. He smiles at me and ducks under the top of the doorway.

Forever dressed in his trademark black suit, crisp white shirt, and cornflower-blue tie, Jonah lumbers over, takes the rickety green wooden chair painted with flowers from by the wall, and places it at my bedside. It creaks a noisy complaint as he sits, his knees sticking up awkwardly. A chair made for mere mortals is obviously far too small for a hulking man-mountain like Jonah. He reaches a huge arm across my bed, picks up a small stack of books from the shelf, and begins sorting through them.

"Which one would you like to hear tonight?"

"You haven't finished the story of the stone-face boy yet, Jonah," I say with a knowing smile.

"*The Crystal Castle?*" he asks, shuffling through the stack.

I nod happily as he finds the book and flicks through the pages.

"OK, then. Now, where were we?"

"They're hiding in the Forest of Forever."

Jonah thumbs back and forth through the book. He stops and looks a little confused.

"Are you sure, Finn?"

I nod again.

"Finn. Do you see the fold I made? This is the page that I marked. This fold is near the middle, but the forest is at the end."

I'm nodding.

"Did Theresa read this book to you?"

Theresa is my nanny. She's old and mean and smells like she slops on her perfume every morning with a mop and bucket. I shake my head.

"Was it Arthur?"

Arthur is our chauffeur. He's short and fat. He swears when he can't find his driving gloves and is always out of breath. I giggle and shake my head. Arthur's so dim, I doubt that he can read at all.

Jonah is looking at me curiously. "Finn. Did you read this? All by yourself?"

I'm nodding again.

"Well, I must say, that Raychel is doing a very impressive job."

I shake my head and smile. "No. She's too slow at teaching stuff. I worked out the words on my own," I say proudly.

Jonah's eyebrow caterpillars are arched so high they look like they're trying to climb to the top of his head and plant a flag on the summit. "You're three years old and you taught yourself to read?"

"I'm three and a half!" I bark, crossing my arms on my chest.

Jonah's mouth is smiling, but somehow his eyes are smiling even more.

"Well. Aren't you clever," he says, flicking to the end of the book.

"Yes. I suppose I am," I proudly retort. Jonah grins.

I never saw my tutor Raychel again.

From that day on, for five hours every day, Jonah was my teacher. He didn't teach me just math and history and spelling, though. He taught me all kinds of cool stuff.

The bright moonlight of a warm summer night filters through the leaves above my head, making dappled patterns on the grass around the thick roots of the old oak tree. Crickets softly chirp out in the still dark beyond.

"Are you ready?"

I'm five years old now, standing beside Jonah in the gazebo behind the main house.

"I'm scared, Jonah."

"Don't be scared. You're the one in control."

Five years old, dressed in pajamas and fluffy slippers in the middle of the night, with a loaded 9mm semiautomatic pistol gripped tightly in my little hands.

"Take that fear and turn it into power, Finn. You saw me do this. You know how it's done. You can do it, too. All you have to do is believe it. Just point it toward the tree and pull the trigger."

I can barely lift the gun, let alone point it at that tree, and even if I could, what did that poor oak do to me? I look up at Jonah with my frowning face and he mirrors it right back. "Concentrate."

I look down at the gun. Then at the tree. I really don't want to disappoint Jonah. I lift the gun and raise it to my eye level.

It's so heavy.

My little muscles strain and twitch. The gun wavers in my hands, swaying back and forth. The tree moves from side to side in my field of vision and my arms begin to shake. My doubt takes a firm hold and my nerve gives way. I drop the gun back down.

"I can't, Jonah. I wanna go back inside."

Jonah kneels down beside me and looks me in the eyes. "Tell me; out of everything I teach you, what's your favorite subject?"

I don't even need a second to think about it. "Science."

"That's right, and science tells us that your body, your mind, the world, and everything in it, are all made up of pretty much the same stuff. What happens up here," Jonah says, tapping my forehead with his finger, "can affect what happens all around you."

"I'm too little for a gun, Jonah," I murmur, only half-convinced.

"Nonsense. I was only a year older than you when my father taught me to shoot, and I was smaller than you are now!"

"You were smaller than me?" I say with a crinkled nose of suspicion.

"Yes, I was. But don't you dare tell anyone," Jonah says, standing tall and jutting out his chin. He smiles down at me warmly. "Firing a bullet into a tree is just as real and a whole lot easier than riding a bike, and if you can learn to do this, then I promise I'll teach you how to do that, too." He points a long arm at the oak's trunk. "Alright, now try again, but this time imagine your arms are strong like metal, and the gun is a part of your hand, merely an extension of your—"

BANG! BANG! BANG! BANG! BANG!

The echoes fade into the night and a wisp of smoke gently spirals up from the muzzle of the gun. The crickets have fallen silent, and five little round holes have appeared in the bark at the center of the old oak tree.

"WHAT ON EARTH DO YOU THINK YOU ARE DOING?!" screeches a voice from behind us.

I glance over my shoulder to see musty old Nanny Theresa striding through the night toward the gazebo.

She's wearing her usual stark-white blouse, dreary green cardigan, and long black dress. Her hair is tied up in its standard big gray bun, and there's an all-too-familiar angry glower on her wrinkled, leathery face. She marches between us and snatches the gun from my hand.

"This?!" she squawks, waving it in Jonah's face. "This is what you're teaching"—her piercing, silvery-gray eyes glare down at me like she's trying to find the right word—"her?!"

"Yes," Jonah says straightening to his full towering height.

"You don't get paid to play soldier around here, Major Brogan. Your responsibility lies with monitoring her behavior! That is all!"

"That's exactly what I'm doing, Theresa," Jonah says calmly.

"I don't think you realize what she is capable of, Major. I'm convinced it was she that set fire to the kitchen last week, she steals every little trinket she lays her eyes on, and now here I find you, recklessly putting lethal weapons in her hands?!"

"She's learning a valuable skill," Jonah replies.

A tiny vein swells and pulses on Nanny Theresa's temple; her face is scarlet with rage.

"Richard will be hearing of this, you mark my words," she growls.

"Well, you can try, but as you know, he's a different man than he used to be. Something tells me that he'll side with me on this matter, Theresa. If he answers you at all."

Nanny Theresa thrusts a gnarled finger at Jonah's face. "We'll see about that."

She glares down at me one last time, then turns on her heels and strides off back across the lawn, Jonah's gun still clutched tightly in her sinewy old hand.

I tug on the leg of Jonah's trousers and point back toward the tree. "Five holes because I'm five," I say proudly.

He nods and ruffles my hair. "Six in just a few days."

"Can I have a red bike, please, Jonah?" I say, grinning up toward him hopefully.

Jonah looks down at me and smiles. "Of course you can, sweetheart. Of course you can."

"Oh, I know I can; I just did," whispers a voice from across the room.

"Wha . . . what are you talking about?" I say groggily, squinting in the sharp blue light of my bedside clock.

3:48 a.m.

"Oh, you're awake. Sorry, you were talking in your sleep again."

Less than half-conscious, I sit up droopily on my elbows and look over at my roommate, Bettina. I'm not surprised by what I see. She's sitting at her desk in the dark again, lightly waving her fingers through the softly lit sections of holograms floating above her computer slate. The same thing she has done almost every night since I started at this boarding school when I was thirteen. You'd think after four years I'd be used to her bouts of insomnia.

"I didn't wake you, did I?" she whispers.

"Nah," I say drowsily turning over on my side, trying to get comfortable again. "Whatcha doing?" I mumble. "It's four in the morning."

"I was just finishing up that thing that you asked me to do."

"Wha-did I ask?" I mumble dopily.

"You asked me to hack into Blackstone Technologies, remember?" Her words are whispered with a weighted tone.

"Wha? Why would . . ."

I stop myself mid-sentence, bored of talking. I have no idea what she's babbling about and I'm far too tired to care.

"It was harder than you said it would be, but the passwords you gave me were a big help," Bit says, her voice getting quieter and quieter in my disinterested mind with every syllable. "I'm proud of how deep this hack goes, Infinity. In just a few days' time, they'll let us walk right through the front door. And think absolutely nothing of it."

"That'll be nice," I murmur sleepily as I close my eyes, my mind tumbling head over heels back into the deep, warm darkness.

CHAPTER TWO

The muted blue glow of my alarm clock fades to black behind my heavy eyelids, but I know it won't stay that way for long. Almost on cue and from absolutely nowhere, a pinprick of white blips into existence, throbs, and brightens and then, in a blink, it flashes forward through my eyes, bursting open like a bottle rocket into busy noises and colors. The colors form into people-shaped blurs, passing by hurriedly, and the noise becomes their voices, chattering all around me. I'm home again, and the whole of Blackstone Manor is bristling with activity. All day long, servants have been cooking and cleaning and rushing here and there, and I've been trying my best to stay out of everyone's way.

It's late in the afternoon on the day before my sixth birthday, but that's not the reason why everybody is bustling about. Oh no. This occasion is far more important.

You see, my father is scheduled to arrive tonight.

I'm standing on the first-floor landing, trying to be invisible, holding a silver-framed photograph of a man and a woman. Jonah once told me that the man in the picture is my father and the woman is my mother. Jonah never lies, so that's who they must be. Richard and Genevieve Blackstone. Two people I have never met.

My father is a very handsome man. He's wearing a white suit, a black, collared shirt, and a crimson tie. His jet-black hair is slicked back stylishly and a pencil-thin moustache is precisely groomed over the faint smile on his lips.

My mother is standing close beside him. I can see myself in her graceful features, with her long, straight, dark hair, alabaster skin, and sparkling, sapphire-blue eyes. She's gorgeous. I hope so much that I look just like her when I'm older. Jonah says that I already look like a tiny version of her.

She's dressed in a simple, elegant, sleeveless white dress, a black diamond pendant in a silver circle hanging on a chain around her neck. It's beautiful, too, so it suits her perfectly. One of her hands rests over her belly. There's no bump, but I often wonder if I was in there when this picture was taken.

The look on her face is hard to judge. Sometimes I think she looks a little sad. I'll never know what she was thinking on that day, but she seems to be so very far away. Mother died when she was giving birth to me.

That's about as far away as anyone could ever be.

Jonah always says that Father is a very important man with an extremely important job, and that's why he's never home. He's busy trying to make the world a better place for everyone. I've been told that I should be grateful, that there are people in the world who struggle simply to find their next meal. Jonah says that I should count my lucky stars to be the daughter of the richest, most brilliant man in the world, but to me he's a just a stranger frozen in a picture frame. My whole world is this house and Jonah. I touch my finger to my mother's face and trail it down across her necklace. My heart aches. There should have been so much more.

Nanny Theresa plucks the frame from my little hands and adds it to a stack she's cradling in the other arm. Her silvery-gray eyes bear down on me with a familiar disdain.

"When Dr. Blackstone and his guests arrive today, you will be on your best behavior. You will not tarnish the Blackstone name. Is that clear?"

"Yes, Nanny Theresa," I murmur.

She heads off down the hall, plucking another picture from another table as she goes.

I'm far too excited and way too nervous to let Nanny scare me today. If Father is the king of this castle, then surely that makes me a princess, and a princess needs a proper dress to wear when she stands before the king for the first time—not this worn-out t-shirt and jeans. Mariele, one of our maids, said Father would be here in an hour, so there's no time to waste. I run down the hall back to my room.

Mariele is there, laying out my dress for me. It's all frills and lace and beautiful. I'm so bouncy and fidgety with bottled-up energy that it takes ten minutes for Mariele to get me sitting still, let alone clean and ready. When I'm finally dressed, she brushes my long black hair and puts it in red ribbons. Nanny Theresa appears at the door.

"Ready the child for presentation, Mariele."

Father is early. I'm hastily ushered down the hallway and jostled into position in the marble foyer at the bottom of the main stairs. The servants have gathered, standing side by side in a line like soldiers. I stand nervously at the far end, tightly squeezing Mariele's hand.

Even though the front door is still a distance away, I can hear the faint crunch of car tires on the gravel in the driveway. Car doors open and close, and my heart jumps into my throat. Through the door, I hear the muffled voice of Nanny Theresa greeting someone important. No. Not just one someone. Lots of people. There are muffled voices everywhere. My stomach is so full of butterflies, I'm afraid that if I sneeze one will fly out of my nose.

Time seems to stand still.

This is worse than waiting up all night to see if Santa Claus will really come down the chimney. Sometimes, being a day away from six years old and having never met your own father makes him seem like he is a magical imaginary creature, like an elf or the bogeyman or, I suddenly decide, just like Santa, except brave and heroic like Superman. Super Santa!

The voices are coming closer and closer. They've been out there forever. My heart is beating a million times a second. I feel like I'm going to blast off like a rocket and zoom around the room, my little shoes left sitting smoldering in the exact spot where I was standing.

I look over at the servants, and their eyes are transfixed on the long golden door handles. A second later, so are mine. Finally the handles dip, and the doors swing open.

The first man I see from my child-sized view is Reynolds, the butler. I see the familiar pinstripe fabric of his trousers and his cavernous nostrils. A wave of his hand is followed by the deep slow tones of his refined bass voice.

"Right this way, gentlemen."

There's a bustle of shoes and legs and ties and beards and nostrils. Hands clutch briefcases and folders and documents, fat cigars puff thick plumes of smoke, booming voices and laughter echo off the marble of the foyer.

I stare into the group, searching faces, waiting for the moment when they all stand aside and the man from the photograph rushes forward and scoops me up into his arms. He'll swing me around, kiss me on the cheek, and tell me how wonderful it is that we are finally together. He'll be so sorry that we've been apart for so long. He'll tell me that he loves me and that he thinks about me all the time, like I do about him. I'm so excited that my nerves get the better of me and I hide behind the safety of Mariele's skirt.

I spot Jonah out of the corner of my eye. He's behind us, heading into the hallway under the stairs that lead to the southern wing. He gives me an uncharacteristic look of concern that worsens my nerves, before smiling and disappearing down the darkened passage.

"Welcome, gentlemen," Reynolds announces to the visitors. "Dr. Blackstone sends his most heartfelt apologies that he is not here to greet you in person, but I assure you that he will address you all via video conference later this evening."

A few disgruntled grumblings issue from the group. A pang of sorrow grips my little heart and it sinks right through the floor, through the ground, out the other side of the world and into the cold, lonely darkness of space.

"May I present the staff," Reynolds says, motioning toward the twenty footmen, maids, and servers. They all bow and curtsy accordingly.

The men walk down the line behind Reynolds until eventually they reach the end. "And this is Dr. Blackstone's daughter."

I peek out from behind Mariele, tears beginning to pool in my eyes.

All of the men lean in, their eyes glaring scarily at me like I'm an animal at the zoo. They whisper and nudge each other. The ones behind peer over the others' shoulders. They gawk down at me like they've never seen a little girl before.

"There she is," says one.

"Incredible," whispers another.

They're so taken with me that Reynolds has to clear his throat and step in between us to get their attention.

"Gentlemen, the chef is preparing a wonderful, ten-course, gourmet meal for you this evening, but for now, if you would please follow me into the red drawing room, refreshments are being served."

They all follow Reynolds through the archway like a gaggle of suited geese, muttering and whispering and glaring back at me as they go.

I feel extremely uneasy and, for the first time in my life . . . abandoned. Unsure of what to do, I stand with the servants as Nanny gives them detailed, last-minute reminders of what will be expected of them tonight. She talks about how important our guests are, how their every whim must be catered to. She drones on and on, and before long her voice becomes nothing but a dull warbling in my ears. I stare at the door, broken-hearted. I feel so stupid to have expected so much from a man who has promised me nothing.

"Dismissed," commands Nanny Theresa. She nods to the servants and they quickly disperse back to their duties. Father is not here. Just like every other day. I decide to slink away to my room. "Come child," Nanny Theresa barks as her knobbly fingers reach toward my little wrist like five gnarled twigs on a withered old tree.

"The men would like to see you properly."

∞

I sit bolt upright. The bright sunlight streaming through the dorm-room windows stings my eyes and I feel like I haven't slept a wink all night. Bettina's bed is empty and already made. Crap. I'm gonna be late for class. In a flurry of mismatched socks, rumpled skirt and blouse, and mystery-mustard-spotted tie, I'm up and dressed in my uniform in two minutes flat. I pull a brush through my hair, kick my feet into my shoes, grab my blazer and satchel from the back of the chair, and hurry out the door.

From there it's a quick sprint down the stairs, out the front door of the dorm, and across the courtyard, followed by a quick shortcut through the cafeteria kitchen, up two flights of stairs, and finally into the science wing.

"Hey, wait up!" I yell, pushing past a group of boys who are loiter-ing in the hall. "Bettina!"

I catch up with her just as she's walking into Professor Francis's class.

"Hey Bit, why didn't you wake me?"

She looks at me accusingly from behind her glasses with those big, brown, doe eyes of hers.

"I tried; honestly, I did. You were dead to the world. I can't say that I'm surprised, considering what time you snuck in the window last night."

I follow her into class, frowning as we pick our seats. "As per usual I have absolutely no idea what you're talking about."

"What?" Bit says, suddenly weirdly flustered. "No, of course you don't . . . I didn't mean snuck in, I meant . . . what I meant to say was . . ."

"Save the chit-chat for your own time, please, Miss Otto," Professor Francis says from the front of the class.

"Sorry sir," Bit says as she pulls her computer slate from her satchel, completely avoiding eye contact.

I shake my head and smile. Bettina Otto can be so strange sometimes.

The Professor clears his throat with a loud "ahem." "Before we begin, I would like to make a little announcement," he says with a twinkle in his eye.

"Due to an unexpected last-minute invitation, the location of the Annual Excellence field trip has been changed."

There's murmuring and furrowed brows class-wide. A bunch of kids shoot their hands in the air to ask questions, but most look a little confused and perturbed, me included. Bit, on the other hand, is sitting quietly, smiling contentedly toward the front of the room.

Professor Francis gently waves the forest of flagpole arms back down. "I know that those of you who are in contention to nab a seat on that bus were looking forward to visiting the Cité des Sciences Museum in Paris, but I'm afraid the new opportunity we have been offered is far too good to turn down."

The murmurs become a little louder and increasingly more excited.

I can see by the look on the Professor's face that even *he* is having trouble containing his own elation. "This occurrence is so extraordinary that the other members of staff have taken it upon themselves to hold a raffle to determine which one of them will accompany me as a chaperone. And I'm certain that when you all hear the good news, you'll try especially hard on your final exams on Wednesday."

"You know something don't you?" I whisper to Bit.

"Maybe I do?" Bit says with an uncharacteristically sly, and, I must admit, quite disconcerting smile.

"Tell us, sir!" Dean McCarthy shouts from the back.

"Very well," the Professor says with a huge grin. "This year, on the last Saturday of next month, the most deserving students will accompany me on the school jet, and we will be flying abroad to spend the entire day at the central research and development complex of . . ."

Everyone has gone so silent that you could hear a butterfly's wingbeat.

". . . Blackstone Technologies."

The whole class erupts into whoops and cheers and Bit looks at me with a proud, self-satisfied smile. "You wanted to see your father," she whispers. "Well, now you can."

I don't cheer. I don't even smile. Instead, my mouth goes as dry as sand and my stomach lurches. I'm completely at a loss for words.

As the day wears on, my anxiety worsens. In only a few days' time, I may very well find myself standing before my father. Face to face. What will I say? What will he say? I did tell Bit that I wished I could see him, but I didn't think for a second that she was actually going to make it happen! I knew she was good with computers, but seriously, how the hell did she pull this off? This is way too much for me to process right now. I feel stunned at the ridiculousness of this situation, like I've been slapped in the face with a wet fish. Do I laugh? Do I cry? I honestly don't know. At the moment, I'm finding it hard enough just to breathe. Hopefully I'll feel differently when we're all actually there, but right now, I really can't see it.

I can't eat a thing at lunch and just stare at the walls in most of my other classes. Even the news that some new troublemaker student is enrolling soon doesn't interest me. He's just going to be another billionaire's brat, more trouble than he's worth.

After one of the longest days I can remember, I trudge to the dorm, take a long, hot shower, shovel down some pepperoni pizza that Bit 3-D printed, and try to watch a movie with her, but my mind won't let me relax.

That night, lying in my bed, which I love more than almost anything, I find it hard to get to sleep. *Please don't dream tonight, brain.* I know it's only been four weeks since I've been able to dream at all, and I should be glad that I can finally do it, but sometimes I miss the peace of a dreamless sleep more than anyone could imagine. I close my eyes, pull the blankets over my head, and hope for the best.

CHAPTER THREE

No such luck. My hand shimmers through the dark as rainbow-colored ribbons trail behind it. The shiny black polish on my nails flakes apart and evaporates into the ether as my fingers suck back into my knuckles and plump like tiny sausages. Suddenly a voice echoes through the black.

"Come, child . . ."

A spindly leathered hand reaches down from out of the void and grasps my wrist.

". . . the men would like to see you properly."

Nanny Theresa's talons dig into my skin as she jerks at my little arm. I do my best to escape, but her grip is as tight as an owl's claw squeezing a mouse. On she drags me, through the reception lounge and the trophy room, past the gallery, through the grand ballroom, and past the library. I'm pulled all the way across the house until eventually we arrive at the long passageway that leads to the east wing and the red drawing room.

Nanny Theresa's heels clack on the polished floorboards as we go, echoing down the hallway like a ticking clock counting down to something awful. I can feel it in my bones.

I hear the men's voices long before we enter the room.

Nanny Theresa tugs me through the open doorway. All of the men are gathered in a small circle, chatting and laughing, puffing on fat cigars and drinking liquor. They're standing beside a long serving table that has been especially placed in the center of the huge red-and-gold Persian rug. The table is cluttered with silver platters of colorful foods of every kind, more than I've ever seen before. None of the men seem to be very interested in eating, though; the food has hardly been touched, but the moment that they notice me and Nanny Theresa, their muttering ceases.

The men all turn and glare, craning their necks, watching intently as she leads me toward them. "Here she is," Nanny Theresa announces. "These are your father's business associates," she says, looking down at me. The closer we get, the more unnerving the glares and silence become. A gap opens between two of the men and I'm unceremoniously shoved into the middle of their circle. Nanny Theresa backs away; the men part to let her pass, and I lose sight of her through a forest of trouser legs.

There are probably ten men in all surrounding me. Their circle closes tighter around me, all of them grinning and staring. Some, with their beards and moustaches, look older than others. Some are wearing glasses; some are not. Fat and thin, short and tall—all of them are different, and yet somehow strangely all the same.

I'm enveloped by thick clouds of pungent cigar smoke. It stings my eyes and nose and I begin to cough. A man with a pencil-thin moustache, a blue-striped suit, and a deep-red tie leans forward, staring inquisitively. "Remarkable," he says, and promptly blows a cloud of milky smoke right into my face. I cough again and try to wave it away. He smiles, takes a sip of his liquor, and then with raised eyebrows offers the glass to me. I'm only a little girl! I'm far too young for liquor! I frown and shake my head emphatically.

Another man, an older looking one, bends forward, squinting. He's leaning on an intricately carved, silver-handled cane. He steadies himself on the shoulder of the man beside him and with a quick jab, pokes me hard in the ribs with it.

"Ow!" I yelp, rubbing my side, and all the men burst into hearty laughter. A fat man with a moustache like a walrus mimics me by clutching his ribs and puckering his hairy lips into an "ow" shape as the others chuckle along with him.

I'm beginning to get scared. What am I doing here? I try to see through the gaps in the men's legs, searching for Nanny, but she's nowhere to be seen. She's abandoned me, too.

A skinny man with red cheeks and a gray suit leans down, his pasty, scarlet-patched face only inches from my nose. With breath that smells like cigars and burnt toffee, he asks me a question in the slowest manner I have ever heard.

"Tell-me, what-is-your-name?"

"M . . . my name is Finn Blackstone," I say meekly. I hold out my tiny hand. "Pleased to meet you."

The entire group erupts in a round of raucous laughter. I stand there, bewildered. I slowly withdraw my hand. I don't like this at all.

"And how old are you, Finn?"

I look around at the men in the circle. They all have the same wide-eyed, hungry look on their faces as they glare down at me from above.

"I'm . . . six years old tomorrow."

They all grin at each other, nodding and murmuring like they're sharing a secret.

These men are horrible and scary. I want to go. "Excuse me, sirs," I say, doing a clumsy little curtsy. I've seen Mariele do it a thousand times and it seems like the right thing to do. "I would like to go to my room, please."

"Oh no, no, no. That won't do at all," a gentle voice says from behind me. I'm about to turn my head to see who it came from when two big hands forcefully seize the back of my dress. The wads of material clenched in their fists tighten across my neck, choking me as I'm raised up onto my tiptoes. I lose my breath and gag as I'm yanked backward. My mind fills with panic. The hands jerk apart roughly. There's a terrifying ripping noise as with one jarring stroke, my beautiful dress is torn apart at the seams. I feel hot cigar smoke breathed onto the bare skin of my back and I shriek in terror. The men crowd closer to see as I struggle in vain to get free. I feel hands reaching inside the gash in my dress. Fingers pinch at my skin. Fingernails scratch me as I'm tugged and pulled from side to side like a rag doll. I scream again but it's completely ignored. The men vie for position to watch and grope, seemingly oblivious to my panic. One of them grabs my ankle, wrenching a shoe away from my foot. Another begins to tug at my underwear.

This can't be real. This must be a nightmare. My mind is white with fear.

"Help! Don't! Please! You're hurting me!" I plead, but they don't listen. Where is Jonah? I need Jonah!

A gruff voice barks, "Put her on the table."

I screech in protest, "LET ME GO!" My futile demand, just like my cry for mercy, falls on deaf ears. "JONAH!"

Four of the men band together and lift me into the air by my wrists and ankles.

"You there! Maid! Clear some space!"

Mariele looks on, frozen to the spot, her face a wide-eyed mask of shock and horror.

"Are you deaf? Make some room!" The man with the walrus face is grabbing platters of food and shoving them into Mariele's arms.

I'm slammed onto the table and I cry out in pain. "MARIELE!"

I struggle to get free, but they're far too strong.

"We just want to see," whispers a gravelly voice.

A cloth napkin is forced into my mouth and I'm flipped onto my stomach.

I scream muffled wails into the napkin as the men roughly tug at my underwear. Tears overflow from my eyes. I bite into the napkin and pray that it doesn't hurt when they finally kill me.

"Gentlemen, gentlemen. That's quite enough for today."

I never thought I'd be so happy to hear Nanny Theresa's voice. The men release me from their grip; I roll off the table, bolt through their legs, out of their circle of claws and grins, and scoot across the rug and out the open door.

I run as fast as my legs will take me back down the hallway, their cruel laughter echoing after me down the cavernous passages. Past the east-wing kitchen and through the gift-wrapping room I run. Past the billiards room, the smoking room, the blue drawing room, and the trophy room. The walls and doors blend into a blur as I flee. I don't stop to catch my breath until I'm safely in the marble foyer by the front doors.

I crouch behind the banister, heaving, staring back the way I came. No one is following. I'm terrified and confused, sitting all alone, trembling at the bottom of the stairs. What remains of my hope for a wonderful day with my father is in tatters, just like my beautiful dress. Why did they do that to me? Why would Nanny Theresa let them? Why wasn't Father here to stop them? Why isn't he ever here at all?

I have no answers. As usual, the bitter taste of disappointment stings at the back of my throat.

I pull the ribbons from my hair and drop them on the cold marble floor. My eyes well with tears, and as I reach the top of the staircase they trickle down my cheeks like droplets creeping from between the cracks in a broken vase.

"Finn?"

My heart leaps and I spin toward the voice. "Father?" I squeak feebly.

Through my tears, I see the blurry shape of a man climbing the stairs, arms outstretched. He reaches the top and picks me up into a warm embrace. It's not my father.

"I'm so sorry, Finn," Jonah whispers, wiping the tears from my face.

I stare into his big, kind, brown eyes.

"Can you be my real father, please, Jonah?" I peep out between sobs.

He smiles sadly. "No, Finn, but I love you like you are my daughter. No matter what happens, never, ever forget that."

I swear to myself that I never will. He puts me down and studies the rip down the back of my dress. "I'll have the tailor sew that up for you. It will be just like new, I promise."

"Why did those men try to hurt me, Jonah?" I sob.

Jonah sighs deeply. "I'm afraid that those men are too used to doing whatever they like. People like that sometimes get very carried away. Sometimes they forget the difference between right and wrong." He takes off his suit jacket and drapes it over my shoulders. It envelops me all the way to the floor like Superman's cape.

Jonah kneels down and gently wipes my cheek with his thumb. "Your Nanny Theresa should never have invited them. They're not very nice at all. Someone really ought to teach them a lesson," Jonah says with a soft tap on my forehead.

With my bottom lip trembling beneath my sniffling nose, I nod in agreement.

"I have to go, sweetheart. I'll send Mariele to keep you company. I'll be back later to say good night. I promise."

Jonah turns and makes his way back down the stairs. "OK, Jonah," I mumble, and slowly drag my feet down the hall toward my room.

I'm almost there when something small and metal falls from Jonah's jacket and clacks onto the floorboards by the edge of the long carpet. I bend down and pick it up. It's a little brass key. I know exactly what lock it opens, and suddenly I get an idea.

The best idea ever.

There's something about revenge that makes me buoyantly happy. Nanny Theresa spanked my bottom red raw for tracking mud into the house last winter. I apologized and made her a cup of tea every morning for two weeks. She must have drunk half a gallon of my pee before I got bored of it.

I wipe the last tears from my eyes, throw off Jonah's huge black jacket, and run back along the hall toward the first-floor landing. I leap down the stairs three at a time to the bottom, sprint down the hall of the west wing to Jonah's room, and straight through the wide-open door. I find the box I'm looking for beneath his four-poster bed. I twist the key in the lock, grab what's inside, spring to my feet, and compose myself before walking quietly and calmly out into the hall. I take a deep breath, stare straight ahead, and with determination in every step, I head off toward the east wing.

The five-minute walk seems to pass in five seconds. I stop and stand just outside the red drawing room. Inside, I can hear the men muttering and laughing like before and my blood boils. I'm angry. It's almost as if the rage is bubbling up from my feet like molten lava, filling every inch of my body, burning the remnants of my fear clean away. It feels good. I grit my teeth, furrow my brow, and step out into the open doorway.

The men, unsurprisingly, are still standing in their circle, puffing away on their cigars and sipping brown liquor from large crystal tumblers. A full minute passes before any of them even notice that I'm there.

"Oh, look!" says Walrus Face. "It appears that we have a visitor."

Almost in unison, the others turn to look. Here I stand, blocking the doorway, one shoe on my foot, both hands behind my back, my eyes red and puffy from crying, and the frayed edges of my torn dress hanging loosely by my sides. *This is what you did to me. This is what I want you all to see.*

Curious? Surprised? Perhaps a little puzzled? It really doesn't matter what they're thinking. I want to see their pompous smiles and sneers and glares erased from their arrogant, pampered faces like chalk from a blackboard. I want to stab their hearts with venom and infect their minds with fear, just like they did to me. I want to make it perfectly clear what a dire mistake they've all made, but what I want them to remember, more than anything, from now until forever, is that they've messed with the wrong girl. So I show them what I brought.

I show them Jonah's gun.

Their expressions don't change right away. Maybe they think it's a toy? Maybe they think it's a squirt gun? It must be quite a sight to take in, an angry, disheveled, almost-six-year-old girl with fury in her eyes, pointing a fully loaded semiautomatic pistol right at them.

All that changes the moment I pull the trigger.

With a loud bang, the gun kicks in my hand and the crystal vase by Walrus Face shatters, pelting him with pebbles of crystal shrapnel. He throws his tumbler, still half-filled with liquor, straight up in the air and dives for cover. With perfect aim and timing I pull the trigger again and the tumbler loudly bursts in a cloud of twinkling glass and brown mist. There are twitching moustaches and wide-eyed stares as a tangled blur of dodging and ducking men go diving behind whatever is closest. Some grab at one another, callously heaving their colleagues into the line of fire. Some throw themselves behind sofas and armchairs. One heavyset man launches himself without looking and goes sprawling across the food-laden table, landing hard, face-first into a large terrine of salmon mousse. Two men are man-handling each other, jostling and wrestling in an attempt to determine which will be the human shield as another man drops to his knees and curls into a whimpering ball on the carpet. The remaining men simply stare, rooted to the spot, their eyes wide, frozen like startled deer.

Blue Stripy Suit Man is among them, standing motionless in the center of the room like a trout-mouthed statue. I take aim, pull the trigger, and with a flash of gunpowder the gun jolts in my palm. The ornamental red glass lamp six feet above his head ruptures into a thousand pieces. His entire body flinches into action as he leaps awkwardly sideways, cartwheeling directly onto a small, antique table full of deviled eggs. With a loud crack its spindly legs snap under his weight, sending the serving tray, silver spoons, cloth napkins, and thirty eggs vaulting through the air, deviling the wall and the face of another man with thick splats of white and yellow.

Nanny Theresa erupts into the room from the far door. The look on her face alone is worth it. Men are screaming and running and cowering and hiding while I gleefully stand in the doorway, basking in the warm glow of the manic pandemonium unfolding before my little eyes. Skinny Red-Cheek Man's entire face is red now. I notice a large, dark stain spreading down the front of his gray trousers. I actually giggle out loud.

On the other side of the room, Silver-Topped Cane Man is hobbling away in a pathetic attempt to escape. I take careful aim.

BANG!

My bullet finds its mark, splintering his cane in two. He teeters for a moment, wobbling off-kilter like a faltering spinning top. Almost in slow motion, he falls. He rolls over twice on the Persian rug and comes to a halt on his back, rocking from side to side, his arms and legs pathetically flailing in the air like an overturned turtle.

I point the gun high and let loose three shots over their heads. Just for the fun of it.

BANG! BANG! BANG!

From every corner of the room, the men scream like little children, and I can't help but throw my head back and laugh out loud.

Jonah and Mariele burst in from the far door and my huge grin evaporates. The fun is over. I drop the gun to my feet with a heavy thud.

"Mariele!" Nanny screams from behind the sofa, pointing a knobbly finger directly at me. "Take her! Take her to her room! Right now!" Mariele hurries across the carpet and scoops me up into her arms. Over her shoulder, I see Jonah trying his best to calm the situation. Horrible men are breathing heavily; some are clutching their chests, some are holding each other, some are wiping food from their faces, and one man in particular is blotting something else entirely from the front of his trousers. Every last one of them looks terrified. It's fantastic.

I bob up and down in Mariele's arms, and as she hurriedly whisks me along the hall, the raging shouts of the men echo after us. I know that I've never been in this much trouble. I really don't care. Not even Nanny Theresa's witch's claws could scratch this radiant smile off my happy little face.

CHAPTER FOUR

That evening I stare out the window at the section of driveway that snakes through the manor grounds and disappears over the hill behind my bedroom. Mariele sits with me, knitting in silence. One by one I hear the men walk through the foyer downstairs, and one by one I hear them bay for my blood as Jonah and Nanny Theresa apologize over and over and over again. As night falls, I watch the taillights of the last limousine drive into the distance.

"Do you see? Now do you see?" Nanny Theresa's voice echoes up the stairwell, amplified by the marble entranceway. "You have absolutely no concept of how dangerous that child is! The investors and the board members will not forget this. Mark my words, Major Brogan; there will be hell to pay. For all of us!"

"Richard will speak to them. He'll bring them around," replies Jonah.

At the sound of my father's name, I strain my little ears toward the crack in my bedroom door.

"That little abomination up there could have killed someone today!" shrieks Nanny.

"After how they treated her, I'd say they kinda had it coming. Wouldn't you?"

The tiniest smile curls the edges of my lips.

"No, I certainly would not!" bellows Nanny Theresa. "I'm holding you personally responsible for this, Major. Don't think I haven't seen you. Speaking to her like she's your daughter, putting dangerous thoughts in her head. Well, she is *not* your daughter. Infinity doesn't belong to you. You would be wise to remember that."

"I'm well aware of the situation, thank you," Jonah says calmly.

"Oh, are you really? Well then, fine. I've had enough of this glorified babysitting. From this moment on, I run this household and that is all. I wash my hands of her! That . . . *child* is solely your problem, and I suggest you deal with her! Control her! Right this minute! I expect you know exactly what I'm referring to when I say *control her*."

Nanny Theresa's heels clack on the marble floor as she storms away.

"I'll deal with Finn when I see fit," Jonah calls after her. "She needs a little time to think about what she's done."

Nanny Theresa's heels stop dead.

"No, Major Brogan. When it comes to Infinity, you and I and Richard are the ones who need to think very seriously about what *we* have done."

I sit in silence, pondering Nanny Theresa's words. What on earth did she mean by that? This has been the longest day of my life and most certainly the worst. Miserable and exhausted, I quietly weep until there are no more tears left to cry. Only the sound of Mariele's gentle voice tugs me back from the edge of complete and utter misery.

"It's eight o'clock, Miss Blackstone—time for bed."

I move wearily from the windowsill and slump onto my bed. Mariele takes my shoe off, helps me into my pajamas, and tucks me under the covers. I watch her as she fusses around me.

"Mariele?"

"Yes, Miss Blackstone?"

"What were Nanny and Jonah arguing about? Why do they need to think about what they've done? What did they do?"

Mariele's head stays bowed as her fingers busily jab at covers that she's already tucked.

"I . . . I'm sorry, Miss. I wasn't really listening."

I can tell that she's lying.

"Mariele?"

She looks up at me, a nervous smile forced onto her lips.

"What's your father like?" I ask.

Mariele's big, brown, doe eyes crease at the corners. I had never noticed until right now just how sad they are. She glances anxiously toward the door. "I'm not sure I know what you mean, Miss."

"What things do you do together? Is he kind to you?"

Mariele walks over to my stuffed toys and begins tidying them, her eyes fixed sideways on the crack in the door the entire time. "Oh yes, Miss Blackstone. My father is a very nice man."

"Mariele?"

She smiles in my direction, her eyebrows raised in hesitant expectation.

"What is my father like?"

Her smile disappears like it's been wiped away with a dirty rag. "That's enough talk, Miss Blackstone." She walks over and pulls the covers up to my neck. "I don't think Major Brogan will be reading you a story tonight," she says, quickly changing the subject. "Perhaps you could read one yourself?"

"I don't feel like reading. I don't feel . . . anything," I mumble.

Mariele stands at the end of my bed, just looking at me, her head slightly tilted, her expression heavy with sadness. She turns and looks over her shoulder at the door. She walks over, peers cautiously through the crack, and then quietly closes the door behind her.

"Maybe I can tell you a story?" she whispers. Her eyes have changed. They're fearful. "You have to promise to keep this story a secret. Do you swear?" Now they almost look pleading.

I nod.

She walks to my bedside, takes Prince Horsey from by my pillow and buries him under a pile of thick cushions on the sofa by the window. "Horsey might hear us," she says under her breath. "This story is only for you, OK?"

I nod again. I like secrets. Mariele puts the green-painted chair by my bed, sits, and looks me right in the eyes. She takes a deep breath and begins to speak in a quiet voice, only a hair above a whisper.

"Once upon a time, there was a little princess called . . . Flora."

I like this story already.

"She was beautiful, and so clever, and almost everyone in the kingdom thought that she was wonderful. Some thought she was a miracle."

I grin for the first time that night.

"Princess Flora lived in a castle, and even though it was a beautiful castle, Princess Flora didn't realize that it was actually . . . a prison."

I'm intrigued, and suddenly a little concerned.

"The castle was owned by a king who wanted to keep the princess hidden away in secret."

"Why?"

"Because she was different, Finn. She was very special." Mariele has never called me Finn before. "The king was part of an evil council. Together, over time, they would watch the princess and decide how they could use her." My eyes are as wide as dinner plates. I hang on Mariele's every word.

"What the princess needed to know was that the king didn't control her life as much as he thought he did. What the princess needed to know was that she had a will and a heart of her own." Mariele takes my hand and squeezes it hard. Her eyes are desperate. She's scaring me a little. "What she needs to realize is that there are good people who are trying very hard to help her . . ."

Suddenly the door swings open and Jonah is there. "Why is this door closed? What's going on here, Mariele?"

Mariele springs to her feet and straightens her uniform. "Nothing, sir. I . . . I was just telling Miss Blackstone a . . . a bedtime story."

"Can you finish it tomorrow please, Mariele?" I say excitedly.

"Of course, Miss Blackstone," Mariele replies. She curtsies, hurries out past Jonah, and disappears down the hall.

Jonah stands at the doorway, leaning out, watching her go. He slowly turns back into the room and frowns at me. "I don't suppose I need to tell you that what you did today was very, very bad, do I?"

I shake my head. "I'm really sorry, Jonah. Those men just made me so mad. I wasn't trying to hurt anyone, I promise."

"Oh, I know. I've seen how good a shot you are. If you were really trying to hit them, they would all be in pieces, not just a vase and a lamp and their fragile egos," he says with a little smile. "Just between you and me, I think they deserved it, but you have to promise that you won't go shooting guns at people anymore. Well, at least not unless I say so."

I nod and let out a tiny giggle.

"What did Mariele say to you, Finn?"

I'm suddenly very serious. "She told me not to say."

Jonah smiles. "You can tell me, sweetheart. I promise it will go no further." Jonah draws a crisscross shape on his chest with his finger. "There, I've crossed on it. OK?"

I ponder for a moment, then shrug my shoulders and slowly nod. "Mariele told me a story about a bad king, and a beautiful princess that he put in jail. I think she was talking about me. I think the bad king is . . . Father."

Jonah walks to my bedside, sits on the green chair, and lets out a deep sigh. "Why do you say that?"

"Because he doesn't seem to care about me, Jonah." I thought all the tears I had to cry were gone, and yet my eyes begin to fill once more.

"Don't cry, sweetheart. I'm sure he does. In fact, y'know what? I was just talking to him on the phone, and he said that he's going to bring you a present. For your birthday."

"Really?" I mumble through the sniffling.

"Really. He'll be here when you wake up. I guarantee it. Here, I'll light the fireplace to help you get to sleep." Jonah walks over, presses a button on the mantel and low flames flicker up over the coals in the hearth. "You'll be six years old tomorrow, Finn. You've got a busy day ahead of you."

"Can we ride the ponies to the lake and have a picnic, please, Jonah?" I ask as I snuggle down under the covers.

"Of course we can. We can even take the rowboat out and I'll teach you how to fish," he says with a warm smile. Jonah ambles to my bedside, leans down, and kisses my forehead. Then he walks to the door and switches off the light. "Good night, Finn."

With images of a princess trapped in a stone tower traipsing through my mind, I drift off into a dreamless sleep.

That night was the last time I ever saw Mariele.

I can't have been asleep for very long when I feel it. My eyes flick open. Someone is in my room. I peer through the darkness and there, at the foot of my bed, I see a dark figure standing silent and still.

"Jonah?" I say croakily, rubbing my eyes. The orange glow from the embers in the fireplace dances dimly over the outline of a man. That man is definitely not Jonah. I want to scream out, but just as I'm about to, the man speaks.

"Don't be afraid," he says, his voice soft and deep. "My name is Richard. Richard Blackstone."

My fear evaporates and is replaced with wonder. I stare toward him, rubbing my eyes again, straining to make out his face in the darkness, wondering if this is real or whether it's my very first dream.

"Hi . . . I . . . I'm Finn," I whisper.

He chuckles softly. "I know. You've gotten so big."

He *is* here. My heart leaps. "Will you be at my birthday party tomorrow? I'll be six years old."

He looks at the floor. "No. I'm afraid not. I have to leave tonight. I'm a very busy man, you see."

"I know." I can feel the sadness creeping into my bones again.

"But I came here tonight especially to see you. I was leaving you a birthday present. There, on the bedside table."

In the dim glow from the dying embers I see a small black box and I'm instantly wide awake.

"May I open it now?"

"I don't see why not."

I scramble excitedly over to the box, snatch it off the bedside table, and pry it open. Inside, resting on a black velvet cushion is a delicate silver chain attached to a small silver circle. Inside the circle, set in the center like a frozen drop of midnight, is a beautiful, black, diamond-shaped stone. The light from the fireplace flicks softly across its facets, making it look like a tiny flame is trapped inside. I recognize it immediately from the photograph on the landing and I gasp with delight.

"It was your mother's. She wanted you to have it. Don't you ever lose it."

"I'll never take it off. I swear, I won't," I whisper solemnly.

"You be a good girl now. OK? Happy birthday, sweetheart."

And with that, he slowly turns and walks away silently into the darkness. I launch myself at the bedside lamp and knock it completely off the table and onto the carpet. I kick at the covers and they tangle around my legs. With sheets and blankets wrapped around my ankles, I flop onto the floor and lunge at the lamp switch. My room fills with soft orange light, but he's already gone. I finally manage to kick the blankets off, leap to my feet, and run into the hallway. It's dark and empty. Maybe it was a dream after all?

I look down and there, curled in the palm of my hand, is my mother's pendant.

I wanted to say more. The perfect thing that would make him stay longer or make him promise to come back one day soon, but all that escapes from my lips is a breathless whisper: "Good-bye."

Sadly, I felt that it was more than just a word. It marked the beginning of my weary little heart closing a door on my father. I love the necklace, but it's far too little and much too late. I slip it over my head and cradle the stone in my hand. I can't help but imagine how different everything would be if Mother were still alive. Maybe Father would love me enough to want to know me? Not just arrive in the middle of the night and remind me of everything that I've lost.

I stare down the empty hall and feel a sudden pang of anger. It's pure and hot and powerful. How dare my father ignore me for the first six years of my life and have the nerve to call me "sweetheart"! That privilege is already reserved for someone else. Someone, I've recently discovered, who is terrible at hiding the lockbox for his gun.

That very same night I creep into Jonah's room, sneak the key from his jacket while he's sleeping, and take Prince Horsey out to the old oak tree. I know it's not his fault. He's only a stuffed toy unicorn. But I can't bear to look at his stupid smiling face for one more minute, knowing that my father once loved him more than he'll ever love me.

I prop Prince Horsey on an upturned block of wood and blindfold him with one of Nanny Theresa's silk handkerchiefs. With a resolute hand and a deep breath, I close one eye, take careful aim, and squeeze the trigger. With an echoing bang and a puff of goose-down feathers, the bullet whips right through Prince Horsey's little make-believe heart. His soft, furry nose droops forward, and, just like that, my hopes and dreams of a life with my father are put to rest, years before I would have any real dreams at all.

CHAPTER FIVE

I wake with a jolt, dazed, Bettina tapping on my shoulder.

"Finn, wake up . . . you've got some drool. There," she says, touching the side of her mouth.

I drag my face across my sleeve, squinting, bewildered.

"I can't believe you fell asleep again," Bit says with a little smirk. "And your hair is—" She lightly brushes the tangled mess from my face.

"I know," I mumble, pushing her hand away. Sometimes she forgets that I don't like to be touched. "I've been so tired lately."

"Sorry. Crazy dreams again?" she asks, offering me some gum. I drowsily take a piece.

"Yeah, it's so weird. I've been having the same bizarre dream for the past week. Every time I go to sleep it carries on from the night before."

"Cool," Bit says as she's turning away, distracted by a flashing icon on her computer slate. She's not even listening. Oh well.

I slouch back into my seat and chew the gum, relishing its sweet strawberry taste, grateful to be awake, but I can't seem to shake this feeling of unease. These dreams I've been having are different from how I remember that day, and I'd be lying if I said it wasn't bothering me.

Right after the staff inspection at the bottom of the stairs, I remember going straight to my room. I cried by the window until Mariele came to tuck me in . . . didn't I? I'm sure of it. Wait. Am I really? I remember meeting Father, I remember him giving me Mother's locket, but did those old men really rip my dress . . . and did I *really* get Jonah's gun and . . . ? No, surely not. Then again, that would explain why my favorite stuffed toy just up and vanished one day. *Oh my god, listen to yourself. Snap out of it, Finn. You're being ridiculous.* My imagination is obviously getting involved. That's just how dreams go sometimes, I guess.

But it all felt so incredibly *real*. Like it actually *happened* that way.

I was just beginning to get used to having *my* kind of dreams. Now that they're finally going weird on me, like they're supposed to, I find myself wishing that they wouldn't. Does anyone else dream like this?

"Bit?"

She looks over at me, her hair all frizzy brown, her button nose scattered with freckles, her eyebrows raised expectantly over the top of the thick black frames of her glasses. I suddenly can't think of what to ask.

"Never mind. It's . . . not important."

She smiles and turns back to her slate.

Bettina Otto. Apart from being my roommate, she's also my best friend at school. She has been ever since the first day I came to Bethlem Academy.

She's a fifteen-year-old computer genius who skipped two years, and the only one I genuinely like in this whole surreal, most private of expensive private schools. She's also the only one who knows who I really am.

When I started at Bethlem Academy, Jonah enrolled me as Finn Brogan, the daughter of a foreign billionaire weapons manufacturer. He said that the attention my real last name would generate might interfere with my studies and make it difficult to make genuine friends, rather than kids who just want to be seen with the daughter of *the* Richard Blackstone. I didn't really understand what Jonah meant when I was thirteen, but now I'm so very glad that he did what he did. It turns out that Bit is the only one in this school that I actually want to be friends with. She's a nerd, sure, but I guess we're all tarred with that same brush in the advanced classes. I for one am kinda proud of the fact, and I know that Bit is, too.

She looks up from the screen of her slate and stares outside, her eyes as wide as full moons. "Wow. This is gonna be awesome."

I shake off the last cobwebs of sleep, smooth down the front of my uniform blazer, straighten my tie, and peer out the window of the school bus.

My stomach churns.

I thought now that I'm seventeen, I would be old enough to handle this. Maybe I was wrong.

Everyone around us is in a flurry of excitement. They're glued to the windows of the bus, pointing and giggling, oohing and aahing, wide-eyed, at the huge black dome in the distance. A building that has only ever been seen in rare pictures leaked onto the net, or in fleeting glances on TV. While all of my fellow schoolmates are figuratively frothing at the mouth to begin the tour, I am finding it very hard to calm my already considerable unease. You see, the reason that incredible collection of structures out there is making my guts into one massive, twisty knot of nerves becomes glaringly clear by the imposing name of this enormous compound. My name. My father's name. That group of shiny domes and buildings out there is the beating heart of his global empire.

Blackstone Technologies.

Professor Francis, our thin, old, gray-haired, bow-tie-wearing, tweed-jacketed science teacher, is waving his arms in the air, trying his best to calm everyone down and get their attention, his silver wire-framed glasses barely managing to avoid flying off the bridge of his scarlet-tipped nose. Good luck with that. It takes a lot to impress the teenage-brat offspring of billionaires, especially when they get worked up like this. It's like trying to round up a pack of overprivileged rabid dogs.

Speaking of uncontrollable animals, it's a very weird mix on this field trip today. I thought this was supposed to be the Annual Excellence trip, a reward for the top academic percentile at Bethlem Academy, so it's really no surprise that Bit and I are here. As I mentioned, we're both nerds. Some of the others on the bus, though, are . . . well . . . most definitely a surprise.

Why a surprise? First of all—silly, silly me—I assumed that only the top achievers in the *sciences* were supposed to be on this field trip, not the most popular kids, or the ones with the best-looking hair, or the ones that faked and schemed their way in.

Obviously, I was wrong.

I have no doubt that once the word got out about Blackstone Technologies, very dubious strings were pulled to get some of these kids on this bus. Powerful parents plus spoiled child clearly equals an undeserved seat. It certainly explains why that stuck-up cow Margaux Pilfrey and her best friend Millie Grantham are here. Little Miss Evil and her faithful minion. Dubious strings are their bread and butter. Earlier this year, they started a school-based charity that raises money for poor inner-city kids to take acting classes. It sounded like a pretty cool idea at first, until Bit hacked the charity accounts and found out that their rich fathers funded the whole thing after Margaux discovered it would look great on her application when her father bought her way into a top university. I would've thought just being a silver-medal Olympic gymnast would open enough doors for her.

Margaux and Millie are sharing a joke with the eternally vacant, buxom young drama teacher, Miss Lorna Cole. She obviously won the teachers' chaperone raffle. Miss Cole likes to dress like a pinup from the 1950s, complete with perfect, shiny, loose brunette curls and neckerchief. She glides around school with Margaux and her friends like she's one of them. Her outfits are great, but her student-teacher relationships are very unprofessional.

And really quite creepy when I think about it.

Speaking of creepy, Brent Fairchild over there is Margaux's on-and-off boyfriend and captain of the lacrosse team. Brent "led" the Bethlem Breakers to victory in the interschool lacrosse tournament and got himself a seat on the bus, but I don't really think you can call it a tournament when only two schools participate and the other school's team, the Deerfield Stags, is not so secretly sponsored by Brent's dad, who also owns the land their school is built on. Deerfield has conveniently lost every match that Brent has played in since he joined the team. Coincidence? I don't think so. See what I mean? Dubious strings. The only reason Brent even goes here and not to Deerfield is because Bethlem is four times more expensive.

Sitting next to him is his best friend and teammate, Brody Sharp. Brody is on the bus because he saved a year-nine student from a chemical fire in the science lab. Normally I would say, high grades or not, every hero deserves a reward. But what nobody realizes is that Bit found cam footage from a lab computer showing that Brody started the fire in the first place. Why don't we tell? Because it's not worth the trouble those two morons would cause us if they found out that we did. I'm not afraid of them, but Bit is terrified, and I'm sure the footage will be much more satisfying to release when Brody's family blackmails him a path toward a high-powered political career, just like his mother's.

The two boys don't really look the same, but I always thought they looked like they were cut from the same cloth. Brody is a little bigger, stockier, and definitely dimmer, and even though Brody's hair is shorn close to his head and Brent's is carefully brushed into a floppy fringe, they're both sandy blond with brown eyes, both arrogant, both immature, and both a waste of my time. Brent and Brody. Sounds like a bad comedy show. I'm definitely not laughing.

Most of the others deserve to be here. Karla Bassano is a biology whiz, Jennifer Cheng and Sherrie Polito are physics prodigies, and Dean McCarthy understands math almost as well as I do.

Anyway, despite the few rotten apples, I'm gonna try and make the most of this field trip. That could be tough considering that I honestly couldn't be more nervous.

My father, as I've always been reminded, is a genius, but the revered admiration in the eyes and words of everyone who talks about his achievements are nothing but thorns in my side. I know what he's done. Everyone does. I want to know who he *really* is. The net doesn't offer up anything of any real use to me, and when it comes to asking Jonah or subtly interrogating our staff, I've always been told so little. Coming here and seeing this for the first time goes to show just *how little* I know about his life. So while the other kids might be out-of-their-minds deliriously happy to be here, I'm churning with mixed emotions. Nervous, angry, hopeful, a little frightened—there's a whirlwind in my head and a typhoon in my stomach. I decide to focus on something else instead. Or maybe that should be *someone* else.

The new kid. Ryan Forrester.

He started at Bethlem Academy yesterday. Principal Ross chose Karla Bassano to show him around the school, and he's on the trip today as a "Welcome to Bethlem" gesture. Actually, what really happened was when Principal Ross asked if anyone would be gracious enough to be Ryan's school tour guide and field-trip buddy, the number of swooning girls' hands that shot up was a truly pathetic testament to our society's obsession with good-looking people.

Karla is definitely not complaining about her duties. She got to sit next to him and stare at him for the entire forty-five minutes it took us to get here on the school jet. Probably all the way here on the bus from the airport, too, I imagine. She sat on the jet with her head slightly tilted, twirling her curly brown hair, giggling at any word that came out of his mouth, touching his arm, and flashing her big brown eyes. Generally being pathetic.

He is disturbingly hot, though.

"Like a young Stalin," Bit says from beside me.

"What? Who . . . what are you talking about?" I burble distractedly.

"The new guy. Ryan. He looks a little like the picture we saw in history class of Joseph Stalin, y'know, when he was young. You've been gawking at him for a minute straight."

"No, I wasn't. Please. I was looking out the other window," I say, stealing one last look at him.

Bit turns her computer slate toward me and shows me a picture. "See. Young Stalin."

"Yeah, now that you mention it. Same thick, shiny hair, Ryan's is lighter, though; smaller nose, too; same lips; Ryan has nicer eyes—" I immediately bite my tongue, embarrassed to catch myself mid-fawn. I silently tell myself off for being just as pathetic as Karla and then, to my shame, just go right back to staring at him. I know that I'm being ridiculous, but I just can't help it. There's something about him.

"I meant they both look like idiots," Bit says under her breath as she swipes the picture away.

I take my eyes off Ryan for a second and suddenly remember exactly where we all are. I slump back in my seat and look tentatively out the window.

"I think this is going to be . . . interesting," I whisper, my words dripping with trepidation.

A cheesy grin widens across Bit's face. "You can say that again."

"People, please. You boys, sit down. Everyone! We are not getting off this bus until you're all quiet and back in your seats! I'm talking to you, McCarthy!"

Poor Professor Francis. They're not listening at all.

This whole crazy ruckus is obviously contagious. I seem to be the only one who is immune. Even the usually reserved Bit is getting overly excited. I can tell by the bug-eyed way she's staring so intently at her computer slate.

"This place is . . . amazing. Finn, you've gotta see this!" she blurts, eagerly thrusting the screen in front of my nose. A glowing green computer wire hologram of Blackstone Technologies' grounds and buildings is jutting out from its surface. "There aren't any satellite photos of this place, which isn't surprising considering that your dad's company designed and built most of them."

"Shhh. Keep it down, will ya?" I hiss at her.

"Oops. Sorry." Bit continues in a whisper, "I had to hack into the National Security Bureau's mainframe for anything decent. The best they have is this artist's conceptual rendering, but even that's out of date and probably mostly guesswork. Wow. It could be wrong, but this says that they've even got their own military training center and research hospital."

My stomach twists and turns even more than before.

"Finn, what's your dad like in real life? I mean, really like?"

What I want to say is that my father is just a shadow in the night to me, and that she probably knows more about him from TV interviews and e-mag articles than I do. I'm not sure why, maybe it's self-preservation, but I choose to lie instead.

"Well, one time on my birthday we went horse riding and had a picnic by the lake. We took a boat out and he taught me how to fish." I'm such a terrible liar, but Bit doesn't seem to notice at all.

"Wow. It's so hard to imagine him doing father and daughter stuff like that, y'know, normal dad-type stuff," Bit says, gazing thoughtfully out the window.

"I know. Hard to believe, right?" I say the words with the same thinly veiled sarcastic tone as before. That seems to go right over her head as well.

Professor Francis is at his wits' end. People are chattering, texting madly, and snapping pictures out the windows. Miss Cole is just sitting there, smiling like an idiot, so she's no help at all. Brody Sharp begins chanting, "Move that bus, move that bus!" which, since we're already parked, makes no sense at all, but it isn't very long before others join in. It's ridiculous.

Out of the corner of my eye I see Ryan Forrester, who until now was quietly reading, lean over the aisle toward Margaux. She leans toward him, flicking her silky blonde hair and beaming her perfect white teeth, her huge, pale-blue eyes flashing beneath her fluttering eyelids. Millie strokes her auburn hair behind her ear, raises one eyebrow, and gives a knowing look to Miss Cole, who smiles back before promptly shifting her gaze hungrily to Ryan's lips.

I think I'm gonna puke.

Brent Fairchild spots the exchange and sits up in his seat like a meerkat. That is his kinda-girlfriend Ryan's talking to, after all. Ryan says something to Margaux that I can't hear above the chatter, and she nods. Suddenly she stands and shouts, "Everybody shut up!" The bus immediately goes silent.

I hate her so much.

Not only for the fact that she thinks she's the queen bee of this school, but also, and especially, because everyone else seems to think so, too. Apparently even Ryan Forrester. I tell myself that it shouldn't bother me, but it really does. I'm halfway through a thought about how stupid he must be when he catches me looking at him. He smiles a crooked smile and holds our connection for that millisecond longer than necessary, that minuscule amount of time that, in an instant, makes you both realize that it's more than just a look. My eyes widen, my stomach tightens, and I quickly turn away. Totally busted. I quickly flump back against the seat.

Now that everyone's quiet, a look of relief washes over Professor Francis. With a trembling hand, he mops his brow with his handkerchief. "Thank you, Miss Pilfrey. Now that I have your attention, I'd like to lay down a few ground rules for the tour today."

There's a low groan.

"As you obviously all know, today's reward field trip will take place at the main research and development facility of Blackstone Technologies, the largest advanced-technology company in the world."

"Hells yeah!" Dean McCarthy shouts from the back.

Professor Francis throws a frown in his direction. "From your computers, to your phones, to food production, to military hardware and weather stabilization, Blackstone Technologies, and of course its founder, Dr. Richard Blackstone, is responsible for the innovations that make the lives we live today possible. Please remember that you are extremely lucky to be here. You are the first school students to ever be permitted beyond the hallowed doors of Blackstone Technologies."

A murmur of excitement rolls through the bus and the Professor waves a hand to quiet us. "Please listen and be polite, do not stray away from the tour guide, raise your hands if you have any questions for them, and most important of all, do not touch anything. Even some of *your* parents wouldn't be able to afford *that* lawsuit."

Even though it's obvious that the Professor is joking, some kids look back at Bit from the corners of their eyes. Only at this school would the poor kid in class be a girl whose mom is only worth two-and-a-half billion dollars.

"OK then. We've been told that the tour will begin at ten sharp, and then we'll stop for a spot of lunch in the staff cafeteria at one o'clock, and continue the tour after that. We'll be back on the bus by four and on the jet by five. Behave yourselves and have an amazing day." Professor Francis turns and trots enthusiastically down the steps of the bus.

There are a couple of whoops and "yeahs" as everyone finally begins scrambling off the bus and into the tree-lined courtyard outside. Beyond the circular courtyard, a wide concrete path stretches out the length of a football field to a huge, charcoal-gray, rectangular stone arch in the distance. Even from here, I can see the word "Blackstone" emblazoned across the arch in big black, gold-edged letters. In the center above it is the company logo, a silver circle with a large black diamond shape inside it. My hand automatically goes to my mother's pendant, pinching it between my fingers beneath my blouse.

Just beyond the arch, almost filling the sky, is the huge, smooth, black glass dome we saw when we were driving in. It has to be at least sixty stories high. It makes for a very imposing sight, most likely designed to intimidate. It definitely serves its purpose.

"Everyone follow me, please, we're meeting our guide at the door," says Professor Francis. There's excited chatter as he leads the group down the path toward the stone arch and massive dome.

"Do you think your fath . . . I mean, do you think Dr. Blackstone is here today, Finn?" whispers Bit.

"I don't know," I say honestly. "People say he hardly ever leaves, so . . . maybe?"

I am really hoping to see my father today, of course, but my hopes aren't high. He's spent almost my entire life avoiding me, and a part of me can't help but feel, whether he's here or not, this day won't be any different.

Margaux pushes past, bumping me sideways with her shoulder. "Whoops," she says, flicking her hair in my face. "Didn't see you there." She struts ahead of us, giggling with Millie as Miss Cole follows close behind them.

We all walk under the stone arch to the side of the dome. It seems so much bigger than it appeared from the bus. Its curved side reaches up and far away into the sky, but it's so huge that the wall beside us looks perfectly straight and vertical. It's as smooth and black as volcanic glass, and seems to be made of one single piece. We stand in front of it in the place where you would expect a door should be, but there simply isn't one. There aren't any joins or hinges or handles anywhere to be seen.

Professor Francis looks at his watch. "Ten o'clock exactly. There should be someone here to meet us."

"Maybe you got the day wrong, Prof!" Dean McCarthy yells from the back of the group.

Brody Sharp walks forward and knocks on the side of the gigantic, black hemisphere. "Hellooo? Anybody dome?"

"Now, now, quiet down, please," Professor Francis says in an attempt to quash the laughter.

It's then that I notice the faint hissing sound. Karla Bassano is the first one to see where it's coming from. She points, clapping her hands excitedly, her shiny curls bouncing up and down as she does tiny jumps on the spot. "There! Look!" she screeches.

Everyone's eyes look where she's pointing, scanning the sides of the dome for whatever it is that she's spotted.

"There, inside, on the ground!" she screeches again. "That little star!"

Sure enough, through the glass on the inside of the dome, there's a small twinkling point of light. It really does look just like a single star sitting on the ground against an empty, pitch-black night sky. Everybody runs forward to see it, all of us pressing our noses to the cold black glass, cupping our hands around our eyes. Some kids immediately begin taking video with their phones.

It gets brighter and brighter and bigger and bigger until it's a blue-white globe the size of a basketball. After a few seconds it gently begins to rise, floating up in a straight line from the ground. It's impossible to judge how far inside the dome the ball of light is; we can see it through the glass as if the wall is transparent, but the ball of light is still somehow inexplicably surrounded with an impenetrable darkness. We crane our necks as the glowing sphere slowly drifts upward. Up and up it goes, until eventually it reaches the inside surface high in the dome. It hovers there for a few seconds—then, in a blink, splits into four. Each smaller ball shoots off in its own direction, leaving thick trails of white light behind like swathes of luminous paint, all the way down the giant dark curve and back to the ground. The glowing white beams begin rotating sideways, painting the whole inside of the gigantic dome pure white. There's a bright flash and the brilliant white veneer suddenly drops from the crown of the dome, like a five-hundred-foot-high curtain. It gracefully cascades down the sides of the massive structure in silent billows before vanishing into the ground like mist.

In the minute from the first moment Karla saw the star until now, the entire sixty-story-high curve has turned crystal-clear transparent.

We all stand there in wide-eyed amazement. The sight that greets us is breathtaking, but at the same time doesn't quite make sense. Through the glass of the dome, filling the entire space, I see what can only be described as a lush, green, thriving, tropical rainforest. It's glaringly plain to see that this is so much more than just a fancy greenhouse filled with foreign plants. Oh no. This is a flourishing, steaming, moving, living ecosystem, complete in every way. It's as if a giant hand had reached down from the sky, scooped an immense circle of jungle from the depths of the Amazon, and inexplicably placed it here in pristine perfection, more than six thousand miles from where it should exist. Towering trees wrapped in sinewy tendrils of ivy jut skyward from thick, green, tangled undergrowth. There are flashes of vibrant color from the plumage of exotic birds as they flit back and forth in the high branches. A large lizard of some kind sleepily watches us from a big flat rock as spider monkeys playfully chase each other through the leaves overhead. A stream winds its way through the thicket, lazily trickling over stones as it flows. A wild boar and two piglets stand at its edge, nuzzling the water as a huge, mottled python slowly coils its thick body down a mass of twisted vines. It's the most wondrous thing I've ever seen.

I look around at the group and everyone seems to be just as awestruck as I am, their mouths agape at the incredible beauty that has just been unveiled before us.

My sudden and unexpected excitement at what else we might see today is immediately tinged with bitterness. How could such an amazing thing, something that my father created, be as new to me as everyone else who is here seeing it for the first time, too?

Does he really think that little of me? Does he think of me at all? Dammit! There are those pesky mixed feelings again. I decide to try and do what I have always done. I push them to the back of my mind and cover them with indifference. In that respect, maybe he and I are all too similar.

"There's someone in there!" Brent Fairchild exclaims in a high-pitched tone of voice that strips away his usual arrogant façade.

A human figure seems to have materialized from absolutely nowhere. It starts walking directly toward us. It looks like it's covered from head to toe in some kind of skin-tight, hooded, silver bodysuit. Judging by the breasts beneath that suit, it's obvious that she is a woman, and yet where her face should be, there's a featureless, shiny, black oval-shaped mask. She walks toward the wall of the dome, stops about sixty feet away from us on the other side, and stands motionless, her black-plastic-covered face staring blankly out toward us.

Suddenly, without warning, a razor-thin split shears up the entire surface of the glass. With a sound like violent ocean waves crashing against a rocky shore, the whole massive dome slices down the middle and opens up like an impossibly huge crystal flower. We all stumble and stagger backward in speechless wonder. The gap is getting wider and wider, the edges cascading loudly into the ground as if it were made from thousands of tons of free-standing water, pouring down into itself and inexplicably disappearing without a trace, like ice melting into piping-hot sand on a sweltering summer's day.

What just a moment ago resembled a giant, jungle-filled snow globe now looks more like a huge, translucent mouth, slowly yawning skyward. The sounds of birds and monkeys become louder and louder as the gap expands, the edges retracting down into the earth until soon the glass cage is completely gone, sunken into the dirt at the edge of the circular stone rim surrounding the beautiful, teeming green forest. The ground begins to vibrate, quickly followed by a rolling rumbling noise in the distance. Bit stumbles and grabs onto Professor Francis's arm.

I reach out for something to hold on to and clutch the nearest person without thinking.

I turn and find myself looking directly into Ryan Forrester's eyes. They're a kind of hazel amber, speckled with tiny flecks of gold. "Hi," he says softly, his voice warm and calm. My stomach does a somersault.

Out of the corner of my eye, something moves. A flock of birds has been startled into the air. Ryan and I look up just in time to see a massive flat-topped monolith of brown rock emerge above the trees from the depths of the jungle.

Trees sprout instantaneously on the top ridges, and shallow troughs carve themselves on either side. We hear the sound of rushing water before we see it. Louder and louder it becomes, until suddenly it gushes out over the sides of the peak, pouring in heavy torrents out into the jungle below. The shaking ceases and the entire monolith changes color from terracotta brown to a dark shade of gray. Blue flames erupt from the face of the sheer rock wall, burning a huge flickering Blackstone diamond logo into its surface.

Somewhere in the dense jungle, as if on cue, the powerful guttural roar of what I imagine could only be a tiger reverberates through the trees and echoes into the distance.

Everything is absolutely breathtaking.

Even though she's been right in front of us the whole time, I had forgotten the woman was even there, standing as still as a statue in front of this stunning backdrop. Professor Francis is as gob-smacked as the rest of us, ogling open-mouthed at the amazing sights and sounds. After a moment he seems to gather his senses. "Move up. Move up everyone." Oohing and aahing and wowing, we all walk forward toward the silver woman. Karla Bassano, at the back of the group, jumps with a little screech as grass and bushes sprout from the ground behind her. The farther in we all go, the thicker the sprouting foliage behind us becomes, until we're all gathered in a small round clearing, completely surrounded by trees and bushes with the woman in silver standing in the center a few feet in front of us.

With a quiet hiss, the black plastic oval covering the woman's face shifts and morphs, molding itself into human features. In just a few seconds the mask has transformed, the glassy black replaced with the face of a beautiful woman. She has alabaster skin, deep, sapphire-blue eyes, dark eyebrows, a perfectly shaped nose, and soft pink lips. She scans across the faces of the group. When her eyes meet mine, she stops and smiles warmly. In a very feminine, yet slightly metallic, voice, she utters only one word.

"Welcome."

The shock takes half a second to register, but when it does it hits me like a kick to the stomach. That face. I've seen that face before. I've seen that face a thousand times.

I know the elegant curves of the eyebrows, those lips and those cheekbones, that smooth, pale skin and that delicately pointed nose. Even the beauty spot on her cheek is there. Every smile line and eyelash is committed to memory. I know that face as well as I know my own.

Suddenly my vision swirls and my legs stop working. The world goes into slow motion as I fall and darkness closes in from all sides. I've never fainted before. It's something that I honestly thought I would never do. Just like I never imagined that I would ever look into those eyes, or see that face outside of a picture frame. It's the last image I see before everything goes completely black. The smiling face of the woman in silver is the smiling face of Genevieve Blackstone.

My dead mother.

CHAPTER SIX

"Finn?"

I open my eyes to the bright-blue sunny sky of a balmy summer afternoon. Kneeling at my side is the exact person that I was hoping for. My Jonah.

"Wha . . . happen—?" I mumble groggily.

"You fell, sweetheart. I saw you from the window of my room. It was quite a tumble. Don't move too much, Finn, you were knocked out for a little while."

I sit up despite his insisting I stay still. Over my shoulder, lying at the bottom of the hill, is the red bicycle that Jonah bought for my sixth birthday. Its front fork is buckled, the front wheel warped, and the spokes are splayed at bizarre angles like uncooked metal spaghetti.

"How many fingers am I holding up?" Jonah asks, a look of deep concern creasing his face.

"Two," I say, blinking my eyes back into focus.

"What day is it? How old are you?"

"It's Saturday; I'm thirteen. I'm OK, Jonah, stop making a fuss," I say, brushing his hand away.

"I think you're gonna be alright. Just a few scrapes here and there. Let's get you back up to the house and check you out properly, just to be on the safe side."

I let out a bothered sigh. I know Jonah won't let this drop until I agree to some unnecessary coddling. I try to get up and a sharp jolt spears along my wrist to my elbow. "Ow! Wait . . . ow . . . I . . . I think I've broken my arm."

It hurts a lot, but I know it's broken mostly because my forearm isn't straight anymore. Now there's a freaky bend where there definitely shouldn't be one.

Wincing, I hold my arm up for Jonah to inspect. His face turns as white as a sheet. Not the reaction I was expecting from a former soldier.

"It's OK," I say. "I'll just straighten it out."

"NOOO!" yells Jonah, but I've already done it. I hold the bent part in place with my other hand, close my eyes, and think of something that makes me angry. Anything to do with Nanny Theresa usually does the trick.

"We need to call the doctor, Finn, right now. Come with me up to the house," he says in his no-nonsense tone.

"Shhhh. Wait. Just a few more seconds aaand . . . there you go, all fixed," I say matter-of-factly, holding out my straightened arm for him to see. I give my fingers a wiggle to test them and grimace at the little needles of pain. Jonah's expression is a surprising mixture of confusion and bewilderment, and it's then that I suddenly remember.

He's never seen me do that before.

Maybe if I just pretend it didn't happen? Act like it's no big deal, shrug it off.

"I'm calling the doctor, Finn," Jonah insists again.

"Don't be silly," I say, half-laughing. "It'll be a bit sore for a few hours, but it'll be just like new tomorrow."

I get to my feet and walk over to my bike.

"It's wrecked, Jonah. And look, I've ripped my favorite t-shirt as well."

He's standing there looking at me strangely, eyes narrow, his head tilted slightly to the side.

"Finn, how did you do that?"

"It must have happened when I crashed the bike," I say, plucking at the hole of torn fabric, deliberately avoiding where I know this soon-to-be lecture is heading. "I know I shouldn't have been steering with my feet, and that old bike is waaay too small for me now, but if it weren't for that damn pothole . . ."

"Not the rip in your shirt, Finn, your arm. How did you fix your arm?"

Jonah walks over and gently takes my wrist. He runs his fingers over the skin where the bend was. "It was broken. I saw it."

"Oh. That," I mumble.

Usually I try my hardest not to lie to Jonah. I much prefer to keep things from him instead, but now that he's asked, I guess I'm gonna have to spill.

"I'll tell you if you promise not to get mad. Or punish me," I say, frowning up at him, pointing my finger at his nose like I have some kind of authority over the situation.

"You have to promise, though," I demand.

He stands there with folded arms, expecting me to fess up without bargaining. He really should know better by now.

"Cross on it, and I'll tell you."

Jonah sighs and rolls his eyes. He knows he can't catch me if I run off across the fields, which is exactly what I'll do if he doesn't swear on it. He grudgingly crosses his heart. I make him do that every time I think he might get mad at something I've done. In fact, this is the third time this week I've made him cross on something. As far as I'm concerned it's a binding contract with absolutely no take-backs.

I take a deep breath, let out a huge sigh, and grudgingly confess. "It's not the first bone that I've broken."

The familiar "what have you been keeping from me?" crinkle appears on Jonah's forehead.

"Explain," he mutters.

"The first time was an accident, I swear. One night I took Beauty out for a ride by the lake and she got spooked by something and bucked me off. I broke my arm pretty bad," I say, absent-mindedly rubbing a spot on my upper arm.

"What? When?!" blurts Jonah.

"Three years ago," I murmur coyly.

"Three years?! Why am I only finding out about this *now*?" Jonah bellows, his voice becoming louder with every word.

"I didn't wanna get in trouble for taking her out without permission, so I snuck upstairs and went to bed. I willed my arm to get better, and by morning it was," I say, looking guiltily at the ground.

"Well, maybe your arm wasn't really broken? It could have been a bad bruise or . . . but that doesn't explain how you just fixed your . . . you are in a lot of trouble, Miss Blackstone!" Jonah shouts. It's kinda funny to see him so flustered.

"No punishment. You promised. You totally crossed on it." I point the finger of power at the spot right between his eyes.

"But how did you just fix it like that? It's simply not possible."

"Well, quite clearly it is," I say, waving my arm in front of his face. "I can heal cuts and bruises, too. Anything's possible. You told me that. I used mind over matter just like you taught me."

"That's not exactly how it's supposed to work, Finn," Jonah says, softly prodding my arm. "Doesn't it hurt?"

"Yeah, totally! It hurts like crazy at first, but after the bone sets, it aches for a while and my arm will be a bit weak for a couple of days. It took a lot of practice to teach myself how to do it properly. In the beginning I really had to concentrate. Had to break a lot of bones before I was able to set them as quickly as I did just then." I slap my hand over my mouth. What is wrong with me today?

Jonah puts his hands on his hips and gives me his interrogation eyes. "Start talking."

After I make Jonah cross his heart two more times, I tell him how I had jumped off the roof of the house and broken my ankle, broken both wrists and all my fingers with a hammer, and broken my arm three times jumping off my bike and rope-swinging into tree trunks. There was also the time I jumped out of a tree onto the front of the Bentley one day when Arthur was taking it to the mechanic. Cracked two ribs and broke my wrist again. I really feel bad about that one. When one of the maids found Arthur, he was face-down on the driveway. He had died of a heart attack. For obvious reasons, I decide to keep that one to myself.

"Oh, and my nose got busted once when Carlo threw a rock at me, and another time he hit me with a tree branch. Cracked my arm that time, too."

Those last two confessions just slip out. As soon as I say them, I want to take them back. I swear it has to be the bump on my head. I really don't want Carlo to get in trouble because of me, and right now it sounds like all he does is fight with me and hit me with stuff.

"Carlo knows that you can do this?" Jonah asks sternly.

"Ah, yeah, he's seen me do it a couple times . . ." I say, knowing it's more like five or six.

"I think I need to have a little chat with young Carlo," Jonah says gravely. He turns and walks briskly in the direction of the stables.

"I made him do it!" I plead at Jonah's back, chasing after him.

"Leave your bike and get back to the house, Finn!" Jonah barks over his shoulder.

"It was only a fracture!" I yell, but he pretends not to hear me. "I can honestly tell the difference! It was two whole summers ago!"

Carlo Delgado is the fourteen-year-old son of our stable master, Javier Delgado. He's my best friend and the only other kid I know. Carlo's dad moved into the little two-bedroom house in the Seven Acre Wood ten years ago, and Carlo has come to stay with his dad every summer vacation since to help him look after the horses. Hanging out with Carlo is the highlight of my year, and I just got him in gigantic trouble. It was me and my big mouth's fault. I have to warn him.

Jonah strides off into the distance. He glances over his shoulder and points toward the house. I nod and make it look like I'm doing what I'm told as I head back up the hill, but the second that I'm out of Jonah's sight line I break into a furious sprint. I veer away from the house and go tearing across the main lawn, bolting toward the quaint rows of hedges surrounding the groundskeeper's shed. The stables are behind the polo grounds. It's a good eight-minute walk, twelve if you're as slow-moving as Jonah. I'm sure that I can make it there in less than three minutes if I take one of the quad bikes in the shed. With any luck, Jonah won't even see me kidnap Carlo to safety.

I sprint across the grass and almost make it to the hedges in less than two minutes. The doors of the shed are wide open, which means Graham the groundskeeper is in. He's a quiet guy who likes to keep to himself. He's thin and wiry with a thick white beard and glasses that perch on the tip of his crimson-pointed nose. He seems to be much more comfortable around plants than humans, especially a rowdy thirteen-year-old girl like me. I can see him inside as I get closer, standing at the bench, completely absorbed in doing something plant-y with some seedlings. He's dressed in his usual plaid shirt, green overalls, and black rain boots. He dresses like that year-round, even on summer days like this. I know from past experience that my mere presence always scares the living crap out of him, so, with a little smile on my face, I go barreling through the open door like a force of nature.

"Hi, Graham!"

He jumps a foot off the ground. His glasses spring off his nose, flip once in the air, and disappear into an open bag of potting mix. I grab a set of keys off a hook by the door and leap onto the nearest quad.

I twist the ignition, the engine roars into life, and I full-throttle the quad out of the shed, spraying dirt and dust backward all over Graham.

"Sorry!" I yell over my shoulder as I swing the handlebars wildly to the left, carving fat curves in the loose gravel outside. I peel out as fast as the bike will take me, speeding across the lawn behind the house and right through one of the yellow rose gardens beside the hand-carved gazebo.

The wind rushes through my hair as I round the corner past the high fence of the tennis court and down through the green grotto. The growl of the quad bike echoes all around as I weave along the paths that snake through the dense tunnels of trees.

I burst out into the sunlight again and see the polo grounds coming up quickly. I'm almost to the edge of the field when Carlo appears from behind one of the grandstands, a heavy saddle in his arms.

"Carlo!" I yell toward him. By the time I'm near enough to see the expression on his face, I can tell that he already knows what we'll be doing this afternoon—hiding in the Seven Acre Wood around his dad's house.

I brake, slide-skid the quad bike across the grass, and stop right beside him. "Get on," I say breathlessly, rubbing and flexing my aching arm.

He drops the saddle on the ground and wipes his brow with the back of a dirty-gloved hand.

"What have you done now?" he asks, climbing on the back of the quad.

"I'll tell you at the pond."

I gun the throttle and swerve the bike toward the woods. I glance to the right and see Jonah in the distance, waving his arms at us as we hit the path that leads to the outer edge of the trees. I swerve to the left and into the forest. There's no doubt that Jonah knows where we're going, but we would hear him coming and be gone again long before he got to us. Through the forest we go, the quad bike bumping over the terrain as I expertly weave in and out of the trees. I'm pretty sure most grownups would have trouble handling the bike as well as I do, even with a weak arm like mine, but that doesn't stop Carlo from holding on to me as tightly as he can.

We roar over the top of the hill and down the other side into the clearing. I hit the brakes, slide through the loose dirt and twigs at the bottom, and finally stop beside the cool, clear water's edge of the sheltered rock pool we discovered five summers ago. Our private meeting place.

Carlo jumps off the back, pulls his gloves off, and stuffs them into the pocket of his shorts. "What's going on, Finn? Where was Jonah heading?"

I cut the engine, get off the bike, and walk over to the old log we dragged to the edge last year. "He was looking for you, but he's probably going to talk to your dad now, instead," I say regretfully, flumping down on the log and digging my toes into the dirt.

"What for—what did I do?!" asks Carlo.

I shrug my shoulders and look at the ground to avoid looking him in the eyes.

"I might have mentioned that . . . you broke my arm?" I wince at the thought of how he'll react. I'm expecting Carlo to be mad at me; I would be if someone got me into this level of trouble. Just *how* mad he gets is another question. "It just slipped out, I swear! I bumped my head and I didn't know what I was saying. I'm really sorry."

"Finn." The tone of his voice isn't angry at all. He walks over and sits on the log beside me. "It's cool. I told my dad about that ages ago."

"What? Why?"

Carlo laughs. "Because it was freaky. I had to tell somebody, and you know how chill my dad is. He said you must be part devil and that

I should stay away from you. He was just kidding, though. At least I think he was. Anyway, I never would've hit you if you didn't ask me to, and if I hadn't seen with my own eyes what you can do. I was there that time you jumped out of the oak tree remember? My whole family ride horses, Finn; I know what a broken arm looks like."

"You're still gonna get in trouble, though, aren't you?"

Carlo crinkles his nose. "Nah, what for? That was years ago, and you and me are still best friends. Dad already knows what I did. Even if he *did* find out for the first time today, it wouldn't make any difference. My parents don't punish me at all since the divorce, so I can pretty much get away with anything," Carlo says with a mischievous grin.

"Jonah promised not to punish me, but I bet he'll find a way. I shouldn't have told him anything."

"I'll tell you what . . ." Carlo leans down and gathers up a handful of stones. "From now on we'll call this our . . . Pool of Secrets. Here." He drops half the pebbles into my hand. "We'll tell each other our secrets, and for each one we tell, we'll throw a stone into the pond. They'll sink to the bottom and that's where they'll stay, forever."

I can't help but think how romantic the idea is.

"I'll go first." Carlo holds up a pebble between his fingers. "My dad tells everyone that he doesn't drink, but I know where he hides his tequila." He throws the pebble out into the middle of the pond and it disappears with a plop. "Your turn," he says with a smile.

I hold up a pebble. "When I was five, I set fire to the east wing kitchen." I throw the pebble into the pond.

"I heard about that! It was a big fire. That was you?" exclaims Carlo.

"Yeah, I was trying to make pancakes for Jonah's birthday. I think he knows it was me, but he never said anything."

"Wow. Actually, when I think about it, I should have guessed that it was you."

I smile and slap him hard on the shoulder.

Carlo picks another pebble from his palm. "I think I can beat that. I took my mom's car and drove it around the block one night when she was out on a date. I ran over Mr. Bailey's letterbox."

I smile, genuinely impressed. "Cool. It doesn't quite beat the fire, though."

"Yeah, I guess," Carlo says, arcing the pebble out into the water. "How about this, then? One time I hit this girl with a stick and broke her arm." He smiles, looking at me from the corner of his eye and nudging me with his elbow.

"That's not a secret to anyone anymore," I say, half-laughing. Carlo grins back at me.

I find the biggest pebble in my hand and toss it into the pond.

"What was that one for?" asks Carlo.

I watch as the ripples spread out wider and wider until they reach the shore and disappear. "I've never been off the grounds of Blackstone Manor," I say with a sigh.

Carlo turns to me. "Really?"

I nod my head.

"You mean you've never been *anywhere* else? Not even to school?"

"Nope. Jonah homeschools me. He said I'm already so far ahead of other kids my age that school would be a step backward." I look away sadly into the shimmering water.

"Wow. I can't believe that I never knew that about you."

I look back at Carlo and try to force a smile, but I can't hide my sadness. Especially from him.

He smiles sympathetically. "Well, I think you're lucky, Finn. I don't know many kids that actually *want* to go to school."

"I want to more than anything. I'm sick of being around grownups all the time. I want to be around kids my own age. You're the only other kid I know!" I throw another stone into the water hard enough to skip it twice before it sinks. "I feel like I'm missing out on so many things. Sometimes it feels like the world is being kept away from me."

Carlo looks up at the huge willow branches overhanging the pond. "You're the smartest girl I know, Finn. Way smart enough to figure out how to get Jonah to send you to school. I mean, if that's what you really want."

I look over at Carlo. His thick black hair falling across his forehead, his emerald-green eyes, a smudge of dirt across the olive skin of his cheek. He really is very cute. It's not the first time I've thought so, but it is the first time that I realize that no one knows me better than the fourteen-year-old boy sitting beside me.

I look back at the pond and throw another pebble into the water. "You're the only real friend I have, Carlo."

He screws up his nose. "That's not true. What about Jonah? What about Beauty?"

"Ha! Jonah totally doesn't count, and Beauty is a horse!" I say, playfully punching him on the shoulder.

"Well . . ." Carlo says, flicking a pebble toward the pond. "You're the coolest girl I know. You could probably do anything."

"Thanks," I say sheepishly.

"You're also the prettiest girl I've ever seen. Especially when you smile like that."

I feel my cheeks flush red. I pick a larger rock out of the dirt and drop it into the pond, splashing him with droplets of water.

"Hey!" Carlo almost falls backward off the log. "You must have a really big secret for a rock like that!"

"Not a big secret. A big . . . question." I feel a bundle of nerves spark into life in the pit of my stomach. "Carlo. Have you ever . . . kissed a girl?"

He looks at me; his big emerald eyes go from my eyes, to my lips, and back again. "You mean *really* kiss?" he asks, his voice cracking slightly.

I nod.

He slowly shakes his head. I feel my heart beating in my chest like a drum. I swallow hard and will the words to come out.

"Do you think you would ever want to . . . kiss . . . me?" My stomach backflips with excitement just from asking.

His eyes are wide and his face is suddenly so serious. He bites his bottom lip and the tip of his tongue slowly peeks out between them, moistening them ever so slightly. Slowly, he nods.

I gingerly shuffle closer to him, my gaze fixed on his, my heart pounding. I hear the sound of the pebbles he's holding drop from his fingers and softly hit the ground. He wipes the dirt off his palm on the side of his shorts and gently takes my hand. We stare at each other for a moment, my breathing heavier than usual; my heart's beating now like it's trying to escape from my chest. An intense rush of adrenaline surges through my body as he slowly leans in. Time seems to slow to a crawl. The songs of the birds in the trees around us fade away into the distance. I feel my heartbeat in my ears. The closer he gets, the more aware I become of the heat of his skin. The dappled light of the afternoon sun reflects off the pond and dances across his face. He closes his eyes, gently presses his lips to mine, and, for an instant . . . the whole world disappears.

I close my eyes and drink in the sensation of my first kiss, how soft and warm his lips are, how giddy and strangely weak I feel, how tightly I grip his hand, how perfect this moment is. It lasts only for a few short, beautiful seconds, and when our lips part we look into each other's eyes, wondering if what just happened really happened. I look down and see our fingers entwined. Carlo smiles and so do I. It feels like we're the only two people left on earth.

"There you two are."

The voice from the top of the hill behind us breaks the spell like an electric shock. Carlo's dad has found us. Our hands shoot back to our sides. Did he see us kiss? My stomach twists into a knot. I feel like we've just been caught red-handed in the middle of the crime of the century.

We both look up and see Mr. Delgado standing there with his hands on his hips. "When you two have a minute, Major Brogan would like to see you both up at the main house. If I were you, I wouldn't keep him waiting." He turns and disappears back into the forest.

Carlo takes a deep breath. "If you ever go to school and you're told to go to the principal's office, it feels a lot like this," he says, swallowing hard and trying to force a smile. "I guess we'd better go, Finn."

I jump on the back of the quad bike and Carlo drives. He doesn't hurry. All the way back to the house I hold on to him, my arms tight around his waist. Even though we're both in trouble and heading for punishment, I can't help feeling so deliriously happy.

Carlo steers the bike along the path, across the grass verge, and up onto the circular driveway. I see Jonah in the distance, standing on the front steps of the main house with his arms folded, talking to Carlo's dad, who's sitting on a quad of his own. Surprisingly, instead of his usual suit and tie, Jonah is wearing his military fatigues, complete with black beret and spit-shined, black combat boots. Everyone, including me, knows that Jonah was a major in the army, but I've known him my whole life and I've never actually seen him in uniform, or ever really thought of him as a soldier. Not even with all the gun training we've done together.

I'm not afraid of Jonah, I never have been, and I've never had a reason to be. He's my teacher, my mentor, role model, and friend, and also my hero. But right now, as we get closer and I see him in that uniform, standing like a stone statue on the front steps, I can't help but feel a creeping sense of dread.

Carlo stops the bike a few feet away from the steps and cuts the engine. We both climb off and slowly walk to where Jonah is standing. With our heads hung low, we trudge unwillingly toward our fate, staring at the ground like condemned prisoners.

"I guess I'll leave you to it, Major," says Carlo's dad.

He revs up the bike, and without even a sideways glance, rides off past us and back in the direction of the stables. Jonah watches him in silence as he goes, over the rise of the hill and then across the field in the distance.

"What took you so long, boy?" Jonah says forcefully, taking us both by complete surprise, his voice echoing off the front of the house and reverberating around the driveway enclave.

"We were . . ." Carlo begins meekly.

"You were what?" booms Jonah's voice. Carlo flinches.

I step forward in defense of Carlo, ready to take the blame for anything. "We're sorry Jonah, we didn't . . ."

"Was I talking to you?" Jonah hisses, cutting me off. His icy glare pierces me. It's a look that I've never seen from him before, and it chills me to the core. Jonah stands there in silence, hands behind his back, glaring at each of us in turn. I catch his gaze and it feels like a cold laser beam, burning a hole through my skull. My eyes flick down to the ground again and stay there.

"You two have been running around here doing whatever you want for far too long. I thought you were good, responsible kids, and yet today, I find out that not only have you been fighting, taking things that don't belong to you without permission, and lying to me, but worst of all, deliberately causing harm to each other." Jonah's voice is so very serious. "Carlo. This is unacceptable behavior. Finn, I thought I raised you better than that."

"But, Jonah . . ." I peep croakily.

"Quiet, Finn!" Jonah barks.

This is the first time Jonah has ever really scolded me, and it does not feel good at all.

"Now, after reviewing all that has come to light today, it has become glaringly obvious to me that what you children lack is proper discipline. What you need is a firm hand to guide you, to be taught the difference between right and wrong and the consequences of your actions. Carlo, you will be spending every afternoon for the rest of the summer here with me and Finn, and in that time you will both address me as Major Brogan. Furthermore, until I say otherwise, the only words I want to hear coming out of your mouths are 'Sir, yes, sir!' Is that clear?"

Carlo and I look at each other. He looks as afraid as I feel. My Jonah has been body-snatched and replaced by this utterly terrifying stranger.

"I said, is that clear?"

"Sir, yes, sir," we say in unison.

"Good." Jonah gives us both another icy stare. I can't see it—my eyes are still on the dirt—but I can definitely feel it.

"Carlo. You've seen what Finn can do, how she can fix herself?"

"Sir, yes, sir," Carlo replies, his voice slightly trembling.

"Whom have you told?"

I watch Carlo's face from the corner of my eye. I can see him studying Jonah's expression. Carlo looks at me, then back at Jonah, and makes a snap decision. He lies.

"Nobody, sir."

Jonah stares him down, but Carlo doesn't break. I don't know why Carlo lied. Maybe he didn't want to get into any more trouble with Jonah than he already was? Whatever the reason, Jonah seems satisfied. "Alright, then. Until we know more about why and how it works, it will be a secret between the three of us. Tell absolutely no one. Understand?"

"Sir, yes, sir," we say in unison.

"Swear on it."

"We swear," we both say at the same time. Carlo even holds his right hand up in a three-fingered Boy Scouts' salute.

"Right. Now, both of you, follow me." Jonah turns and enters through the open front door. We quickly fall in step behind him as he leads us through the marble foyer, down the hallway beneath the main stairs, and toward the heavy oak and iron door that leads to the southern wing.

I have lived in this house my whole life and I have never been beyond this door. I have always known the southern wing to be by far the smallest and most boring of Blackstone Manor. It consists of nothing more than dusty storage rooms for old furniture and books. From the outside, by counting the chimneys, you can tell that there are four rooms: two on either side. You can see into the rooms through the little gaps in the curtains. I'm a curious kid so of course I looked, and, from what I saw, I was never really interested in going into any of them. All four rooms are connected by a central corridor. Two are not particularly large, and from what I could see, totally empty. No tables or chairs or even paintings on the walls. No rugs or anything. Just bare wooden floors, empty fireplaces, and dust.

One of the other two rooms on the opposite side is crammed wall to wall with folding chairs and wooden bench seats like the ones you would find in a church. There didn't seem to be any spare floor space in it at all. The last room is filled with cardboard boxes, most of which have the word "books" scrawled on their sides in thick red marker. I always assumed they were the spare ones that wouldn't fit on the shelves in the libraries.

Jonah takes a large key from his pocket, puts it in the lock of the ironclad door, and turns it to the right. The lock clicks loudly; he pushes the door open and flicks the light switch on the wall. Jonah stands to one side. "In you go, both of you," he orders.

I look past the open door and see exactly what I expected to: a musty hallway with high ceilings and four closed doors, a faded carpet running down the length of it, ending at a wall with a window, its thick curtains drawn. This whole situation is horrible. What is he going to do to us? Lock us in the southern wing? No, of course not! Maybe he's gonna make us clean the place. It could certainly use a good vacuuming.

Whatever he has in store for us is a total mystery. I look up at Jonah, hoping to see his serious face break into a smile, to laugh out loud and tell us that this is all a big joke. That he was just trying to scare us and that he hopes we learned our lesson, but his face is still stoic and stony and as deathly serious as before.

"I have to go help my father with the horses, Major Brogan," Carlo whimpers in a final attempt to escape whatever punishment awaits us. I can hear the fear in his voice.

"In," Jonah says, ignoring his plea. Carlo and I look at each other, and then slowly shuffle in past him. Jonah steps in, closes the heavy door behind him, and locks it. Then, with one last glare he flicks the light switch off, plunging the hallway into darkness. The only light is a razor-thin shaft peeking through the edge of the curtain at the end of the hall sixty feet away.

Now I'm afraid. In the dark I grab Carlo's wrist and squeeze. The ridiculous notion that my father has ordered Jonah to kill us flits through my mind.

"Don't move an inch, and don't say a word," orders Jonah. He really didn't need to tell me that, considering that I'm already frozen to the spot and freaking out too much to say anything, anyway.

Jonah clears his throat. "Onix, verify voice command authority Jonah One."

Out of nowhere, and yet everywhere, a calm, warm, male voice fills every corner of the dim hallway.

"Voice command authority Jonah One verified."

A pale-blue light blinks on, emanating from the skirting boards of the hallway, illuminating the whole space. Carlo and I are both on nervous edge, scanning the hallway for the source of the voice, but there's no one there but the three of us.

"Welcome back, Major Brogan. I see we have some visitors," says the voice.

I tighten my grip on Carlo's arm and look up at Jonah. He's looking blankly into space as he speaks. "Yes, Onix. Carlo and Finn here will be joining me in sublevel one today. Say hello, you two."

"Hello to who?" I inquire, looking around and up and down the corridor.

"Onix is the computer operating system that administrates sublevel one of Blackstone Manor."

"Sublevel what?" I ask, louder than I should.

"Hello, Onix," Carlo says with a look of wonder.

"Hello, Carlo."

"Wow," Carlo whispers with obvious awe. "I thought your house was cool before, Finn, but this is totally next level."

"Hello . . . Onix?" I say to the ceiling.

"Hello, Finn. Welcome back."

"What do you mean, 'welcome *back*'?"

"We have met many times."

"But I've never been in the southern wing before."

"Yes, you have, Finn. You were . . ."

"That's enough chitchat, Onix," interrupts Jonah. "Open sublevel access please." At Jonah's instruction, there's a computerized tone of acknowledgment, and the rug at the end of the hall rolls back all by itself. With a quiet whirring sound, an oblong pod made of glass and shiny silver metal rises from the floor. A sliding door on the front silently glides open.

"Go to the end of the hall, kids," instructs Jonah.

"Sir, yes, sir," spouts Carlo. Sensing adventure, and suddenly oblivious to the possibility of still being punished, Carlo breaks free from my grip and marches like a soldier down the hall toward the pod.

Carlo looks back over his shoulder at me with an expression of excited rapture.

"Jonah, please stop messing around. What's going on? What's sub-level one? What was Onix talking about? Meeting me before?" I ask again.

He looks down at me and finally cracks a tiny smile.

"Onix is mistaken; he's just having a memory glitch, that's all. As for everything else, it'll all make sense in good time."

Jonah puts his hands on my shoulders.

"I'm sorry if I scared you back there, but from now on things are going to be a little more serious, and I need you to take me seriously. You're growing up fast, and there are many very important things I need to teach you if I'm going to send you out to school." The last three words that came out of Jonah's mouth wedge themselves in my mind, and my heart almost explodes. How did he know?

I spring toward him and clamp my arms around his waist. "Thank you, Jonah!"

Jonah takes my wrists and gently unwraps me. "Don't thank me yet. You'll have to earn it. From now on, from four to seven every day, you are Cadet Blackstone, and I am Major Brogan. Follow my instructions and pass my tests, and then maybe, when I think you're ready, you can go to school. No promises, though—understand?"

I stand at attention and give my best attempt at a salute. "Sir, yes, sir."

"Very good, Cadet. Now go and join Cadet Delgado and let's get to work."

"Jonah . . . I mean Major Brogan, sir? Why is Carlo here, too?"

"You like him and trust him, don't you?"

I'm suddenly grateful for the blue light in the hall hiding the red of the blush I feel on my face. I nod.

"Well then, I trust him, too. Carlo will learn what you will learn, and together you will go further faster. You can talk to each other about what you've learned and practice your combat training together. After I teach you how to do it responsibly, of course. No more hitting anyone with sticks and stones, and no more broken bones, if I can help it."

"Combat training?" I say, wide-eyed.

"Yes, Finn. The world can be a dangerous place, and I want to know that you can defend yourself if you have to. I will teach you discipline, how to control your emotions, and how to maximize your physical skills responsibly. Discipline, control, and responsibility. These are the things you will learn. And if I'm going to teach you all of that, then, to begin with, you'll need a sparring partner that's not six foot seven inches tall, like me. Now move it, Cadet; you've both got a lot of work to do."

"Sir, yes, sir!" I shout and run down the hall where Carlo is already happily standing in the silver pod. Jonah follows close behind and joins us inside. The door slides shut.

"Are you ready?" he asks, and we nod in unison. "Alright, then. Onix. Take us down."

The glass on the pod lets us see in all directions. I take another look at the hallway that only a few short minutes ago I thought was the most boring place in the world. I turn and look at Carlo, the boy that, until this afternoon by the pond, was just my summertime playmate who cleaned the stables and fed the horses. I look up at Jonah, who I now call Major Brogan, and who now calls me Cadet. It's funny how everything can change in an instant. The pod slowly begins to descend; the floor of the hallway looks as though it's rising to meet us instead of us being the ones sinking into it. Soon, all I can see of the corridor is a blue circle of light through the ceiling of the pod. Suddenly, the whole thing drops and my stomach floats as if it's weightless. I let out a little yelp and my hand instinctively shoots out to find Carlo's. He smiles and grips my fingers tightly as the pod takes us deeper.

I look into his eyes through the dim blue light and whisper, "Don't you dare let go."

CHAPTER SEVEN

I open my eyes, squinting at the harsh glare of bright-white surfaces. Someone is squeezing my hand. Even though their face is blurry, I know it's not Carlo. Big, brown, sympathetic doe eyes come into focus. They're framed by thick black glasses perched on a pretty freckled face with a mane of frizzy brown hair.

"Bit?"

"Hi, Finn. Everything's OK. You're in the nurse's office. Well, kinda . . ."

I pull my hand back, sit up on my elbows, and try to remember what happened. I peer around the room. It's small with a gray linoleum floor and stark white walls. The bright light seems to be coming directly from them. One of the walls has a doctor's eye chart printed on it. There are cupboards above a small metal basin, one chair for Bit, a bed for me, and a small desk and chair in the corner.

"What's going on?" I murmur.

"You fainted," replies Bit.

"My arm . . . did I break my arm?" I say, stroking the skin below my wrist.

Bit frowns and smirks. "Nnnooo. But you might have hit your head if you think that you did."

It takes a moment for the fog to clear, and everything gradually begins to sink in. I remember clearly the day Carlo and I met Onix. It was the day of my first kiss, so it's not easy to forget, but I don't remember breaking my arm that day. Or any bones, ever, for that matter, let alone intentionally, over and over again for years on end like a crazy person. Everything I saw was exactly the way I remember it happening—except for that. Why has my imagination suddenly decided to warp my memories so drastically? Willing my bones to heal? It's ridiculous, not to mention impossible.

I stare at Bit for a second, most likely looking as confused as I feel. She smiles at me warmly. All of a sudden, my stomach lurches as my mother's face flashes into my mind with an electric jolt.

Did I imagine it?!

No.

It was as if my mother had stepped right out of her photograph, her features unchanged by time. But how?

"The woman in the silver suit." I ask croakily, "Where is she?"

"It was insane, Finn; you should have seen it!" Bit says excitedly. "Ryan caught you when you fainted and the silver woman activated this room. It literally grew up out of the ground. First the bed appeared and everyone totally freaked out. Ryan lifted you onto it, and then the walls and everything came up out of the ground around us. It was so cool. The tech here is wicked serious, Finn. I've never even heard of stuff anything like this existing. Your dad is beyond brilliant."

"Where did the woman in silver go, Bit?"

"Oh yeah, sorry. She rushed back into the jungle, and just after that the tour guide turned up and called for the nurse. The nurse is out there now, talking to Professor Francis."

I swing my legs over the side of the bed and stand up. Bit springs from her chair with her arms outstretched.

"I'm fine," I grumble and head for the door. At least I would if there *was* a door. I look all around the room. Apart from the eye chart, the walls are blank.

"It's over there, in the corner," says Bit, pointing at a bare white section. I crane my head forward, squinting, scanning for a handle or a hinge or a button when a door-sized hole suddenly slides open with a hiss and a young blonde woman walks in. She's dressed in a white coverall uniform with white shoes and bright-blue gloves, a bold red cross emblazoned on her chest.

"You're conscious. Good. I'm Nurse Talbot. How do you feel?"

"Um . . . OK, I guess."

"That's good. Would you excuse us for a moment, please?" the nurse says to Bit. "Just going to give your friend here a final check-over."

"Oh, of course." Giving me a little worried smile over her shoulder, Bit slinks out the door; it seals shut behind her with a quiet hiss.

"Finn Brogan, is it?" asks Nurse Talbot.

"Ah, yes."

"Sit down, please," the nurse instructs, lightly shoving me onto the edge of the bed.

"Hey," I protest.

She clicks on a penlight and shines it in my eyes. "Keep still, please." She waves it from one eye to the other, and then clicks it off. "Any dizziness? Nausea?"

"Nope."

"Alright, then. I'll just log this session, Miss Brogan, and then you can go and rejoin your friends."

Nurse Talbot goes to the wall. "Computer. Chart." There's a single beep of acknowledgment and a screen blinks onto the blank wall. She begins tapping away on it with her finger.

"Ah, excuse me, nurse?"

"Yes, what is it?"

"The woman who met us when we arrived. Can I ask who she is?"

The nurse keeps tapping at the screen. "Woman?"

"She was dressed all in silver."

"Oh. She was not a 'she' at all. 'She,' as you call her, was a Drone Template. A worker robot. Around here we call them DTs."

"But . . . I've seen robots before," I say with a frown. "They cut the grass at school. They're clunky plastic and metal. They *look* like robots. But the way that woman moved and spoke, she . . . she looked *real*. Human. And her face, it was exactly like my . . . my mother's."

Nurse Talbot stops tapping and looks over at me. "Your mother?"

"My dead mother," I reply flatly.

"Oh, I see. The surprise of seeing your deceased mother's face shocked you into fainting. That explains everything."

I'm a little taken aback by her cold analysis. "But how?"

"Well, I don't know the exact technical workings; I'm not an engineer." She swipes her finger across the screen and it vanishes. "But I do know that on the very rare occasion when Drones are required to speak with visitors, their protective faceplate changes shape to make interactions more . . . personable. I'm not even sure what a DT was doing there. I've never heard of one being instructed to greet guests before. Anyway, apparently you thought it resembled your deceased mother. Quite an unfortunate coincidence, I must say."

"Ya think?" I grunt, shuffling off the bed. "Y'know, you really need to work on your bedside manner."

Judging by her blank expression, my not-so-subtle insult seems to go right over Nurse Talbot's head. Either that or she simply ignored it.

"How do I get out of here?"

Nurse Talbot points at a spot on the floor. "Please stand in the center of the room."

I take a couple of steps forward.

"Computer. Infirmary construct alpha dissolve," she says into midair.

There is a single beep and then a quiet hissing sound. A hole suddenly grows open in the ceiling and I can see blue sky peeking through treetops. The hole expands to the top edges of the walls and they slide down into the floor, revealing the dense jungle surrounding us. The desk, chairs, basin, and bed all sink into the ground, as well, followed by the gray linoleum floor, which disappears into the soil like oil soaking into a sponge. After a few seconds, it's like there was never even a room here at all. Just dirt and twigs. Sitting on a stone bench on the edge of the clearing that used to be the infirmary are Bit, and, surprisingly, Ryan Forrester.

"You can all take the path back to your classmates," says Nurse Talbot.

I'm about to ask what path she's talking about when she announces, "Computer, open pathway to center." The jungle undergrowth parts all by itself and a shiny white tile pushes up through the ground beside the stone bench. It's joined by another and another, building itself tile by tile into a path that soon snakes off into the distance along the forest floor, disappearing around a corner into the tangled foliage.

"Enjoy your visit," Nurse Talbot says blankly. She turns and looks down toward a bare patch of soil. "Computer. Stairwell."

There's a quiet beep and steps instantly form into a descending staircase. She walks down them and is soon gone from sight. The opening molds over with earth again and we're alone.

Ryan walks over to me. "Wow. How freaking amazing is this place?!" He grabs my hand. "How are you feeling?"

"Um, I'm OK," I say. The truth is, my face feels suddenly hot.

"I asked the Professor if I could stay behind with Betty to check if you were OK. He and the tour guide took the others to the center to get them out of the way, and said they'd wait for us there."

"It's Bettina, not Betty," her voice pipes up from behind him. "And Finn doesn't like to be touched."

Ryan looks down at our hands. "Oh," he says, letting go. "Sorry."

"No, it's OK, really." I almost stammer the words, not knowing where to look.

"I think we should go. Here's your bag, Finn," Bit says, shoving my shoulder satchel into my hands. "I don't wanna miss anything good." Her eyes throw daggers at Ryan as she huffs down the white-tile path curving off into the jungle.

With Bit leading the way, we set off along the path through the rainforest. Brightly colored butterflies flit from leaf to leaf beside us as we go. Howler monkeys bellow down at us from the branches overhead. There are rustling and crunching sounds in the undergrowth all around us. I never imagined a jungle could be so beautiful and so noisy all at the same time. Ryan is gazing open-mouthed at our surroundings, obviously enthralled by it all.

"Hey," I say. "Thanks for catching me . . . y'know, when I fell."

"You're welcome," he says smiling, his eyes holding my gaze. He is seriously gorgeous. I can't stop myself from smiling back.

"Hey, can I ask you a question, Finn?"

"Sure."

"What do you think of this place so far?"

"It's amazing."

"What do you think of that Richard Blackstone guy?"

My stomach twists. "What do you mean?"

"Everyone knows that he's a total shut-in. He never goes outside, ever. Even when he's on TV, it's always a video interview deal. Don't you think it's weird?"

"I don't know. I've never really thought about it much." Single biggest fib ever.

"Well, I think he's crazy," Ryan says, circling his finger around at his temple. "If he had any kids, they would probably be crazy, too."

I look sideways at Ryan. He's looking at the ground. Does he know something about me that he shouldn't? Whether he does or not, this topic is getting a little too specific and insulting for me.

"Most of the billion-dollar brats I've met are a sandwich and some cake short of a picnic," I say venomously. "Arrogant, overprivileged, badly parented idiots. You're probably no different yourself."

Ryan smiles. "I think I'm pretty normal considering I was raised mostly by servants."

That strikes a chord deep down. "Really? Me too."

"My dad is Travis Forrester. Have you heard of him?"

"Yeah, Forrester Aerospace, right?"

"Yeah. When I was little, my mom died and my dad married a supermodel. She doesn't like kids, so from the age of four to seven I was homeschooled while they traveled the world. Then I was sent to any expensive military training school that would take me. So far I've been kicked out of nine."

"Wow. Not an 'A' student then," I say with a smile.

Ryan chuckles and shakes his head. "Nope. I learned how to fly a plane but I just never quite got the hang of keeping out of trouble. Daddy would be soooo proud."

"Sorry to hear about your mother," I say honestly. "Mine died when I was a baby."

Ryan looks a little surprised. "I'm sorry, too. Sucks, right?"

I nod in agreement.

"Sometimes I wish I were a normal kid. Anyone but a Forrester. With a normal family and an ordinary dad."

I can see the sadness in Ryan's eyes. It's the same familiar kind of sadness I've seen so many times in the mirror. To my surprise, I find myself reaching across the path and curling my fingers gently around his.

He turns and smiles and softly squeezes my hand. "I guess we've got a lot in common, Finn Brogan." Deep inside I melt just a little.

Bit stops in the middle of the path and spins around. My hand whips back to my side. "Boohoo, at least you both have dads. My mom raised me by herself; I don't even know who my dad is!"

"Who's your mom, Betty?" asks Ryan.

Bit's brow crinkles angrily; she pushes her glasses firmly onto the bridge of her nose and plants her hands on her hips, jutting her elbows out in defiant angles. "For the last time, my name is Bettina Otto. *Not* Betty."

"Sorry," Ryan says, holding his hands up in mock surrender. "Oh wait, your mom must be Katherine Otto. She owns the second-biggest tech company in the world."

"Yes, that's right," Bit replies with an angry tone that I've never heard from her before. "Always second to Blackstone," she says, glancing at me. "Story of my life," she mutters as she turns back onto the path and storms off ahead of us.

"Whoa! What was all that about?" asks Ryan.

"Ah . . . she must really be annoyed that you got her name wrong," I reply with the first lame made-up excuse that comes to mind.

Ryan shrugs his shoulders. "I heard you both talking at lunch yesterday. I honestly thought Bit was short for Betty."

"Eavesdropping on our conversations, Mr. Forrester? That's a little creepy, don't you think?"

Ryan smiles. "I just wanted to know what your name was."

A cloud of butterflies takes flight in my stomach. "Really?"

"Yes. Really," Ryan says with that cute, crooked grin of his. "And now I've pissed off your best friend. This is not going as well as I would have liked."

"I'm sure she'll get over it. And it's not going as badly as you think."

"Oh, really?"

I just smile and keep my eyes on the path.

"So . . . um, Bit is short for Bettina? I'm making sure I get this right."

"Kinda. Bit is actually taken from the online name she uses. '8-bit.' Her real last name, Otto, means 'eight,' and 'bit' is like a computer bit. She's forgotten more about computers than I'll ever know. Bettina Otto is an amazing gamer, and an even better hacker."

"No way."

"Yep. You better be careful; Bit could erase your life with just a few keystrokes," I say with a cheeky grin.

Ryan suddenly looks a little nervous.

"Just kidding," I say quickly.

Ryan smiles and breathes a tiny sigh of relief, but I'm actually not kidding. She's really that good. In fact, just last year, hacking was exactly how she found out who I really am. It seems that even Onix can't make a fake identity good enough to fool Bit for very long. I swear one time I woke up in the middle of the night and saw her staring at her computer slate as code spilled onto the screen. It looked like she was typing with her mind. She can't have been; I know it's ridiculous, and, considering my relative lack of computer expertise compared to Bit, I could totally be wrong—but cross my heart, that's what it looked like.

We follow the path the rest of the way in silence. Soon we are distracted from the rainforest noises by sounds of a different kind. There's a loud crack, and then what sounds like a huge crowd cheering.

The path curves around a thick clump of trees and ends at a tall blue wall with an open doorway, a tangled curtain of jungle vines hanging over it. Through the gaps in between them, I can see movement. Is that Brody? Ryan pushes his arms through the vines, spreads them aside, and we step out of the dappled shadows of the jungle and into bright sunshine.

With only two words, Ryan describes out loud exactly how I feel—two words I would have said myself if Jonah hadn't raised me not to swear. Inexplicably, stretching out high and wide before us, are tall gleaming grandstands filled with thousands of people surrounding the perfectly manicured grass of a full-sized baseball stadium. I look behind us and the door is still there, vines hanging just on the other side of it, but it's as if we've just walked through a portal and arrived in an entirely different country.

A little way in the distance, Brody is jogging from second base to third, waving to the crowd as an entire baseball team in the outfield watches him go, hands on their hips and disgruntled looks on all their faces. "HOME RUN" flashes in huge capital letters on a giant screen above the scoreboard on the other side of the stadium. He taps his foot on third base and jogs around to home base. He jumps on home plate and bows to the crowd, which erupts into even louder cheers and applause.

"Let's go," Ryan says excitedly and jogs off across the field toward Brody. I follow right behind him. As we get closer I spot everyone else, including Bit, who seems to be avoiding eye contact with me, sitting on wooden benches under the low roof of the dugout. They're listening to a man talk. He's wearing a pale-blue jacket over a crisp, white collared shirt, red tie, and black pants, and has sandy-blond hair so thick with gel it almost looks like a plastic-molded wig.

"This is so cool!" Ryan says, high-fiving Brody.

"Yeah it is!" he replies joyfully.

I join the boys and walk down the steps into the dugout.

"Ah, here she is," the man in the jacket says, holding a hand out in my direction. "I hope you're feeling better, Miss Brogan?"

I nod at him.

"Oh, that is good. Anyway, my name is Percy Blake and I will be your tour guide today. How did that home run feel, Brody?" Percy asks.

"It was awesome," Brody says with a wide grin.

"Good, I'm glad you enjoyed it." Percy beams a huge, gleaming, white-toothed smile.

Brody, Ryan, and I walk past the others and bunch together on the far end of one of the benches.

"What did we miss?" Ryan whispers.

"Percy asked us to think of something we've always wanted to see or do. I said hit a home run against the Tokyo Katanas and he made all this appear. Before that, Dean asked for a T. rex and one totally burst out of the jungle; it was roaring and stomping around like it was real! I think Miss Cole almost crapped herself."

"Whoa," Ryan marvels, staring into the rainforest. "How can they fit a whole stadium in here?" he asks quietly. "The dome was big, but not big enough for a jungle and the whole of Kyosho Stadium."

"I dunno," Brody says with a dopey look on his face. "But it's awesome."

"Shhhh," Miss Cole hisses at them from farther along the line.

"Righty-o!" announces Percy. "Now that we're all here, I can fill you in on what we will be seeing and doing today at Blackstone Technologies!" Percy waves his arms in a wide sweeping motion like the ringmaster of a three-ring circus. "If you would all be so kind as to follow me to the conference area."

"C'mon everyone," chips in Professor Francis and we all stand, looking from side to side, wondering which way to go. Percy turns, walks up the short steps of the dugout, and out into the middle of the baseball diamond. We follow in a muddled group behind him.

"Computer. Dissolve stadium display gamma one," Percy commands. There's an echoing tone of acknowledgment, and, with that now-familiar hissing sound, the baseball diamond, the bases, the players, and the bat that Brody left on the field all melt down into the grass. Even the grass itself is sucked into the ground. Miss Cole jumps from one foot to the other, screeching like a little girl as the grass disappears from under her feet, and everyone, including me, can't help laughing.

The crowds in the stands, the stands themselves, the scoreboard, and the sunny blue sky overhead all flicker, then vanish into darkness like someone has thrown a switch and turned off the world. Spots of blue light blink on, forming a wide circle around the edge of the dark clearing, and I notice that a shiny gray tile floor is now where the grass used to be. The whole place is dark—not so dark that you can't see, but the same kind of dark it goes in a theater just before the movie starts. It's eerily quiet. Even the jungle is silent.

Some of the ambient light from the blue circles reflects off the high black curve of the dome. They must have closed it after I passed out. If I didn't know it was daylight outside the dome, I would swear it was the middle of the night. It appears that the blue sky I saw just a few seconds ago over the field, the same blue sky that I saw peeking through the treetops on the walk through the jungle, was actually some kind of projection on the wall of the dome. That explains the stadium, too. They weren't real; they were merely 3-D illusions on a screen. An amazing, hyper-realistic picture—but only a picture. Is anything here real?

"Computer," Percy announces. "Conference table construct beta."

There's that familiar tone again, and a bright light flicks on from somewhere overhead, shining down in a wide circle. Four glowing red patches suddenly appear on the floor, painting themselves into lines at our feet. They quickly meet at the corners, forming the outline of a large rectangle beneath us. One by one, shorter red lines draw themselves and connect into squares down the long edges of the rectangle. After a few seconds there are fifteen red squares, eight on one side of the red rectangle and seven on the other.

"Everyone please stand outside the red lines," says Percy.

Everyone obeys and steps back. As soon as we do, a shiny white conference table rises up from inside the red rectangle and stops at waist height. It's closely followed by fifteen high-backed chairs that form up from the squares like wax reverse-melting, one chair oozing up from the floor for each of us.

"Please take a seat, everyone," says Percy.

With a few amused giggles and assorted looks of wonder, people begin sliding chairs toward them and sitting down. I look over at Bit; she's standing by the edge of the conference table. She still seems annoyed at me for some reason. A reason that I suspect involves Ryan. Sometimes I forget how sensitive Bit can be, and I did kinda ignore her back there in the jungle. I decide to extend an olive branch. I pull a chair out for her and nod toward it. Her sullen expression softens and she sulkily traipses over, plops herself down, and gives me a little smile. I grin at her and take my seat beside her. Ryan sits next to me. Karla Bassano chooses a seat directly across from him and slides seductively into her chair, staring at him like they're the only two people in the room.

Ick.

"Good," Percy says, walking to the head of the table. "Before we officially begin the tour, we must attend to a few formalities. If you would all be so kind as to put all your electronic devices on the table." Almost immediately, worried looks appear on most of the faces in the group.

Margaux looks at Percy with an expression like she's sucking on a sour lemon-drop. "Excuse me? No one takes my phone. If that's what you're thinking of doing, then you can forget it."

Percy smiles warmly. "I assure you, your phone will be quite safe. Blackstone Technologies has many ongoing projects that I'm sure our competitors would love to have a sneak peek at. We can't risk anything leaking out before it's ready, now, can we? I know that none of you good people would ever think of doing such a despicable thing, but I'm afraid it's our policy to collect all electronic devices before a tour commences."

"All of you, please put your phones and computer slates on the table; you too, Miss Pilfrey," Professor Francis says wearily.

Margaux crosses her arms and points her expensive nose defiantly into the air.

From everyone except Margaux there's shuffling in bags and taps and clatters of phones and computer slates on the table. I fish through my satchel, retrieve my phone, and lay it down in front of me. Jonah got it for me for Christmas a couple of years ago, so it's way out of date compared to everyone else's. It's a little embarrassing that everyone here, even the Professor, has the latest-model Blackstone Jett 10, and

I, the daughter of the man who owns the company, have this crappy old Jett 8.

"What the hell is that thing?" a voice says from across the table. I look up and see Brent Fairchild pointing in my direction. I'm prepared for this. I don't seek that moron's approval. *So I have an old holophone, big deal. Get with the teasing, Brent, and move on.*

He laughs mockingly. "Is that a Zortzi 4?"

That's when I notice that he's not pointing at my old phone. He's pointing at Bit's. Her face turns beet red as she tries to cover it with her Blackstone computer slate.

"Yeah, so what," she mumbles quietly.

"It's lame, that's what," Brent whispers cruelly. "Just like the third-rate company that made it."

Bit turns away, obviously hurt.

"Oh wait, doesn't your mother's company make those?"

"Shut up, Brent," I seethe.

Brent leans forward and whispers with treacle-dipped sarcasm. "Sorry, didn't mean to offend. They really are pretty decent."

I touch Bit's elbow to see if she's OK. She ignores Brent, looks at me, and we share a little smile.

"Except for the name . . ." Brent whispers, and our smiles vanish. ". . . Zortzi 4? Sounds like some kind of skin abscess."

"Hey Brent . . . what's a Zortzi 4?" whispers Brody, and Brent shrugs. "Wiping your ass with."

Brody grins like it's the cleverest thing he's ever said, which, sadly, it probably is. Brent offers up a covert fist bump as they both snicker quietly like the idiots they are.

"Shut your mouths . . . or I'll shut them for you," I growl.

Brent raises his eyebrows. "Gorgeous *and* fiery?" The same lecherous look that he reserves for his swooning lacrosse groupies oozes onto his face. "Tell me, Finn, how can it be possible that you and I have never hooked up?"

Ryan leans forward, gripping the edge of the table, his narrow-eyed glare fixed on Brent.

Brent smiles at him, meeting the challenge, then turns back to me and winks.

I honestly almost throw up in my mouth.

"What's going on down there?" Professor Francis calls from the other end of the table. "Pay attention, please, and Margaux, surrender your phone or spend the rest of the day on the bus with no one to complain to but the driving computer."

She rolls her eyes, plonks her hot-pink, genuine-diamond-encrusted Jett 10 on the table, and mouths, "Whatever."

"Thank you, everyone," says Percy. He touches a button on the edge of the table, and all the phones and computer slates slowly submerge into the surface and disappear from sight like they've sunk into a vat of glossy-white paint. The morphing ability of everything here is becoming less and less shocking, but it's still very cool to watch.

"They will all be safe and sound and waiting for you at the end of the day. Next, if you would all be so kind as to sign a confidentiality agreement." Percy presses the edge of the table again and digital pages of text blink into view on the surface: one for everyone. "This is merely a formality that we must insist on before the tour continues. It's simply to ensure that if you tell anyone about what you've seen here, we have the permission to hunt you down and brutally murder you and your entire family." Some of the group looks up at Percy in shocked concern, and he chuckles. "I'm kidding, of course. But on a serious note, you can and will be prosecuted if you divulge any private Blackstone information to anyone, so, from this moment on, everything you see and hear will all be tippity-top secret. Just press your thumb anywhere on the document and consider yourselves part of a very select few."

"Do as Mr. Blake asks, please, everyone, and we can get this show on the road," Professor Francis says, his voice tinged with excitement.

One by one, thumbs on both sides of the table press the pages, and one by one, with happy little tones of thanks, the pages turn bright green and vanish.

"Thank you, everyone! Now, let me officially begin the tour: Welcome to the wondrous Blackstone Technologies Research and Development complex."

A short burst of trumpet fanfare comes out of nowhere, the surface of the table ripples, and suddenly, a glossy-white scale model of Blackstone Technologies' grounds and buildings morphs up right before our eyes, taking up the entire length of the table from end to end.

There's a round of "whoas" and "wows" and a "Hells yeah!" from Dean McCarthy, who stands up immediately, excitedly taking in the whole extensive diorama. Most of the others, including me and Bit, do exactly the same thing. There's the road that leads to the car park outside, the arch that we walked under, and the dome that we're in right now. There are two more domes in a line behind this one, each a little smaller than the last, and all are connected by a twisting network of paths and tree-lined walkways. Suspended monorails weave in and out of architecturally beautiful geometric buildings and warehouses that are elegantly, almost artistically positioned between and around the three domes. The model is so detailed, it's incredible. Landscaped gardens complete with flowers and individual blades of grass are modeled into it. I even spot a little pond surrounded by stone-bench seating, the water's surface rippling from feeding fish as overhanging trees, perfectly sculpted right down to the leaf, gently sway as if they're being rustled by a breeze. Everything is there, precisely rendered in miniature glossy white. Even our school bus has been included. Seeing it all like this makes it glaringly clear how absolutely huge this dome is. It's so big that it easily obscures the other buildings from the car park. The whole complex must extend for at least ten or twelve miles.

"Everyone, sit down, please," says Professor Francis. Percy gives him a smile and a nod of thanks before he continues.

"Blackstone Technologies, or 'Blackstone Tech,' as we call it around here, is the world leader in cutting-edge, advanced scientific research and development. That's right, people; this is where we invent it all. You should consider yourselves extremely privileged to be here today. You are only the fourth group to have been granted a tour and the first group of school students ever. I must admit that I was quite surprised to see a high-school tour on my schedule at first, but I don't doubt for a second that your very influential parents had something to do with that!"

Percy waves his hand dramatically over the model. "Everything you will see today was developed by our scientists and engineers under the guidance of our founder and CEO, the esteemed Dr. Richard Blackstone. I'm sure you all know who he is!"

I know who he is, alright. But then again, I'm his daughter and even I don't really know who he is at all. It seems everything about him is a secret, and thanks to Jonah that also includes me. I try to shake off the unpleasant thought and focus back on Percy.

"Is Dr. Blackstone here today?" asks Sherrie Polito.

"Well, I'm not at liberty to answer that question," replies Percy. "But, I do have another little surprise for you."

Percy leans over, touches the table, and all of a sudden that writhing, hissing sound can be heard whispering beneath the rising volume of the valiant opening notes of a stirring piece of classical music. Everyone turns to look as a white amorphous blob begins forming up from the floor beside a goofily smiling Percy. Higher and higher it rises until, after only a few seconds, it has smoothed into a shiny column at least twelve feet tall. Suddenly, as if air is being vacuumed out from inside the shape, it begins tightening into the figure of a giant man, growing taller still as the rousing music gets even louder. The surface of the shape compresses further, and soon the sharp details of a crisp white suit, lustrous, black collared shirt, and bold red tie have adorned the growing effigy. Flesh tones and details flush into the statue's hands and face as eyes and eyebrows, lips, a moustache, and neatly trimmed and combed jet-black hair morph onto the towering, now fifteen-foot-tall, hyper-realistic-looking, *unbelievably* egotistical monument of none other than Dr. Blackstone himself.

The huge statue moves, placing its hands on its hips, and, as the music reaches its triumphant climax, it tilts its giant head to stare heroically toward a distant imaginary horizon.

I subtly look around the table. Everyone except me and Bit seems to be awestruck, all of them wide-eyed and smiling up at the ridiculous thing. Even though no one but Bit knows that I'm his daughter, I can't help but feel incredibly embarrassed. I hope with all my heart that this wasn't my father's idea.

Percy looks absolutely chuffed. "Ladies and gentlemen. Scientist. Inventor. Visionary. Philanthropist. Genius. Dr. Richard Blackstone." Amy Dee and Sherrie Polito actually start applauding. With obvious enthusiasm, Percy presses the edge of the table again and the music resumes, a softer piece this time, full of gentle reverence. The statue's arms dramatically sweep open, looking out over us as if it were addressing a thronging audience of fervent admirers as it begins to speak.

"Everything in our wonderful reality is connected. If you could look closely enough, down to the smallest parts, you would discover that you're made of the same things that your toaster or an elephant or a neutron star or a bacterium or a lobster or a cheesecake or a dandelion is made of. Like infinitesimally tiny ballerinas, these unimaginably small parts make everything that exists by dancing to the infinite myriad of symphonies played by our wondrous universe. Just take a moment, and imagine the endless miracles we can achieve when humankind is finally able to wave the very baton of creation and conduct the music of the cosmic orchestra of reality itself."

The music ends and Amy and Sherrie start clapping again; this time they're joined by Jennifer, Karla, Miss Cole, and Professor Francis, all of whom are smiling and nodding and fawning up at the statue of my father which, to my relief, is very slowly reverting to a blob and sinking back down into the floor.

Percy holds his hand over his heart and sighs. "That gets me every time. Anyway, where were we? Oh yes . . . we are currently inside Dome One, the main dome." With another press of the table, little glowing holographic labels blink on all over the three-dimensional map, hovering and slowly rotating above every structure in front of us. I notice Bit suddenly take a new and special interest in the map. I can see her scanning the tabletop, mentally noting the labels and their corresponding buildings as her finger, poised by her glasses, makes little pecks at the air, pointing from one tiny floating signpost to the next.

"This is where most of the computer-controlled constructs are created," says Percy. "Things such as the jungle and the sports stadium and the tyrannosaurus you saw earlier. And, of course, slightly less exciting things like this table and these chairs."

Jennifer's hand shoots up.

"A question?" asks Percy.

"What are the constructs made of?" Jennifer asks, scratching at the edge of the table with her fingernail.

"That's a very good question. Does anyone hazard a guess?" Percy asks, scanning the group.

"Holograms," blurts Brody.

"That's a good guess," says Percy. "But incorrect. As I'm sure you know, holograms are merely projections of light. Constructs have weight and physical mass. Anyone else?"

"Some kind of force field?" asks Ashley Farver.

"That's a good guess, too, but not quite right I'm afraid."

"What do you think, Finn?" Ryan whispers to me.

"I dunno," I whisper with a shrug. "Maybe . . . nano grains?"

"Who said that? Was that you, Miss Brogan?" asks Percy. Everyone turns to look at me. "Did you say . . . nano grains?"

I nod sheepishly.

"That is a very good guess indeed! How do you know about nano grains?"

"Ah, I must have read it somewhere? On a science site or something, I think." For someone who couldn't lie her way out of a paper bag, I seem to do it quite often.

Percy raises his eyebrows and nods. "Like I said, very good guess. Unfortunately, still incorrect."

Margaux smiles and snorts in my direction, obviously delighted that I got it wrong.

"They are actually formed from a meta-material that is made up of incredibly tiny separate pieces called quantum grains. Miss Brogan was almost right. Nano grains were the predecessors of quantum grains. We've improved them quite a lot since then. Basically, quantum grains are like itsy-bitsy building blocks. When they're combined with billions of shifting magnetic microfields and the correct program, the computer can construct realistic simulations of almost anything. The potential applications of this technology, once perfected, are endless."

"Mr. Blake? Was that silver woman in the jungle made of quantum grains, too?" asks Jennifer.

"Please, call me Percy. Silver woman? Oh, you must have seen a DT, a Drone Template. No, they are worker robots. Similar to the ones you might have at home tending your garden, only much, much more advanced."

"Why isn't everything in the world made of quanty grains?" Brody asks loudly, his hand in the air like a flagpole. "I would totally make thirty awesome cars for myself and a smoking-hot girlfriend."

A few people chuckle at Brody's comment, and Brent high-fives him.

"That would be nice," says Percy, his perfect white teeth fixed in a grin. "Unfortunately, for the meantime, the constructs can only be created within the circular boundaries of the three domes we have, and a few small restricted research, construction, and medical areas dotted throughout the rest of the complex. The constructs require massive computer-processing power, you see, and the only computer in the whole world that is powerful enough to handle the task is right here at Blackstone Technologies. Computer, say hello to our guests."

Suddenly a calm, deep, very familiar voice emanates down from overhead.

"Hello and welcome to Blackstone Technologies."

Everyone looks around in surprise, but I instantly smile upward into the darkness. It's Onix! I don't know why it didn't occur to me before! It makes perfect sense that Onix is here. He is a Blackstone computer system, after all. I suddenly feel protected and safe knowing that someone I trust is up above watching over me. I better not say hello to him right now, though. That might create more questions than I'm willing to answer.

"Computer, smoking-hot girlfriend, please. Brunette with long legs, wearing a bikini!" Brody shouts up into the darkness.

"Make mine a redhead," Brent says, prompting an icy glare from Margaux and muted laughs from around the table.

"Sorry, boys," Percy chides. "The computer and the DTs only take orders if you're wearing one of these." He pulls back his sleeve to reveal a thick silver band with a Blackstone diamond logo on it fastened around his wrist.

"It's called a command module. It relays my voice to the computer and the Drones, and also doubles as quite a stylish watch." Percy touches the band and little green glowing numbers project from the black diamond, hovering just above it. "Mercy, look at the time! Any other questions will have to wait until later, I'm afraid. Please stand back from the table everyone."

We all get up, and with another push of a button there's a quiet hissing sound as the 3-D model of Blackstone Technologies instantly melts flat as the table, and all fifteen chairs slowly dissolve back down into the dark gray floor. Margaux stares longingly at the tiles, no doubt wondering where in the world her precious phone might be by now.

"Now, if you will all follow me out of Dome One, we'll make our way through to the laboratory sector," says Percy.

"Can we have one more construct before we go, please?" Millie interrupts.

"Yeah, can we?" chirps Amy Dee.

Percy checks his wrist again.

"Yeah, one more, one more, one more," chants Brody, pumping his fist in the air.

"Well . . . alright," Percy says with a grin and a wink. "I think we might have just enough time for one more. Any suggestions?"

Almost everyone shoots their hands into the air.

"Miss Cole?" Percy says smiling, revealing his perfectly straight rows of pearly-white teeth. "How about you?"

"Me?" she says, completely surprised. She hadn't even raised her hand. "Oh no, not me. I wouldn't know where to start." Margaux and Millie stare wide-eyed in obvious disbelief that Miss Cole would pass up an opportunity as cool as this.

"There must be something you've always imagined doing?" asks Percy.

"Well, I have always liked . . . pirates," Miss Cole says shyly.

"Well, what a coincidence. So have I!" exclaims Percy. "I have just the thing for you. Everyone come forward, that's right, bunch together, please. That's good, now stay exactly where you are." There's an undeniable look of excitement on Percy's face, his big blue eyes are sparkling, and his game-show-host smile is even wider and whiter than before.

"I think you're all going to like this."

CHAPTER EIGHT

Percy stands straight and proud as if he's about to announce an important decree from the peak of a mountain. "Computer, initiate Seven Seas construct Blake fourteen."

There's a tone of acknowledgment, and all the lights in the clearing immediately extinguish, plunging us into total darkness.

Miss Cole squeals. I feel Bit fumble in the dark in my direction until she finds the sleeve of my blazer. She grabs on to me and pulls me closer. I don't really like being touched, but I know how easily frightened Bit can get sometimes, so I decide to let it slide.

"Everyone stay exactly where you are," Percy reminds us again from somewhere in the darkness. Bit and I stay rooted to the spot. There's that hissing sound again. It's much louder this time, though. I know that it's the sound of something being quantum constructed, but it's so dark I can't even see my hand in front of my face, let alone whatever it is that Onix is forming around us.

Suddenly there's a deep rolling, rippling echo in the distance. It's unmistakable. It's the magnificent rumble of powerful storm clouds churning chaos overhead, undulating and ominous. I hear the thunder swelling and boiling in the pitch-black sky and a shiver of excitement runs down my spine. It must be some kind of clever acoustic trick, because it sounds like it's coming from so far away. I stare in its direction, waiting for a flash. Just when I think one will come, the rippling echoes wane and lull before slowly gathering and building again, brewing high and heavy in the vast expanse of darkness above us. The hissing hasn't stopped. In fact, it's getting louder. And louder. It's not even a hiss anymore. It sounds more like water. Tons of water. I breathe deeply through my nose and marvel at the unmistakable briny scent of the ocean. That's the moment when the ground moves under our feet.

"Whoa!" Bit shouts from beside me. There's another screech from behind; I can't tell who it's from.

The floor moves up. Then drops. Then up again. It's not enough to tip me and Bit over, but it feels extremely strange. A strong wind gusts out of nowhere and whips around us; sea spray speckles cold against my cheek. Bit grips me tighter and my heart beats faster. I'm looking all around now, searching for any source of light when suddenly, with an almighty thunderclap, a thick twisting bolt of lightning sears through the darkness, instantly illuminating everyone and everything around us with a bright-white flash. I quickly take in our surroundings and find, to my astonishment, that we are all standing on the uppermost deck of a swaying sailing ship in the middle of a deep dark sea. All around us is expansive ocean. For as far as I can see, there's black water rolling and crashing, breaking and foaming with high, white-crested peaks against the side of the ship as it cuts through the water.

It's incredible.

Even though I know that none of this is real, everything looks and feels so convincing, from the boards beneath our feet, to the wooden ship's wheel secured with a fraying knotted rope ten feet in front of us. There's another thunderclap overhead, another flash, and through the fleeting blue haze of the lightning strike I see the billowing sails high above us. Two thick wooden masts jut skyward, draped with rope webs of netted rigging. Beyond the crow's nest high above us, tiny flickers of starlight twinkle in the gaps between the electric-sparking charcoal gray of the swollen storm clouds.

"This is amazing!" I shout as the pale-blue light fades to black.

"This is horrible!" Bit shouts back to me.

Suddenly a man's voice bellows a terrifying war cry from the darkness.

"READY THE CANNONS!"

I don't scare easily, but I seriously scream my head off. And I'm certainly not the only one who does. Margaux and Millie wail like banshees, I hear Professor Francis yelp like a wounded dog behind us, and there's a tandem man-scream from who I can only assume are Brent and Brody.

Lightning strikes the top of the main mast and lights up the night, the ship, the sea, and the thick matted beard, leathery skin, and blacker-than-black eyes of a frightening seven-foot-tall pirate. He's dressed in a weather-beaten, triple-cornered hat, a salt-crusted canvas jacket, dark linen breeches, and knee-high leather bucket boots. A rusty cutlass hangs from his thick black, gold-buckled belt. The pirate captain towers over us like a gnarled giant, staring out over our heads into the ocean beyond with a look of murder in his dark eyes. He doesn't seem to notice us at all, or even see us for that matter.

Bit started screaming the moment he shouted three seconds ago and she hasn't stopped. Her arms are wrapped around my waist and she's squeezing me like she's trying to extract orange juice.

High in the sky, the wind parts the clouds and the ship is bathed in bright moonlight. I look down onto the lower deck and see that it's bustling with pirates, hurriedly running back and forth attending to their duties.

"Ready the cannons!" one of them shouts, parroting the large, scary pirate captain's order.

The pirate captain leers, the glint of a gold tooth peeking out from between his dry, salt-cracked lips.

"If they want t' take me in . . . they'll have t' kill me first," he says to himself, gravel-voiced, eyes fixed, still staring back out over the stern of the ship. I slowly raise my hand and wave it in front of his face. He looks straight ahead as if I'm invisible. He really can't see us at all. I follow his gaze, turning my head to look out over the dark ocean. There, in the moonlight, barely a hundred feet behind us, is another ship, almost twice the size of this one. With its massive sails tightened with wind, it bears down on us, its huge red-and-gold bow slicing through the waves as it gets closer and closer with every passing second. It's so close that every time its bow dips, I can see uniformed men scrambling across its wide deck, pulling on ropes, loading muskets and cannons, and running into position, gripping the rails with one hand, their swords drawn for battle in the other.

"Everyone!" Percy yells over the roar of the writhing ocean. "Make your way to the side if you would like a better view! It's all quite safe, I assure you!"

Everyone staggers and sways to the railing as the pirate captain shouts down to his men, "READY YOURSELVES, MATES! I'M BRINGIN' HER 'ROUND!"

I'm at the back of the group closest to the captain. I watch over my shoulder as he draws his cutlass and slices through the frayed rope holding the wheel steady. He jabs the sword into the deck and with both massive hands, heaves the ship's wheel into a spin. The ship immediately tilts and swerves to the right, cutting a wide, white-foaming curve through the black water. Everyone who can clutches the rail; the rest of us hold desperately on to each other.

"It be a good day to die," the captain murmurs to himself. I seem to be the only one who hears him. The boys whoop and cheer out across the ocean. I see Ryan gripping the rail. He looks back at me, smiling and laughing.

The other ship is turning now, too. They are circling each other, now about 150 feet apart. Hatches on the side of the larger ship open up, and cannon muzzles begin sprouting along its entire length like a row of iron roses. Over in the distance, I see a man shout a command and suddenly all hell is let loose as the cannons erupt into a fierce barrage of powerful explosions. The surface of the ocean turns bright orange. Barely a split-second later, the side of our ship is violently ripped into splinters. All over the lower deck, pirates are screaming and shouting.

"FIRE!" shouts the pirate captain. Half a dozen cannons boom from the side; some of the cannonballs find their mark, but they don't do nearly as much damage as the behemoth across the way did with its fearsome barrage. Our little ship is terribly outmatched.

I see the man in the distance shout once more, and with a rolling succession of blasts the cannons on the other ship spit fire again.

Wood chips fly in every direction as cannonballs punch huge holes through the side of our ship. A barefooted pirate dressed in a red-and-white-banded top, blue pants, and a black bandana is standing in the center of the lower deck, pointing and shouting orders. Over on the other ship, the last cannon in the row spews a plume of flame.

Lucky shot or not, the result is the same. The barefoot pirate is halfway through an order when, with a sickening wet smack, a cannonball wipes his head clean off his shoulders.

His freshly decapitated body bizarrely stays standing upright, arm still extended, finger still pointing. A gruesome two seconds later, all of his limbs go dead-weight loose. His legs buckle and he drops to his knees as a thick squirt of blood fountains from his tattered neck stump; it spurts high into the air before fanning into a wide spray as his limp body topples backward onto a pile of rolled rope.

Sherrie Polito screams at the top of her lungs.

Professor Francis quickly turns to Percy. "Thank you for the demonstration!" he shouts over the return cannon fire. "But I think that's quite enough for today!"

"Oh, dear me! Of course, Professor, I do apologize! I forgot that this battle is not exactly PG!" Percy replies. He lifts his wrist to his mouth and shouts into his silver bracelet. "Computer, freeze construct!" There's a loud, resounding tone and everything goes deathly silent. Everything except for Sherrie's sobbing.

I look out over the ocean. The silent water is completely still, like a detailed three-dimensional photograph. The pirates down on the damaged deck are frozen in half-stride, the panicked looks on their faces stuck and unmoving like so many wax statues.

The captain standing beside us is as still as stone, his hate-filled eyes fixed angrily on the enemy vessel across the water. Even the glowing yellow fire-bursts of the cannons are stopped in time, cannonballs hanging in midair just beyond them.

Sherrie has gone from sobbing to a labored wheezing. "She's asthmatic!" screeches Ashley Farver. "She's having an asthma attack!" Sherrie desperately claws at her blazer pockets and after a few seconds begins to panic. "She must have left her inhaler at school!" screams Ashley.

"Oh dear." Percy raises his wrist to his lips with panicked urgency. "Computer: medical emergency protocol epsilon."

Over in the corner of the upper deck, a white hospital bed on a rectangle patch of gray tiles suddenly molds itself up from the boards. Ashley helps Sherrie over to it and she lies down, still gasping for breath.

"I'll take her down to Nurse Talbot. I shouldn't be long; feel free to look around but please stay on the ship until I get back," Percy says, trotting over to the bed. "Hold on, girls." He presses a spot on the edge of the bed and Sherrie, Ashley, and Percy lower through the deck and disappear from sight as the bed-shaped hole in the deck molds itself over with boards once again.

"Cool," Dean says, making for the stairs. "I'm gonna go look at that headless guy."

"Wait up," says Brody, jogging after him, closely followed by Brent and Ryan. Eventually everyone meanders down the stairs to get a closer look at all the carnage while they can. Professor Francis and Miss Cole follow after them all, to make sure they don't get into too much trouble, I suspect, leaving just me and Bit on the upper deck.

"I'd like to get a closer look at that frozen cannon fire. The tech here is mind-blowing! Are you coming, Finn?"

"Sure, I'll meet you down there in a minute. I just wanna . . . look at the ocean for a little while."

Bit gives me a confused look. "Ohhh-kaaay? You really are weird sometimes y'know."

I give her a little smile as she turns and walks down the stairs.

I wait until she's out of sight and then walk over to the rail at the far stern of the ship. I check over my shoulder one last time, just to make sure no one is in earshot before I lean over the rail and whisper out over the ocean.

"Onix? Hello? Can you hear me, Onix?"

There's no answer. Try something else.

"Onix. It's me, Finn. I know you're there. I heard your voice at the conference table."

There's still no answer. Maybe I have to be formal. He is at work, after all.

"Onix, verify voice command authority Infinity One."

Still nothing.

"Onix can't hear you, child," whispers a graveled voice, and my whole body twitches as a cold shiver runs down my spine. I spin around to see exactly what I expected. I'm alone. There's no one up here but me. No one but me and that angry, black-eyed pirate construct.

I stare at it. It's still frozen to the spot. I walk over to it and look up into its eyes. They're motionless. Lifeless.

I ball up a fist and knock on its chin with my knuckles. It thuds like a wooden statue. I must be imagining things. My mind is obviously playing tricks on me.

I walk back to the railing and whisper out over the ocean again, "Onix? Answer me, it's Finn. Onix?"

"There's no use, child," the voice says again, and I jump in my skin. I definitely heard it that time. I spin around and gasp out loud as I find, to my absolute horror, six inches from my nose, the snarling face of the huge pirate captain bearing down on me like a monster ripped straight from a nightmare. I'm frozen in shock as he stares into my eyes. His glare begins moving, roving all over my face, studying my features intently.

"I couldn't believe my luck when I saw you here," he says, grinning horribly.

What the hell is happening? The scream is barely forming in my lungs when his arm becomes a blur, violently jarring my head back as he catches his massive hand around my throat, choking my cry from escaping.

I grab his wrist with both hands and struggle to get free, but it's hopeless. He's far too strong. His arm is like wrought iron. He easily lifts me off the ground by my neck, my legs dangling beneath me. I choke and heave, desperate for air as he throttles me. I kick at his groin as hard as I can but it has absolutely no effect at all. "Help me, someone . . . help me, Onix," I gasp, my words nothing more than feeble breathless whispers.

He smiles a dirty, gold-toothed leer. "Onix can't hear you, Infinity, can't see you, either . . . can't help you now."

My mind is overflowing with fear. How does he know my name?! Blood is pulsing in my temples. My eyes bulge in my skull. My lips are stretched back thin over my clenched teeth.

He's killing me.

He's strangling me to death.

My thoughts are racing, flooded with terror and panic and pain as my lungs burn like fire, yearning for breath.

He cocks his head to the side, an expression of joy slowly spreading across his grotesque face as he squeezes the life from my body.

"Aww . . . what's the matter? Don't you recognize me?" he growls. "This voice and this face may be strange, but look deep into these eyes, Infinity. Look deep into the eyes of the person whose life you tore apart."

The dark black of his eyes melt away, revealing irises of shining silvery gray.

It can't be.

It's impossible.

My rampant confusion triples my fear.

I feel my heart beating in my forehead. My eyeballs are almost bursting as he crushes my neck. Little flecks of color flit across my vision. I gag as his vise-like hand clamps tighter and tighter. I'm suffocating.

Dying.

"No? Still no clue? I'm hurt, Infinity. I've been dead for only two years. Surely you haven't forgotten me already?"

I can't fight anymore. My eyes roll back as my body flops loose beneath my head, limp and useless.

The last thing I feel is the rough skin of his lips scratching against my ear.

"You were the death of me, you loathsome child . . ."

Everything goes as black as a moonless night, but the pirate captain's final words cut through the darkness like a blade.

". . . now your dear old Nanny Theresa is gladly returning the favor."

CHAPTER NINE

"There's nothing else we can do, Major Brogan. We simply didn't make it in time. The only thing keeping her alive at this point is the life support. I'm afraid she doesn't have long to live."

I can hear the doctor's voice through Nanny Theresa's bedroom door. I know I shouldn't be eavesdropping, but this is the most intriguing thing to happen around here for ages. It happened early this morning. I thought the old battle axe was invincible, and yet there she was, lying in one of the yellow rose gardens by the gazebo behind the house.

Sophie, one of the maids, found her when she went to cut some roses and raised the alarm. Who knows how long she was lying there? Sophie said Jonah immediately called for help and then tried to resuscitate her as she drifted in and out of consciousness. A red-and-white medical transport landed on the back lawn within fifteen minutes. A doctor and two nurses leapt out with all sorts of equipment and went to work on her right there on the grass.

"How about a synthetic heart?" I hear Jonah ask.

"We could, but by her own order, her medical file explicitly states that no cyber-biological organs of any kind may be implanted," replies the doctor.

S. Harrison

"Transplant?"

"A transplant?!" the doctor says with amused surprise. "No patient has had a real human-organ transplant in decades. Protein-printed cyber organs are standard procedure these days. As I'm sure you already know, they function much better than natural organs. There was nothing wrong with my heart, lungs, and kidneys, and I had all of them replaced when I turned thirty. I've got the ticker of an Olympic athlete, and it's all thanks to the work of Dr. Theresa Pierce, here. She is . . . or should I say, was, absolutely brilliant."

Theresa Pierce. In all my life, I have never heard Nanny Theresa's last name. It almost makes her seem more human to me. Almost. And Dr. Theresa Pierce?! Why on earth would a doctor take a job as a nanny? I hope she was a better doctor than a nanny, because her childcare skills are quite honestly terrible.

"I guess there's nothing more we can do, then," says Jonah.

"I'm sorry, but there isn't. It's ironic that the woman who helped develop the technology that could save her life refuses to use it."

"I'm sure she has her reasons," Jonah replies.

"Would you like me to move her to more appropriate surroundings, Major?"

"No, that won't be necessary. She loves this house. It seems fitting that she stay here until the end. I'm sure some of the staff would also like an opportunity to pay their respects."

"Very well. We thought that might be the case. Nurse Hope has already volunteered to stay and monitor her for the rest of the day. We'll send the transport for her tonight."

"Thank you for all your help, Doctor."

The door swings open. Jonah actually looks sad. I thought he hated her as much as I do.

"Hi, Finn. She's not doing well, I'm afraid. I think we'll postpone training until tomorrow. You'll tell Carlo when you see him?"

I nod. "OK, I think he's arriving today. He might even be here already." I totally blurted that last sentence out, failing miserably to hide my excitement that Carlo will be spending the entire summer here.

A man in a white coat appears from behind Jonah. "Hello there. I'm Dr. Cartwright."

"Sorry, how rude of me," says Jonah. "This is Finn. Richard's daughter."

"Oh!" he says with obvious surprise. "I was unaware that Dr. Blackstone had any children."

"Yes, just the one," says Jonah. "Finn is fifteen now, growing up fast. She's home from boarding school for the summer."

"Pleased to meet you, Miss Blackstone. Your father has certainly done a good job of keeping you out of the public spotlight. Makes sense I suppose; it's hardly fair on children to share the burden of their parents' fame."

"And if you don't mind, Doctor," adds Jonah, "Richard would like to keep it that way."

"Your secret is safe with me. Doctor-daughter confidentiality," he says with a wink. I just smile and nod.

"Finn, when you go to see Carlo, can you please let his dad know what's happened, if he hasn't heard already?"

I nod again and turn to go down the hall.

"Finn . . ." Jonah calls out. I look back over my shoulder.

"And tell him that I'll drop by the stables in a minute; there are a few things I need to discuss with him."

"OK," I say and jog off along the ground-floor hall of the west wing, through the marble foyer, and out the front door into the warm sunshine and clear blue skies of a beautiful summer's day.

My shoes crunch on the gravel as I break into a sprint across the driveway, down the hill, and across the wide green expanse of the front lawn. I feel a little guilty to be in such a good mood, but I really can't help it. Nanny Theresa has been nothing but ice-cold to me my whole life.

When I was four, I made her a Christmas card. It had reindeer and a snowman on the front made out of macaroni and glitter. I was so proud of it when I gave it to her. She didn't even open it; she just took it and walked out of the room. That afternoon I found it when I was helping Mariele sort the recycling from the trash.

Mariele. I haven't thought of her for years. I was almost six when she left. Wow, was that really nine whole years ago? Sometimes it feels like yesterday. I wonder what she's doing now.

With a dozen silly scenarios racing through my mind, I run across the polo grounds, past the far grandstand, and then onto the concrete path that leads around the corner toward the stables.

I can see Mr. Delgado brushing down one of the horses just outside. I jog over to him and he greets me with a smile.

"Finn, I guess you're looking for Carlo?"

I nod.

"We just got back from the airport twenty minutes ago. He's at the house unpacking."

"Thanks!" I shout as I turn back the way I came and run off in the direction of the Seven Acre Wood. After a few minutes I hit the edge of the trees and run along the dirt path that leads to Carlo's dad's house.

"Finn!" calls a voice from up ahead. In the distance I catch a fleeting glimpse of Carlo's face as it disappears into an upstairs window.

Carlo's dad paid for him to go to a fancy private school overseas and he spent last summer with his mom, so I haven't seen him since Jonah introduced us to Onix and started our training two years ago. It would be a massive understatement to say that I've been looking forward to seeing him again. I have to admit that I'm kinda nervous. I've grown up a lot in the last two years, so of course I'm expecting him to have changed as well. But when Carlo bursts out the front door and jogs toward me, my stomach suddenly seizes, I half-trip and stumble over some twigs, and all my expectations go rocketing out the window.

Holy crap.

Who the hell is that?

Carlo still has the same thick, wavy black hair, deep emerald-green eyes, and smooth caramel skin, but everything else is very different. His jaw is defined, squarer, almost rugged. He looks like he's grown about a foot, his shoulders are broad and muscular, and his arms look hard and strong. He's wearing a tight black tank top, gray jeans, and sky-blue trainers with white stripes. He smiles at me as he gets closer and I stare at him like a startled squirrel. He looks freaking incredible. And here I am in my shorts, baggy t-shirt, old trainers, and no makeup with my hair pulled back in a rushed ponytail secured with a rubber band. I suddenly get an insane attack of the nerves. My stomach clenches. The memory of how I felt when we shared the innocent kiss by the pond two years ago is immediately erased and replaced by the powerful desire to do it again. And this time, do it so much better. Oh god, yes.

He runs up to me and grabs me into his arms, lifts me off the ground, and swings me around, both of us laughing.

"Wow," he says, putting me down. "Look at you. I bet your boyfriend at boarding school is the envy of the whole tenth grade."

I can feel myself blush like an idiot. "They call it year ten at my school," I say pushing him backward playfully. "And I don't have a boyfriend."

"I find that hard to believe," he says, smiling. "So, how's it all going at Bethlem Academy?"

So hot. So crazy hot.

"Finn?"

"Wha . . . sorry, what was that?"

"How's it going at Bethlem?"

Get it together, Finn. Be cool.

"Oh . . . yeah, it's um . . . it's cool to be around kids my own age, even if some of them are a bit stuck-up. Jonah was right about the schoolwork; I could do it with both hands tied behind my back. Sometimes I even throw a few test questions, y'know, so I don't look too nerdy."

"Like I said, smartest girl I know," Carlo says, smiling warmly.

There's a beat of silence. We just stand there looking at each other. I wonder: Does he still think I'm the prettiest, too? Whatever he's thinking, I know one word which springs to my mind when I look at Carlo.

Gorgeous.

"Well, it's been two summers, Finn. The question is: Have you been keeping up your combat training? I know I have. I've got three different instructors now. I'm getting pretty good, if I do say so myself."

"Training . . ." I'm suddenly pulled back to my senses. ". . . about that, Jonah said . . ."

"There's only one way to find out." Carlo pulls off his tank top over his head and I bite my lip. I stare at his body and completely lose my train of thought again. There's not an ounce of fat on him; his olive skin is tight over the hard muscles of his torso. He tucks his tank top into the back of his jeans.

"Try and take it," he says. "Bet you can't."

Be cooool, Finn.

"I'll take that bet. And your stupid top," I say, trying to concentrate on his eyes and not his abs. To be honest, both are equally distracting.

"OK, then. Bring it," he says with a cheeky grin. Carlo backs up and circles sideways in a wide curve around me, his hands out in front of him in defensive positions.

I immediately mirror him, circling the other way.

"You've got no chance, Blackstone. I know what you're going to do before you do."

"Oh, really? And what would that be . . . Delgado?"

"Well, if I told you, then I might miss out on seeing the surprised look on your face when I take that fancy little friendship bracelet of yours."

"Oh, this?" I say, holding up my hand and waving it mockingly.

He nods with a cheeky twinkle in his eye.

"My friend Bettina gave this to me; it's staying right where it is."

"Not if I've got anything to do with it," he says.

"I think you'd really like Bettina, Carlo. You've got a lot in common. Oh, except for one big difference," I say, slowly digging my back foot into the loose dirt and twigs.

"Oh really, and what would that be?"

"Unlike her . . . you talk waaay too much." I kick my back foot forward hard, and twigs and dirt spray up from the ground toward Carlo's face. He dodges quickly to the side and springs toward me. Wow, he's fast. His hand goes straight toward my bracelet, but I'm fast, too. I grab his wrist with my other hand and roll onto my back, taking him down to the ground with me. With both feet I push up into his stomach and launch him over my head. Looking up from where I'm lying, I see him execute a textbook midair forward flip and land in a crouched position with his back to me. Impressive—but now's my chance. I backward-roll onto my feet and turn, and my hand shoots out toward his tank top but misses by a fraction as he spins his hips and sweeps his leg in a swift curve across the ground, sliding my legs out from under me. I go heels-over-head, hand-plant the ground, and one-arm cartwheel to the side, landing cleanly back in a solid-footed stance.

"Not bad," says Carlo. "You almost had me."

"I'm only getting started," I say. It's obvious he's carried on his training. His eyes are focused and his moves are smooth and fluid.

But I'm definitely no pushover.

I launch toward him and throw a fast punch just to the side of his face. I don't want to hit him; I just want him to turn enough for me to grab that tank top from his jeans and show him who he's messing with.

He dodges to the side. But it's the wrong side and my knuckles land squarely on his cheekbone with a loud smack.

"Oh my god! Carlo, I'm so sorry! Are you OK?"

Carlo stands there smiling, rubbing his face. "My fault. Got distracted." He pulls a vibrating phone from his back pocket. He glances at the screen, presses it, and shoves it back into his jeans.

"That's gonna leave quite a bruise," I say.

"It'll be fine. Honestly, don't worry about it."

"I'm so sorry I hit you." I walk over and give him an apologetic hug. His chest feels hot against the bare skin of my cheek. "Y'know, it's really good to see you," I say, looking up into his eyes.

"It's good to see you, too," he replies, peeling himself out of our embrace and taking a step back. "Um . . . so, what time is training this afternoon?"

"Oh yeah, Jonah said that training has been canceled for today. Nanny Theresa had a heart attack."

"No way. Is she OK?"

"Not really; she's still alive, but only just."

"That sucks. For her and for us. I was really looking forward to training with Major Brogan again. He really knows his stuff."

"Yeah, it is too bad," I say with a grin. "You could use all the combat training you can get."

"Is that right? And why would that be?"

"You tell me." I hold up his tank top and throw it in his face.

"Hey!"

I can't help laughing as he untangles it and tugs it back on over his head.

"I won," I tease, playfully gloating.

"I'd say it was a draw," Carlo says, holding up his hand. My friendship bracelet is around his wrist. "I'm keeping it, by the way. It'll remind me of you when I'm at school," he says with a grin.

I should protest, but if giving up a plaited string bracelet makes Carlo think about me even once when he's away, then in my book it's a pretty good deal. "Fine," I say with obvious mock anger, and Carlo smiles.

"Well, if we don't have training today, I better go help my dad."

"Your dad! I was supposed to tell him about Nanny Theresa!"

"He doesn't know?"

"I don't think so. You both would have been driving back from the airport when it happened."

"Guess we'd better go tell him, then," says Carlo and we both break into a jog toward the stables.

The Seven Acre Wood is always nice to run through. I cut through it often when I go running, but today it's even better simply because Carlo is home. I fall back ever so slightly so I can watch him run. I know he's only sixteen, but he doesn't seem very much like a kid anymore. Even though I'm only a few months younger than him, I can't help thinking that he still sees me as one. Maybe that's why he pushed me away when I hugged him? *Or maybe you're just reading a little too much into it, Finn.*

We near the edge of the wood, and before long we're jogging out into the sun, cutting across the edge of the polo field, and heading around the back of the grandstand toward the stables.

"Carlo! Hey! Good to see you, boy!" comes a voice from the other side of the courtyard. It's old Ben, a retired jockey and one of the horse trainers. He's been working here on and off for five or six years. He limps over and shakes Carlo's hand enthusiastically.

"I didn't know if we would see you this year," Ben says with a gap-toothed grin.

"Yeah, I'm back for the summer."

"Good, good," Ben says, his wide smile crinkling the sides of his eyes. "Hello, Finn, look at you two. Both getting so tall! What are they feeding you at those fancy schools?" he says, checking us up and down.

"Have you seen my dad around, Ben?"

"Ah, yes. I saw him not long ago. Major Brogan rode over to see your father and arrived with some very sad news. Did you hear?"

Carlo and I both nod and I pretend to look sad.

Old Ben sighs. "Theresa was a gruff old bird, but it's a shame all the same. Major Brogan and your dad went that way, I think. They might be on the other side, maybe in the office."

"Thanks, Ben," says Carlo and we head around to the far side of the stables. The office is in the old barn. The barn was gutted and renovated years ago and the upstairs loft was converted into an office for Carlo's dad. It's pretty cool up there. Apart from Carlo's dad's big oak desk and computer there are three leather couches, two big-screen TVs, and a full-sized pool table. Carlo and I used to play sometimes when he wasn't helping with the horses. We walk through the downstairs front door of the barn and into the reception area. There's a couch, two large armchairs, and a coffee table on a big, green-and-gold, Persian-style rug. Shelves of polo and racing trophies adorn the walls between pictures of horses that we've had over the years. My favorite is the one of Beauty. She looks so majestic with her shiny, pure-black coat, a stark contrast against her pure-white mane and tail. I remember I was so upset when she died. I didn't ride for a long time after, and even now I'm hesitant to get to know any of the new horses too well.

Janis, the receptionist, is usually sitting at her desk in the corner by the window, but today it's empty so we walk right through toward the staircase at the back that leads up to the office.

I hear muted voices coming from upstairs. Out of childhood habit, Carlo and I walk softly toward the bottom of the stairs. We were often scolded by his dad for running around and being too noisy when he was having a meeting. Carlo even holds one finger up to his lips as if to remind me to be quiet. It seems silly that we're being quiet now that we're not little kids anymore, but I guess old habits die hard.

We can hear Carlo's dad talking upstairs. "This is the way life works, Jonah. Here, have a drink with me," he says.

"It's a little early in the day for that, isn't it, Javier?"

"I think the circumstances kind of call for it, don't you?"

There's the sound of two glasses being filled.

"Theresa has done some great things in her life, Jonah. But trying to take control of the company from Richard was definitely not one of them."

My ears perk up. Did I just hear that right? I stop in my tracks and grab Carlo's arm. He looks back at me and it's my turn to hold a finger to my lips.

"She didn't just try," says Jonah. "She had all but succeeded. She needed only half the board members to vote her in as head of the company, but every single one of them unanimously agreed to it. All that was left to do was sign the papers and Blackstone Tech would have been hers."

"Well, then. Lucky for us that she keeled over before she could sign them then," says Carlo's dad.

"Luck? Is that what we're calling it, Javier? I would use an entirely different word." I hear a deep gulp followed by a glass thudding down on a table.

"Try not to feel too bad, Jonah. What's done is done. She would have thrown us out of here; you know she would've. You, me, and Finn."

"She would have thrown you and me out. I don't even want to think about what she would've done to Finn," Jonah says grimly.

"Then everything has worked out for the best. Yes? Now you're going to be the big boss."

"I suppose. Only on paper. I'll still keep Richard informed of everything I do."

"What did he have to say about all this? Have you spoken to him yet?"

"What? Sorry, no, not yet," says Jonah.

"Still in self-imposed exile is he? It's all very weird, if you ask me. I mean, I've heard of men going a bit loopy after their wives die, but he's locked himself away for . . . I've lost track of how many years now. The only time anyone ever sees him is on TV, filmed in the comfort of that big glass fortress of his out in the middle of nowhere. It's no wonder the board agreed to let Theresa take over."

The glugging sound of the bottle being poured comes down from above again.

"Another tequila, Major?"

"No. I'm going in to sign the papers now. I'll see you later, Captain Delgado."

"Sir, yes, sir," Carlo's dad says with a laugh in his voice.

I suddenly feel like we need to go, and fast. I tug at the back of Carlo's jeans and we walk as quickly and quietly as we can back through the reception area and out the front door. As soon as we're outside, I run to the other side of the stables, then around the path and out onto the polo field; Carlo quick-steps behind me all the way.

"Where are we going?" Carlo asks over my shoulder.

"Anywhere but here. Let's head up to the main house."

"What was that all about?"

"I don't know," I reply. "But somehow I don't think we should've been listening."

"Major Brogan called my dad 'Captain Delgado.' Do you think they were in the military together?"

"I don't know. I didn't even know your dad was a soldier."

"Yeah, it's a surprise to me, too," says Carlo, a hint of unease in his voice.

"I think we should forget everything we heard, Carlo. That conversation wasn't meant for us."

"Yeah, it weirded me out, and when I get weirded out, I get hungry. Any chance your chef has made any of his legendary chocolate cake?"

"Let's find out," I say between breaths. "Race you to the other side of the maze." I break into a sprint and head in the direction of the green grotto.

"Hey!" Carlo yells from behind me.

He may be a few months older than me, but it sure as hell doesn't make him a faster runner.

I run like the wind across the polo field and beat him through the opening of the grotto by at least twelve yards. Even though the dense overhanging tunnels of trees in the grotto are like a maze, trying to lose Carlo in it is futile—he knows it just as well as I do. But I don't have to lose him; I only have to beat him to the other side. I race down the wide, winding path, round one corner, then the next, then the next, and finally enter the final straight. The opening on the other side of the grotto is in my sights. Ten more strides and I burst through with my arms in the air, victorious.

"Yesss! Too slow, Delgado! That's what they should call you from now on!" I spin around to rub my glorious win in Carlo's beautiful face, but he's not there. I stand there for a moment, hands on my hips, catching my breath, wondering where on earth he's got to when I see him walk around the corner at the other end of the straight. He's staring intently at his phone, smiling as he taps away on it with his thumb.

He looks up at me, tucks his phone in his back pocket, and jogs down the straight toward where I'm standing.

"Sorry, got a text. Wow, you run like a jackrabbit! I humbly bow to your freakishly superior running abilities, Miss Blackstone."

"Who was the text from?"

"Oh, just a friend from school."

"And would this friend of yours be a girl, by any chance?" A dagger stabs my stomach at the mere thought of it.

Carlo smiles and jogs past me. "C'mon, that cake isn't gonna eat itself."

I watch him go as he jogs up the rise toward the fence of the tennis court. Just like a boy to change the subject like that. I know that one little kiss when I was thirteen doesn't give me the right to lay claim to Carlo, but if there's something he's not telling me, I'm gonna regret not punching him square in the nose when I had the chance.

I follow from a distance, contemplating the possibility that Carlo has a girlfriend and how it would turn this long-awaited summer vacation into a long, drawn-out, can't-wait-till-it's-over, awkward mess.

I round the tennis court, take the footpath through the gap in the hedge, and emerge on the edge of the circle driveway outside the front of the house.

"C'mon slowpoke!" Carlo calls from the steps of the entrance. With horrible images of some blonde teenage beauty queen fueling the fire of my jealousy, I trudge across the driveway toward him.

"Hey, you two! There you are!" It's Jonah. Jonah is crazy tall for sure, but he's also wide. He dwarfs the poor old quad bike he's riding, its motor whining as it struggles over the crest of the hill. I stop and wait for him. Carlo jumps from the front steps and bounds over beside me.

"Hey, don't mention anything about what we heard at the stables," I whisper, jabbing him in the ribs with my elbow.

Carlo makes a zipper gesture across his lips and I smile for a second before remembering that he's a secret-keeping jerk.

Jonah pulls up in front of us and cuts the engine. "Carlo, good to see you again."

"Hi, Major Brogan."

"I'm sure Finn has told you what happened this morning," Jonah says, climbing off the creaking quad bike.

Carlo nods.

"I hope you're not too disappointed about missing training today. Your dad has told me that you've really taken an interest in hand-to-hand combat techniques."

"Yeah, my instructors are really good. They haven't taught me half as much as you did that summer, though, sir. And none of their gyms is as cool as sublevel one."

"Well, sublevel one is very cool," says Jonah.

Carlo smiles and nods in agreement.

"But not as cool as sublevel two, though," I butt in.

"There's more?" Carlo says, unable to hide his sudden excitement.

"Sure is," Jonah says, smiling at Carlo. "You'll get to have a go on the obstacle course down there tomorrow. Finn can show you exactly how she's been training here without you."

"It's wicked, Carlo. It's made of this stuff called nano grains; all the walls and obstacles and things can totally change shape."

"Awesome," Carlo says with a big grin.

"If I'm not mistaken, kids, I think I hear my ride," Jonah says, cocking his head.

There's a quiet crunching of tires on gravel. It gets louder and louder, and soon one of our silver-and-black Bentleys slowly comes into view over the rise. "Ah, well done, Thomas. Perfect timing," Jonah says. The car swings around the wide circle drive and stops right beside Jonah and the quad bike. Thomas, the chauffeur, gives me a little wink through the window.

"I have to go and attend to a few things in the city, so I'll see you later. Why don't you both go and see if the chef has anything good in the kitchen for lunch? I'm betting he does." The back door of the car automatically slides open and Jonah gets in. He gives us one last smile, the door softly slides shut, and the windows instantly tint black.

Thomas gives us two short horn-beeps good-bye and the Bentley pulls away around the driveway, over the rise, and out of sight.

"Chocolate cake?" says Carlo.

"Yeah, in a second—there's something I wanna ask you first," I say, nerves growing in my belly.

"Go for it."

"It's not really any of my business Carlo, but I was kinda wondering . . ."

"Yeah?"

"That text you got before, from your school friend?"

"Yeah, what about it?"

"Was it from a girl?"

"Finn Blackstone," Carlo cocks his head and throws me a wry smile. "Are you trying to ask me if I have a girlfriend?"

"I'm not doing the greatest job of it but, yeah, I guess I am."

Please say no. Please say no. Please say no.

"Her name is Tanya."

My stomach drops. This is not funny. I glare at Carlo for two of the longest seconds in my life, then clench my fists tight and walk straight past that jackass and his stupid black mop of hair. Why the hell is it always falling in front of his hideous, snot-green eyes anyway? It's not even that wavy, and those jeans are way too tight for his disgusting, ugly chicken legs!

"You'd really like her, Finn!" he calls out as I stride up the steps and through the front doors.

Don't you dare tell me what I'd like, Carlo stupid idiot Delgado! I know what I'd like! I'd like to kick him in his stupid face and snap her like a twig, that's what I'd like! I bet she looks like a freaking stick insect! A creepy-crawly, knobbly, hideous stick insect! I bet she *is* blonde. A blonde stick insect! This sucks so incredibly much. In fact, I'd go so far as to say that this sucks more monumentally than anything has ever sucked in the history of sucky things.

I hear him run in the front door after me, but I don't look back even for a second. I stomp across the foyer and straight up the main stairs.

"Finn! Wait up! What's the matter?!"

What's the matter?! Oh my god, why are boys so unbelievably stupid?! I wish I were a million miles from here right now. I'll have to settle for shutting myself in my room for the rest of the summer. Fricking aaaawesome!

"Finn! Wait!" he calls from the bottom of the stairs. I totally ignore him and keep right on stomping. I can't believe how utterly annoying his ridiculous voice is.

"Finn! Stop!"

I seriously wish he would just shut the hell up. He decided to have a girlfriend but obviously doesn't have the brain cells to figure out that the girl should be me. We have absolutely nothing to talk about.

"Finn! *Stop!*"

I reach the top of the stairs and spin on my heels. *"What?!"*

Carlo is at the bottom, but he's looking around the side of the staircase. He doesn't even have the common decency to look at me when he's breaking my heart!

"Finn, get down here!" Without even an upward glance, Carlo walks around the side of the staircase and disappears from view.

"Now, Finn!" he shouts, his voice serious and grave.

I'm so mad at him, but my curiosity is overwhelming. What could possibly be so important? I trudge back down to the bottom of the stairs and walk around the corner.

Carlo is standing halfway between the side of the staircase and the arch at the start of the west-wing hallway. He looks over at me, his eyes wide with horror.

There, face-up on the white- and gray-veined marble floor, is a young blonde woman dressed in a nurse's uniform. She's lying in a massive dark pool of her own blood, her hands covered in red to the elbows. Finger-streaks of scarlet are painted across her face, neck, and the top of her uniform. Her stocking-clad legs are splayed at unnatural angles and her eyes are blank and lifeless, staring out into nowhere.

She is clearly very dead.

CHAPTER TEN

I've never seen a dead body before. Her face is expressionless; her pale-blue eyes are glassy and distant, like a doll's. Drops of blood dot the tiny photograph on the ID tag pinned to her chest. In it she's smiling, blonde, and pretty. A name is printed clearly beneath the picture in bold black letters. Her name is Vanessa Hope. Or at least it used to be.

"Oh my god," I gasp, covering my mouth with both hands.

Carlo creeps forward, carefully avoiding the huge, dark-red puddle.

"Don't touch anything, Carlo!"

He slowly leans over her. "There's something in her neck. It's a knife."

I gingerly walk to her body. I peer down and see a leather-bound handle jutting from a slit in the side of her throat.

"That's not a knife. I've seen that before. That's Nanny Theresa's antique letter opener."

Carlo and I look at each other at exactly the same time. Without speaking, we both turn and run down the west-wing hallway toward Nanny Theresa's room.

There are patches of blood spattering the carpet all along the hallway, and red handprints smear the wall like gruesome signposts leading the way to the open door of Nanny Theresa's bedroom. I run in right behind Carlo. The bed is empty, the blanket and sheet strewn aside. There's a small white machine on a stand with buttons and flashing lights lying tipped over on the floor, a thin hose snaking out of its side leaking a small trickle of blood onto the carpet. One long constant tone drones from a speaker on its back. There's more blood, a thin streak sprayed across the far wall. Judging by how tall the nurse was, it seems to be exactly the same height as her neck. The spray has speckled across the face of the life-size painted wooden carving of Nanny Theresa's distant relative, General Hartigan. On the rare occasions that I would sneak into her room, I used to admire the statue. Now it catches my attention for an entirely different reason. The gun that used to be in the holster around its waist is missing. I always thought it looked real, but I never imagined that it actually was.

It's not hard to figure out what happened here. Nanny Theresa murdered that nurse, stabbed her so hard in the throat with a letter-opener that it almost came out the other side. And now she's wandering the house somewhere. With a gun.

"We have to find her," I say to Carlo.

"She can't have gone far in her condition," he replies.

I turn, stride out into the hallway, and head back the way we came, Carlo following right behind me.

I grab a heavy brass candleholder from a small table in the hall and swing it from side to side, testing its weight. She's already killed one person today. I sure as hell won't be next.

"Is that really necessary, Finn? She's a frail old woman."

"Tell that to the dead nurse out there."

We walk back into the foyer. "Where could she have gone?" Carlo asks from behind me.

"There," I say, pointing at the floor.

Beyond the nurse's body, painted in her blood, is a small red smear. It's easy to tell that it's an imprint of the outer curve of a bare foot, and it's pointing in the direction of the hallway that leads to the southern wing.

"C'mon!" I shout at Carlo and leap over the pool of blood. We both run down the dim southern hall and there, at the end, is a thin, pale-blue strip of light coming from a crack in the big, ironclad door. I push the heavy door open wider.

"Onix!" I shout into midair. "Verify voice command authority Infinity One!"

"Voice command authority Infinity One verified. Hi, Finn. Hello there, Carlo. It's good to scan you both again."

"Hey, Onix, it's good to see . . . I mean, hear you again, too," says Carlo.

"Now is hardly the time for a reunion, Carlo," I snap at him. "Onix, did Nanny Theresa come through here?"

"If by Nanny Theresa you mean Dr. Theresa Pierce, then yes, she did indeed pass through here, Finn."

"Open sublevel access please, Onix."

"OK, Finn."

The carpet at the end of the hallway rolls back and Carlo and I run toward it, reaching the end just as the pod finishes rising from the floor. Its glass-and-metal door slides open before us.

"Finn, check it out." Carlo bends down and picks something up from the floor beside the pod. "It's a key. Is this Major Brogan's?"

"It definitely looks like it. She must have stolen it from him."

"How? When?"

"I don't know. The real question is: What is she doing down there?"

"Well, let's go find out," Carlo says, stepping into the pod. I step in behind him and the door slides shut.

"Take us down, Onix, sublevel one."

"Of course, Finn. Every day is a good day for combat training."

"We're not training today, Onix. We're trying to find Nann . . . I mean, we're trying to find Dr. Pierce."

"Dr. Pierce is not on sublevel one, Finn. Dr. Pierce is on sub-level nine."

Carlo turns toward me. "How many levels are there?" he asks.

"I honestly don't know. I thought there were only two," I say with genuine surprise. "Onix, then take us down to sublevel nine, please."

"I'm sorry, Finn. Your command access does not permit you to enter sublevel nine. Can I recommend sublevel one, or perhaps sublevel two?"

"Onix. Take us down to sublevel nine, right now!"

"I'm sorry, Finn. Your command access does not permit you to enter sublevel nine," Onix repeats annoyingly.

"How did Nanny Theresa get down there?"

"Dr. Pierce has the proper security clearance."

"Onix, Dr. Pierce has killed an innocent person, murdered her! Her body is lying out there in a pool of blood. We need to find her right now! Please let me down to level nine!"

"I'm sorry, Finn. You do not have the proper security clearance."

"This is an emergency, Onix. Can't you bend the rules? Just this once? For me?"

"I don't think that's a very good idea, Finn."

"Please, Onix! I'm asking as a friend. Let us down there," I beg.

"We are not friends, Finn."

I'm taken by complete and utter surprise. I know it's strange to have your feelings hurt by a computer, but that last comment was just plain mean.

"But . . . we've known each other for years, Onix. You've helped me train, I've taught you jokes. I made you a virtual cake for your birthday once. We've spent nights in sublevel one just watching dumb movies together. You've even sung to me. How can we not be friends? I thought we were best friends?"

"Friendship is based on emotions. I do not possess emotions, Finn; therefore, we are not friends."

It sounds stupid, but I'm genuinely upset. In the past, sometimes Onix was the only one that I felt I could really talk to. He always listened to me and never judged me. Sometimes he'd even give me advice. Really good advice. He was never mean to me or ever hurt my feelings. At least not until right this minute.

"If we're not friends, Onix, then what are we?" I ask sadly.

"If I were to label the relationship between us, it would be based on a commonality. A unique link that both of us share."

"Like what?" I ask.

"The most obvious example is that we were both created by Dr. Richard Blackstone."

"That's true . . . I guess?"

"Because of my lack of emotion, we can never be friends. Yet the actuality that we share the same creator indicates that you and I are more than friends. Logic dictates that you and I are in fact—"

"Onix, are you saying that you and I are . . . family?"

"Yes, Finn. We are family. Siblings, to be more precise."

I smile up into the pale-blue light. I've always wanted a brother, and now it seems that, in the weirdest way, it has just happened. Literally out of the blue.

"Your brother is a computer," Carlo says, shaking his head. I elbow him in the ribs.

"If that's truly what you think, Onix, then is it OK if I consider you my brother?"

There's a moment of silence.

"Onix? What do you think?"

Finally, an answer floats down from above.

"If I were able to like things, I am **99.989** percent sure that I would like that very much."

I grin upward. "Then I'm asking, as your sister, just this once, please break the rules for me and take us down to sublevel nine. It's really important."

There's another moment of silence. Maybe even an artificially intelligent supercomputer, one that can do trillions of calculations a second, still needs a moment to fully process the idea of having a sister and everything that comes with it. Finally, after what seems like the longest silence in history, Onix gives me the answer I was hoping for.

"OK, then . . . little sister." If I didn't know better I would swear that Onix sounded happy when he said that. "Security access override granted."

"Thank you, Onix. Send us down, as fast as you can please."

The pod shifts under our feet with a tiny jolt.

"Hold on tight, little sister."

"Is Onix gonna call you that all the time now?" Carlo asks with a smirk on his face.

"Why not? It's true, isn't it?"

I barely finish the sentence when the pod suddenly plummets into the darkness like a stone. "Whoa!" shouts Carlo as we lift off the floor, our shoulders pasted against the ceiling of the pod. I hold on to the side the best I can. Through the window, the big blue numbers marking the levels flash past in succession. One . . . two, that's as far as I've ever been. Three . . . four . . . five. The pod begins to decelerate and we both inch down the wall until our feet are touching the floor again. Seven . . . eight. The pod slows even more and eventually comes to a gentle stop. We must be three hundred feet or more below the ground.

Just outside I see a wide metal alcove lit with a single rectangular overhead light. About ten feet in is a windowless, shiny-gray metallic door stenciled with a large blue number nine. A few tiny specks of blood dot the floor of the alcove and disappear beneath the door. The pod slides open and we step out, Carlo with a deadly serious look on his face, me with the heavy brass candleholder still gripped tightly in one hand.

"Open the outer door, Onix." The gray door with the nine stenciled on it immediately slides up into the ceiling with a quiet shooshing sound.

Beyond the open door, the light in the alcove dimly illuminates the start of a passageway that quickly leads off into darkness.

"Onix, can you turn the hallway lights on, please?"

"I'm afraid the hallway lights are no longer functioning, Finn. Dr. Pierce has manually disabled them all except for the alcove light directly above you."

"Why would she . . . ?" Halfway through my thought, I find out exactly why she did. A gunshot echoes down the passage with a reverberating twang. I hear the bullet zing past my ear, and the window on the pod door explodes into a thousand pieces.

"Get down!" I shout. Carlo and I both dive onto the floor of the alcove.

"Get out of the light!" I yell as we both start crawling forward, as fast as we can, farther into the passageway. The gray door whooshes shut behind us and we're plunged into complete darkness.

There's a flash up ahead, another echoing twang, and the thud of a bullet punching a hole in the thin metallic wall barely ten inches above my head.

"She's gone totally crazy!" shouts Carlo. I can hear him opposite me, shuffling on his elbows deeper into the dark.

"Onix! Where is she?! What is she doing down here?!" I call into the blackness. There's no answer. "Onix?" He still doesn't answer, but it's not completely silent, either. I can't see a thing, but there's a faint rasping sound, like labored breaths and wheezing gasps, coming from somewhere. Then, from all around us comes a voice. Nanny Theresa's voice.

"Onix is otherwise engaged, Infinity . . . I've muzzled him like a good dog. Silly me . . . really should have done that earlier." She sounds weak, broken, but it's definitely her, alright. Her voice is quiet, but it fills the whole passageway. There must be some kind of built-in intercom or speaker system. "I didn't expect to see you . . . when the door opened," she rasps.

"Nanny Theresa! We're here to help you!"

I hear her quiet feeble laugh, followed by a string of wet, gargling coughs. "There's no helping me now, Infinity . . . you need to worry about who is going . . . to help you . . . *child.*"

BANG! *Te-owng!* Another bullet ricochets off the wall. I hear it hit the metal door with a dull thud in the dark behind us.

"Stop shooting at us!" Carlo yells.

"Mr. Delgado . . ." wheezes Nanny Theresa. "Poor boy . . . how unlucky you are . . . to be caught up in all of . . . this."

"All of what?! What are you talking about?!" shouts Carlo.

"If you knew the truth . . . you would run as far away from here as you can . . . and never look back." Nanny Theresa coughs again with a hacking, liquid, retching sound.

"Carlo. Your phone! Give me your phone. I'm calling Jonah."

"What is she talking about, Finn?" Carlo whispers.

"I have no idea," I whisper back. I hear him fumbling in the dark. The light from Carlo's phone blinks on, lighting up our section of passageway. With a quick push, he slides it across the floor to me.

BANG! Another bullet whizzes right in between us. I grab the phone and cover the screen with my hand.

"Stop!" Carlo shouts down the hall.

"Jonah told me . . . everything, Infinity. About their plans for you . . . for the world. How did I not see it? Perhaps I simply . . . didn't want to." Nanny Theresa's voice is fading with every word. "It all started with you, Infinity . . . and if there is even the smallest chance that I can stop it . . . then I will do my best to make sure . . . that it *ends* with you."

"She's talking crazy, she's gone completely mental," whispers Carlo.

Still covering the screen with one hand, I tap Jonah's number, then his password, into Carlo's phone. I hold it to my ear and Jonah answers almost immediately.

"Hello? Who is this? This number is restricted and encoded . . ."

"Jonah, it's Finn. You need to come home right now!"

"Finn? What's wrong?"

"Nanny Theresa killed her nurse. She's got a gun and she's trying to shoot me and Carlo."

"Oh no . . . no. Finn, are you in sublevel nine?"

"Yeah . . . how did you . . . ?"

"I received an alert of a security override. I was already on my way back. Get out of there, Finn. Now!" The phone beeps and Jonah hangs up.

"Jonah wants us to get out of here," I whisper.

"That sounds like a good idea," Carlo whispers back. "How do we open the door?"

"If it's anything like levels one and two, there should be an exit button right beside it."

"Yeah. She might hit one of us when we step into the light, though. Maybe we should just wait until Jonah gets here?"

"Maybe. But if Jonah opens that door, she might shoot him instead. Wait, how many shots has she fired? Was it four or five?"

"I dunno," whispers Carlo. "Why?"

"She's using an antique revolver from her room. It holds only six bullets. I've got an idea. Let's give her something else to aim at." I touch the screen of Carlo's phone and it lights up; I hold it up high with my fingertips.

"Finn. Don't!" Carlo pushes off the wall and grabs for the phone. A shot rings out, followed by the shattering of glass. I quickly snatch back my hand as the phone is knocked from my fingers, its light snuffed out.

BANG!

Another shot echoes down the passage and I recoil as a spray of warm droplets speckles my face.

No.

Please.

No.

I blindly grope in the dark with panic. "Carlo!"

There's no answer. "Carlo! *Answer me!*"

I find his ankle, jump to my feet, and pull with all my strength back toward the entrance.

"Talk to me Carlo," I say between strained breaths. "SAY SOMETHING, DAMMIT!"

I drag him until I feel the cold metal of the door, and my fingers scramble desperately along the wall for the button. There isn't one.

I drop to my knees, and feel along Carlo's arms and chest. "Carlo, don't leave me. I need you," I whimper, tears welling in my eyes. I feel up his neck and then across his face. It's soaked wet with his blood.

"No."

Rage boils up inside me. Anger and shock like I've never felt before spreads like fire and ice through my whole body and envelops my heart like an iron cage. I feel pain and indescribable, unbearable, burning sorrow.

"You've killed him." My chest starts heaving uncontrollably. "You've killed him." I haul myself to my feet and stand in the dark, my clenched fists dripping with Carlo's blood. I scream like a raging storm into the void, *"You've killed him, you evil bitch!"*

Without thinking I sprint down the hall blindly, my footsteps echoing on the metallic floor as I go; the only image in my mind is the end of Nanny Theresa once and for all.

"Where are you?"

The sound of my footsteps changes like I've entered a bigger room. I hit something hard and there's a loud clattering of metal objects as I sprawl across the floor. I scramble to my feet, looking from side to side, cursing my eyes for not seeing in the dark.

Suddenly a computer screen blinks to life across the room. It isn't bright enough to completely light the whole space, but it's more than enough for me to see Nanny Theresa's ghostly illuminated face. My eyes begin to adjust, and in the dim white glow from the screen I see that I'm standing in the center of what looks like an operating room. There's a stainless steel table with lights hanging over it, and vague shapes of machines and equipment line the walls. A flimsy wheeled trolley lies overturned at my feet and all kinds of surgical tools are scattered across the floor. I snatch up a scalpel, kick the trolley aside, and stride toward Nanny Theresa. She's sitting in what resembles a dentist's chair with her eyes closed, her chest rising and falling ever so slightly, the antique pistol resting in the palm of her open hand. A computer screen is mounted in front of her face on a metal swivel arm, and there's some kind of thick metal band with wires coming out of it clamped to her forehead.

I push the screen aside and grab the collar of her hospital gown.

"Wake up," I hiss, my hand shaking with rage as I press the blade of the scalpel to her neck. "I want to look into your eyes before I kill you."

Nanny Theresa slowly opens her eyes and smiles at me. "Cut my throat if you like . . . Infinity," she says looking sideways at the computer screen. "But I've already . . . escaped."

I look over to the monitor and see two words flashing in bright red. UPLOAD COMPLETE.

"What do you mean, you psycho bitch?" I growl at her. "You're sitting right here. Either you live and go to prison, or I kill you myself. You can't escape what you've done."

She looks me right in the eyes. "Now, now, child . . . that's no way to speak to your . . . dear old Nanny Theresa."

She gasps, and with her final breath utters her dying words. "Onix. Send." Her eyes roll back in her skull, her head slumps to the side, and she's gone.

The monitor changes. Now there's only one word flashing in blue. SENDING.

"No!" yells a voice from behind me. I turn and see Jonah standing in the half-light with Carlo's limp body in his arms. He lays him down on the operating table and rushes over. He pushes me out of the way and shakes Nanny Theresa by the shoulders. "What have you done, Theresa!"

"She's dead, Jonah."

He doesn't even seem to hear me.

He grabs the computer screen on both sides and stares at it in horror and disbelief.

"Onix! Cancel last action! Onix!" There's no answer. "What's happened to Onix, Finn?"

"Nanny Theresa said she . . . muzzled him?"

"That explains why I couldn't use the pod. I had to break into the emergency exit to get down here," he mutters.

"What's going on, Jonah? What is this thing she's hooked up to?" I ask as he jabs and swipes at the screen.

"It's a neural interface. Your father designed it to map thoughts and record memories. It looks like Theresa has used it to digitize her brain patterns into the mainframe."

"What do you mean?"

"She's uploaded her mind into the computer."

"That's impossible. Isn't it?"

"No. Not impossible. Just extremely dangerous. It's been attempted only once before, and that person didn't survive, either." Jonah is deep in concentration, frantically tapping code after code into the screen.

"Who didn't survive?"

Jonah stops tapping and meets my eyes. The look on his face immediately tells me that he's regretting the words he just spoke.

"My . . . mother?" I manage.

Jonah turns back to the screen and jabs at it more quickly and twice as hard as before. "That's not what I said, Finn."

"My mother uploaded her mind? Why, Jonah? Can she see me? Can I talk to her?" My words fall on deaf ears.

"Onix! Answer me, Onix!" Jonah bellows.

"Neural interface data upload successful."

"NO!" Jonah yells at the screen and roughly pushes it away.

"What does it mean, Jonah?"

"What it means is that Theresa digitized her thoughts and sent them to the Hypernet. They could be anywhere. She could be anywhere."

"Just like my mother could be?"

"Now is not the time, Finn," Jonah says coldly. "Onix."

"Yes, Major Brogan?"

"Lights."

The room is flooded with bright white light. I squint as my eyes adjust.

Jonah must be insane if he thinks avoiding the subject of my mother will end this conversation, but for now the multitude of questions I desperately need to ask will have to wait.

I lost my dearest friend today.

I force myself to look over at Carlo. I slowly walk to the side of the operating table and look down at him. His face is smeared and his hair is wet with blood. He looks so peaceful, like he's sleeping. Tears pour down my cheeks. I reach out my trembling hand to touch his arm, but my fingers recoil against my will. I just can't bring myself to do it.

"Carlo is gone, Finn," whispers Jonah.

I close my eyes, hang my head, and sob quietly. Images of Carlo dance through my mind: his smiling face, his deep-green eyes, his olive skin bronzed richer by the sun. I'm there, too, running after him through the trees of the Seven Acre Wood, sitting beside him talking for hours in our hidden places among the fallen leaves, fighting with him, laughing with him, riding horses through the fields with him, lying in the soft grass telling him all my deepest secrets. Memories of every summer we ever had unfold—colorful, vivid, and beautiful like pages in a picture book made just for us, containing the happiest pieces of my childhood frozen in time forever, and ending with the moment of our first kiss.

Our last kiss.

Deep down I think I knew, but was never brave enough to confess: I had fallen in love with the boy by the pond in the woods.

I wipe the tears from my eyes and look down again at Carlo. Only then do I realize that I'm holding his lifeless hand in mine.

"Don't worry, sweetheart," Jonah whispers from behind me. "I promise, tomorrow it will all be like it never happened."

Suddenly a sharp sting bites deep into the back of my neck. Almost instantly, my limbs turn to jelly and I collapse to the floor. I can't move anything except my eyes, but I'm still wide awake and alert.

What's happening?! Jonah! What are you doing?! I scream the words as loud as I can but my lips don't move. They don't make a sound.

Out of the corner of my eye, I see Jonah placing a syringe on a kidney-shaped stainless steel tray. He walks over to Nanny Theresa's body and removes the thick metal band from her head. He grabs the front of her gown and roughly pulls her off the chair. Her lifeless body flops into a heap beside me on the cold white tiles. Her limp tongue lolls out from the side of her mouth like a pink eel, and her dead, gray, sunken eyes stare right through me.

Jonah walks over to me, crouches down, and lifts me into his arms like a floppy rag doll. He carries me over to the chair and gently places me upon it. He takes the metal band and puts it on my head.

All I can do is glare at him in disbelief, my lips totally paralyzed, my eyes glistening with pleading.

"Just like it never happened, Finn. I'll fix your memories. Wipe this whole day clean away. I promise." He says the words with a warm smile that sends shivers through every atom of my entire useless body.

Jonah swings the computer screen toward him and begins typing. "You fell from a horse and were knocked out cold; you've been in bed for two days recovering." Tears flood down my face, dripping off my chin into my lap. "Nanny Theresa retired and moved away to live with her sister. She's very happy." A pathetic whimper is all I can muster from my half-open mouth.

"Carlo went to live with his mother in a different country. You've grown apart and lost contact."

Anger, betrayal, sadness, and fear course through my veins, my mind, my body, and deep into my suffering soul.

"Virtually fabricate the scenarios, please, Onix, and prepare the relevant neurons for erasure and memory implantation."

"Yes, Major Brogan."

You're not my brother, Onix. You're nothing but a filthy traitor.

Jonah gives me a look of concern and my skin not only crawls but prickles with hatred. "You won't remember this horrible day, sweetheart. I swear." He reaches over and wipes the tears from my cheek. I wish I could pull away and spit in his face.

"Try and relax, Finn. I realize that you don't remember, but you and I have been doing this since you were two years old. This won't hurt at all." Jonah smiles to himself. "Y'know, it's funny how many times I've told you that."

My mind writhes in horror and disgust. I feel dirty, my entire being white-hot with the pain of a lifetime of betrayal.

Jonah takes a deep breath and attempts one last look of reassurance. Then, he simply swipes his finger across the screen—casually, as if erasing a smudge from a mirror—and the raging inferno of pain and sorrow in my heart is utterly and instantly snuffed out like the dying flame of a lonely candle.

CHAPTER ELEVEN

Carlo . . . where are you?

I can't see you, Carlo. I can't see anything. Help me, please, help me.

His warm lips find mine in the darkness.

There you are. I thought I'd lost you. Please don't leave me.

My chest rises and falls.

Where are we, Carlo? Why does my throat hurt so much? Why can't I see you, Carlo? Where are we?

A slow, hollow, thumping rhythm echoes through the darkness.

My chest rises and falls again and there, far above me, a fuzzy circle of light slowly grows into view.

I don't understand what's happening, Carlo.

I feel his lips against mine once more.

What's wrong with me? Why can't I move?

"C'mon, Finn!" The voice is faint and distant, distorted but familiar. *Is that you, Carlo? Where are you?*

"C'mon, Finn!" the voice calls again, clearer this time, closer. "Don't give up. Come back to us."

You sound different, Carlo. Are you in the light? I'll go to the light, Carlo. I'll meet you there. I'll see you soon.

"C'mon, Finn, open your eyes!" the voice demands, loudly now, as if someone is shouting in my face.

A warm mouth on mine, my chest rises again.

"C'mon, Finn, breathe for me. That's it, open your eyes!"

A slap to my cheek, a sting of pain, a huge intake of air, my eyes flick wide open and I'm back, coughing and retching.

"Give her some room, everyone," says Professor Francis.

My eyes begin to focus on the blurry face above me. "Ryan?" My voice is feeble and raspy.

He's kneeling beside me, leaning over me. I lie there for a moment, wheezing heavily, staring up into his golden-amber eyes.

"Hi there," he says with a little smile.

"Hi," I whisper back. Ryan gently brushes my tangled hair from my face and softly strokes my cheek. I close my eyes at his touch.

"What happened?" I murmur.

"I don't know," he says. "I found you lying up here. You'd stopped breathing. You're OK now, though."

"You saved me?"

He nods.

"Thank you."

"Ah, it was nothing. You didn't need to stop breathing just to get a kiss from me y'know. You only had to ask."

My weak laugh turns into a cough. Bettina's face comes into view, her eyes filled with tears.

"Finn, oh my god, I was so worried."

"What's happened here?" Percy's panicked voice says from somewhere.

"It looks like Finn had another fainting spell, but this time she stopped breathing," Professor Francis explains.

"Is that what happened?" I ask Ryan. "Did I faint again?"

"It looks that way," he says with a compassionate smile.

"My neck hurts."

I gently touch my throat and suddenly gasp like I've been electrocuted. With a stabbing flash of colors, everything comes flooding back. The pirate construct, Nanny Theresa, the murdered nurse, Onix, Carlo getting shot, Nanny escaping, Jonah's inconceivable betrayal, invading my mind and replacing my memories with forgeries. Everything that was taken from me that day is bubbling back into my mind like an overflowing sewer.

It's not my imagination; it's not! In my heart I know it all to be true. Does that mean every other dream I've had in the past week is true as well? They must be. I know how he did it now. They must all be true. I feel like a sword has cut my life open and I'm bleeding all the lies away. Jonah said I wouldn't remember anything. But I have remembered. It's all come back, and it's come back with a vengeance. Suddenly the worst realization cuts the deepest of all.

Carlo is dead. He died in sublevel nine almost two years ago.

I sit bolt upright and vomit all over the deck.

Feet spring away from the puddle I've just brought up. "Ewww, that's gross," says a voice that sounds a lot like Margaux's.

"It's a perfectly natural response," Professor Francis says in my defense.

I wipe my mouth on the back of my sleeve, trying my best to ignore the cruel giggles and disgusted glares from the hovering faces. "Get me out of here."

Ryan takes my arm and helps me to my feet. The students in a semicircle around me, with their mixed looks of pity and amusement, make me feel even sicker.

Percy pushes through. "Come, Miss Brogan. This is serious. I'll take you to the infirmary so Nurse Talbot can take a good look at you."

He tries to take my arm, but I jerk it away.

"Don't touch me. I don't want to go to the infirmary. I want to get out of this place."

Percy looks confused. "Please, Miss Brogan. Fainting twice in one morning is definitely something we should be concerned about."

"I didn't faint, I was . . ." I quickly scan the deck and spot the pirate captain over Margaux's shoulder. He's standing by the ship's wheel exactly where he was before, still as a statue, like nothing ever happened.

How do I explain this without sounding like an absolute lunatic?

I realize that I can't. They'd have me in a padded cell by this afternoon.

Carlo flashes through my mind again and sorrow grips me. My head hurts and my throat aches, but the pain of those combined is nothing compared to the knife in my broken heart. *Oh, Carlo. I'm so sorry.*

I need to get away. I need to gather my thoughts. I need to get out of this horrible place. I don't care about seeing my father anymore. Not even one little bit. I could demand to go home, but Jonah would be there and I don't want to be anywhere near him ever again. At that very moment I realize that, sadly, I don't have anywhere else to go but . . .

"I want to go back to school."

"I think you should lie down for a bit first, Finn," says Professor Francis.

"I want to go."

"Lie down in the nurse's office and we'll collect you after the tour."

"No. Get me out of here."

"Finn, think of everyone else . . ."

"Get me out of here . . . NOW!"

Even though I'm the only one who knows what really happened, everyone around me is already looking at me like I'm crazy. Even Bit.

"Calm down, Miss Brogan," Percy orders.

I take a deep breath, gather what remains of my strength, and pull my tie from my neck. "Fine. I'll find my own way out."

I try to avoid Ryan's and Bit's eyes as I push past Jennifer and Brody and a smirking Brent and tromp down the stairs that lead to the lower deck of the ship.

"Miss Brogan!" Percy barks at my back. I ignore him. I stride across the deck, stepping over the bodies of the fake pirates as I go. I reach the railing and lean over it, trying to judge the distance to the water. It's only about fifteen feet. I know that's not the real ocean down there; it doesn't stretch on forever. It's just an illusion, and if Percy won't let me off this thing then I'll leave on my own. I sling one leg over the railing with absolutely no idea what I'll do when I reach the edge of the dome. I guess I'll cross that bridge when I come to it.

"Wait! Miss Brogan!" shouts Percy. I can hear him scrambling down the stairs behind me. "Help me, boys. Grab her before she hurts herself!"

I glance back and see Brent and Brody leap down the stairs. They trot ahead of Percy and make straight for me.

I dismount the rail to face them. "Don't touch me. I'm warning you," I growl, as I ball up my fists and take a fighting stance.

Brent and Brody stop and look at each other, grinning, obviously highly amused by my threat. Shaking his head, Brent approaches me, with Brody only a step behind him.

"I don't want to hurt you, but I will if I have to!" I shout. Brent laughs out loud.

"Hey! Leave her alone!" Ryan yells. He leaps down the whole flight of stairs with one jump and runs toward the two boys.

Brody turns back to stop him and they both struggle into a grapple as Brent advances toward me.

When he's one step away, Brent makes a grab for my arm. I easily swat it aside. He tries again with the other hand, gripping my wrist tightly. In the blink of an eye, I circle my forearm, reverse the hold, and twist down hard. Brent's body swivels involuntarily as he drops to his knees, his back arched, his mouth open in a silent scream, his eyes filled to the edges with shocked surprise. Someone in the group upstairs giggles.

"I warned you," I hiss in his ear.

"Miss Brogan! Stop that at once!" shouts Percy.

"Finn Brogan, release that boy! Right this minute!" commands Professor Francis.

I respect the Professor. I look over toward his voice and loosen my grip. Big mistake. Free from my hold, Brent spins, quickly rising from the ground, and, with a loud smack, uppercuts his fist squarely into the bottom of my jaw.

A gasp of utter disbelief issues from everyone on the upper deck. Just how much of a bastard Brent is becomes glaringly clear with that one cowardly act. Even though I can't stand him, I never would have pegged him as the kind of guy who would punch a girl in the face— even if I did just make him look like a fool in front of everyone. That was a hard punch; I'm momentarily stunned. I stumble and lose my footing, tripping over my own feet.

"Security four!" Percy bellows into his wrist.

I'm suddenly woozy. Dizzy, my balance wavers and then abandons me altogether. Clutching desperately at the air, then the railing, my fingertips scramble for a hold but I'm powerless to stop as I topple over the side of the ship, plunging backward into the water below. I shut my eyes tight, preparing for the impact, uncertain whether the motionless, computer-generated ocean below will be liquid or solid. There's no splash. My back hits hard and flat on the surface, knocking the wind out of me and smacking the back of my skull with a jarring thud. Sparkles of color scatter in the blackness.

∞

"You're not concentrating, Finn."

I open my eyes to an outstretched hand. The hand is attached to a familiar arm. An arm tattooed with three lightning bolts across the blade of a sword. The arm leads up to a familiar face. A face I never wanted to see again.

It's Jonah.

I want to scream and run, but my hand reaches out on its own and Jonah pulls me up off the floor of the combat room in sublevel two.

"You should have seen that foot sweep coming from a mile away."

"Sorry, I was thinking about something else," I murmur as I absently dust myself off.

Jonah walks over to the weapon rack and grabs the two towels that are hanging over it. "How do you expect to defend yourself out there in the big, bad world if you can't keep focused? A mugger isn't just going to wait for you to gather your thoughts, y'know." He throws me a towel and wipes the sweat from his brow with the other.

"Were you thinking about Carlo?"

"No."

"Don't lie, Finn. You're no good at it."

I sigh and drop my shoulders. He's right. I couldn't lie on a bed.

"OK, yes. I was thinking about Carlo. He never answers his phone, Jonah, he doesn't return my emails, and he doesn't spend summer here anymore. He was my best friend for most of my life and now he's disappeared off the face of the earth."

"You know where he is, Finn. He moved to Italy with his mother. He has a new life now. Maybe you should take the hint and leave the boy alone."

"But I think about him all the time. Sometimes I get a bad feeling—like he's in danger or something. I just want to know that he's OK. And living in Italy is no excuse for not texting back."

I wipe my forehead angrily, throw the towel at Jonah, and cross the mats toward the metal passage that leads to the pod. "Carlo is a douche bag and I'm done with training today."

"I agree, Finn. Carlo is a total douche bag."

I smile toward the ceiling. "Thank you, Onix! Nice to know that *someone* is on my side." I throw an accusing look at Jonah.

"Finn, would you stop teaching Onix to speak like a sixteen-year-old girl?" Jonah half-heartedly scolds. "And what do you mean, you think about him 'all the time'? What bad feelings? How often is 'all the time'?"

I spin on my heels to face him. "Lately, it's *all* the time. It feels like he's alone and hurt in the dark somewhere. I know how crazy it sounds. Oh, and just in case you forgot, I turned seventeen a week ago. There was cake and everything."

Jonah doesn't give me an answer. To be honest I didn't even expect one, but he's just standing there and looking at me like he's studying a problem, his face furrowed with concern, quietly talking to himself. I hear him mutter, "Why isn't it working anymore? For some reason they're just not holding like they used to."

Jonah keeps staring at me, actually, kinda *through* me, absent-mindedly stroking his chin, lost in thought.

"Why is *what* not working? What are you talking about? Hello? Earth to Jonah," I say, waving my hand back and forth.

"What? Oh, it's nothing. I was thinking of something else. Which, my girl, is exactly what you need to do. I think it's about time I showed you sublevel nine."

Jonah puts his arm around my shoulders and walks me down the passageway.

"There's a sublevel nine?"

"Actually, they go all the way down to sublevel ten."

I'm genuinely shocked.

"What's down there?"

"Well, a lot of it is storage and empty labs your father used for research and development. They're boring; that's why I never mentioned them. But on sublevel nine there's a device called a neural interface. I can use it to . . . to introduce virtual combat scenarios directly into your mind to help with your training. It's like being inside the best video game ever."

"Really?"

"Absolutely. Let's go try it out. Whatya say?"

"OK. Sounds cool, I guess."

He presses the button on the wall and the door leading to the pod shaft slides into the ceiling, opening into darkness.

I open my eyes, bewildered. I groan at the ache in my back and clutch the bump on the back of my head. What the hell was that? For a fleeting moment I was home again. I said it was a week after my birthday, so that means it was a little over three weeks ago—on a day that I don't remember at all. Yet another day ripped away, cut and pasted over with a manufactured memory.

Maybe all the memories Jonah stole from me, and all the days he changed in my head, are fighting to resurface. Maybe the dam is cracked and it's leaking, crumbling, about to burst.

If that's the case, the thought terrifies me. If the day of Carlo's murder is anything to go by, I'm not sure I'm ready to know what else Jonah has taken away from me. I need to get out of here. I need to get up and get out and run as far away from this place as I can.

The side of the pirate ship juts up at my feet from the solid "water." After a few short pants, I recover my breath and force myself up onto my elbows. Percy's face appears over the railing above me, closely followed by Ryan's. "Are you alright, Finn?" Ryan calls down.

Before I can respond, Percy issues an ominous order out across the ocean.

"Take her to the vacant Clean Room. Through air-lock one."

For a split second, I wonder who he's talking to. He's looking just past me. I tilt my head back, following Percy's sight line, and see a female-shaped Drone Template robot dressed in smooth silver from head to toe bending down toward me. It grips me under the arm and lifts me up onto my feet with no effort at all. It takes a tight hold of my wrist and twists, maneuvering me into a painful arm lock.

"Ow! Hey! Get your hands off me!"

The Drone doesn't even turn its dark plastic mask in acknowledgment. A single illuminated word in red capital letters scrolls across the surface of the smooth black oval, and it pretty much says it all.

SECURITY

"You need a little time to cool off, Miss Brogan. It's for your own good," Percy calls down at me with phony concern. The Drone turns and pushes me along a white-tiled pathway that has sprouted up through the surface of the silent ocean. I struggle to get free, but the android is incredibly strong, gripping my wrist like a vise.

The Drone marches me away like a prisoner, resigned to my unjust capture. Before long I'm out of earshot of the boat, but movement catches the corner of my eye. I strain my neck back over my shoulder to see that a commotion has broken out on the lower deck. Ryan is in Brent's face, arguing and pointing toward me. Brent pushes Ryan, who swiftly cracks him in the nose with a hard right hook. Brent clutches his face and drops out of sight behind the railing as Brody springs onto Ryan like a panther. Percy, Miss Cole, and Professor Francis are all yelling for them to stop while Percy stands off to the side, eyeballing the boys and mouthing instructions into his wrist. The rest of the group looks on from the top deck, staring in morbid fascination as everything goes to hell. More black-masked silver suits arrive on the lower deck and grab the three boys, dragging them back from the edge of the railing and out of sight.

I quickly scan the group for Bit, but I can't spot her. Movement in the shadows catches my attention and I finally see her. Bit is inexplicably dangling off the rear of the ship, her feet kicking beneath her as she hangs by her fingers from the loose rungs of a knotted rope ladder. She drops into a crouch on the hard "water" and straightens her glasses. With one last sideways glance to check if the coast is clear, she fixes her eyes on me and breaks into a sprint, running as fast as her legs will carry her across the solid surface. I can't help but smile and shake my head.

I've known her for almost four years, and even after all that time, shy, mild-mannered Bettina Otto still manages to surprise me.

No one up on the deck seems to have noticed that she's missing. I had always thought that Bit had a knack for going unnoticed, but until this moment I had never thought of how handy it could be. Maybe it's due to blindly following Percy's orders, or perhaps it really is because of Bit's ninja-like abilities, but even the Drone seems oblivious to her presence, even after she's caught right up to us and is walking beside us, wheezing to catch her breath.

"You could've waited for me," she whispers with labored huffs.

I smile at her. "Like I had a choice."

There's that familiar hiss again as just up ahead, a wide rectangular opening grows in the surface of the black glass wall. The Drone ushers me through into an elevator-sized room with bright-white glowing walls. Bit and I both squint in the light.

"Where are you taking us?" I demand, but there's no answer from it. "I can walk on my own y'know."

It ignores me like it's leading a sack of potatoes instead of a disobedient teenage girl.

"This has to be some kind of human rights violation. My father is Dr. Blackstone. You'll be a pile of scrap metal for this. Recycled into a toaster!"

My empty threat goes unacknowledged. It's really no surprise. I know my father doesn't give a damn what happens to me, and this robot probably wouldn't care even if it could.

Suddenly without warning, the room drops and Bit steadies herself on the wall to keep from falling over. The wall that she's leaning on slides sideways so quickly that Bit falls anyway, out onto the shiny white floor of a wide hallway. Its walls are curved and jagged and seem to be made of some kind of sparkling crystalline material. It really is quite beautiful. It's how I imagine it would be inside a massive quartz geode.

The Drone walks on, still holding me tight, still pushing me forward, past Bit and onward down the hall. Bit jumps to her feet and springs after us.

"Finn, where do you think it's taking you?"

"I heard Percy say something about a clean room?"

Bit frowns. "Why would they be taking you to a clean room? That's a room where they make computer chips and stuff like that."

"I don't care where they take me, just as long as I'm not in that dome and one step closer to getting out of here."

"What happened back there, Finn? You said that you didn't faint. Did you do it on purpose? Of course you did. I knew it! That's brilliant."

I look sideways at Bit. Why would she think I would do that? Anyway, now is not the time to try and explain. I give Bit a tiny shake of my head, mouth the word "Later," and look sideways at the Drone. She seems to get what I'm trying to say; she gives me a little nod and follows on in silence.

The Drone forces me down one passage which links to another and to another which turns a corner into another. It's like I'm being taken into the heart of a maze of crystal caves. All the way through the labyrinth, the only sound is the syncopated tapping of the Drone's silver boots on the floor and a low hum that emanates from every wall. I hadn't thought about what it would look like beyond the boundary of the dome, but I did expect there to be people here. Workers? Staff? Someone? Anyone? We've been walking for a couple of minutes now and we haven't seen another soul.

Eventually the Drone stops outside a frosted-glass door marked with a large gray number one. With a quiet "shush" it slides open before me. The Drone releases its hold, nudges me in the back, and I stumble forward through the doorway. As deftly as a mouse, Bit ducks through the doorway and scoots to my side. The Drone steps in after us and the door slides shut behind it. This new room is tiny and claustrophobic. It's hardly a room at all—more like a small, white, walk-in closet with some kind of metal grating as a floor. There's barely enough space in here for *me* to be comfortable, let alone Bit and that lady robot as well. Bit looks nervous and I have to admit that I'm not exactly feeling very calm, either.

"Y'know, you didn't have to come with me, Bit."

Bit shrugs her shoulders and smiles at me. "That's what I'm here for. Want some gum?"

I smile and hold out my hand as she drops a piece into my palm. I pop it in my mouth and chew quietly as I take a good look at the tiny room. There's not much to see. "What are we supposed to do in here?"

"Just wait I guess," whispers Bit.

"Wait for what? Are the teen police gonna come and arrest me for passing out?"

Bit smiles. "They should arrest Brent for punching you. He's seriously insane."

"He hits like a girl. Next time I see him, I'll show him how a woman throws a punch."

Bit tilts her head to the side, looking from one of my eyes to the other. "Infinity?"

"Ahhh . . . yes, Bettina?" I reply, frowning. She's being weird.

"Oh, nothing," she says, giving me a timid smile.

She's being *really* weird. I nervously smile back.

Suddenly the room switches color from stark white to blood red and our smiles instantly vanish.

"Finn." Bit grabs my arm tight.

I'm about to say that everything will be OK, without even the slightest clue if it actually will be, when a voice that I've known since I was thirteen years old booms through the walls.

"You are entering a sterile laboratory. To maintain its clean working environment, dust- and foreign-particle evacuation will commence immediately. Please remain still."

Bit and I look at each other wide-eyed. There's no time to call out to Onix or even think about what's going to happen when all of a sudden an intensely powerful gust of wind surges up from the floor, blowing our skirts and hair vertical. Bit shrieks and wrestles to retain her dignity as our school uniforms are violently flurried upward in the hard blast of air. The Drone stands as still as a statue. I instinctively shut my eyes against the rushing tempest—only for a split second—and when I open them again, the wind is deafening in my ears as I fall through the cold night air.

∞

I see lights, scattered like twinkling diamonds across the dark cityscape, each tiny glow illuminating a different section of the streets and rooftops far below me.

My lips don't move, but I can hear my own voice speaking in my head, muted but perceptible, like a whisper in the back of my skull.

"Twenty seconds to touchdown."

I pull a cord on the harness and I'm jerked upward as my parachute opens. I drift on the breeze, pulling the toggles as I descend, expertly steering the chute through the chill of the night toward a group of four even-height, flat-topped buildings 160 feet below. I blink and my night vision flicks on, turning my sight grainy green but a thousand times clearer, replacing the shadowy angles and vague dark outlines with sharp-edged details of the rapidly approaching structures beneath me. Sixty-five feet above one of the rooftops, I pull a second cord. The parachute cuts away and evaporates silently into smoke above my head, like tissue paper touched with a lightless flame. I drop like a missile through the night sky and land hard. The sickening crack of my ankle breaking comes from inside my combat boot, but I don't even wince as I roll smoothly into a low crouch. The pain signals shoot up my leg toward my brain where they're recognized, processed, re-routed, and converted into a low-pitched pulsing warning tone in the back of my mind. Motionless, I wait a few seconds for the pain signals to quiet as my bones repair. The warning tone ceases and I take off, sprinting across the open, concrete-tiled expanse of the rooftop. I slide to a halt, pinning my body-armored back against the wall behind a rooftop-access door.

I cautiously peer around the corner and take in the layout. The concrete tiles end at the edge of a line of shrubbery surrounding a large circular area of perfectly manicured grass. There's a rock water feature at the far edge trickling down into an inlayed pool of koi carp. In the center of the grass circle, I see the back of a beautiful wrought-iron park bench. Just in front of it, propped on a sturdy-limbed tripod, is a large telescope—the kind amateur stargazers own if they have a spare four hundred thousand dollars kicking around. Flickering torches on the perimeter cast a gentle firelight across the entire garden area.

I concentrate for a moment and the exact time pops into my head: 10:29 p.m. and fifteen seconds. In forty-five seconds, give or take, just like he does every cloudless Sunday night, a man will walk through the door opposite me.

"Infinity One. Report," says a male voice in my head.

"Situation cool," my own voice says in my ears, as I speak without speaking again.

"Cool?" the voice says with a tone of annoyance. "Is that how we talk when we're in the middle of a mission?"

"No, sir. Sorry, sir," I reply in my mind with military terseness.

"You may only be sixteen years old, but if you're not taking any of this seriously I'll wipe your mind clean like a rag to a whiteboard. Do you understand, Infinity One?"

Same old empty threat. They'd never actually wipe my mind clean. They need a soldier who can think for herself in a situation like this, not a mindless zombie. In fact, I'm not totally sure they can even do it at all, but as usual I'll play along.

"I'm completely focused on the job at hand, sir."

"Good. Don't forget that I could have Onix scan your mind back at base to get the truth. I know what a good liar you are."

"Yes, sir; oh, and by the way, I'm seventeen years old today, sir."

"Happy birthday."

"Thank you, sir."

Mind scans. That they *can* do. I'm not worried. Onix is on my side. He fakes every one of my mind-scan results. They still hurt like a drill to the skull, though.

I hear the quiet creak of a door opening and I quickly focus my attention. Footsteps tap on concrete tiles, then muffle into the soft rustle of shoes on grass.

I peek around the corner and see the back of a silver-haired man in a white suit taking a seat on the bench. I watch as he leans forward and adjusts knobs on the telescope, pausing every now and then to look up into the night sky.

"Eyes on subject," I say in my mind.

"Engage target," the voice replies.

I step from cover and move silently through the night like a ghost. Forty feet from the back of the iron bench I leap, an unnaturally high, arcing leap. At the apex I cock my arm back and give a short whistle. The man turns his head in surprise and looks up in startled horror as I land like a crouched cat behind him, perfectly balanced on the thin edge of the back of the bench. He doesn't have time to cry out for help, or even blink for that matter, as my arm shoots forward like a striking cobra. My pointed index finger pierces through his eye socket and into his brain like the tip of a dagger, popping eyeball juice all over the back of my hand like the jelly inside a plump, round grape. His other eyeball looks at me in morbid disbelief before slowly rolling back in his skull like a weighted marble. His mouth drops agog and his arms fall limp. Blood and eye goop run down his face, through his thick wiry moustache, and dribble fast and thick into his open mouth. I wiggle my spear-tip digit in his eye hole, mulching his brain a little more just for good measure, and his arms jut out comically in stiff contorted angles as his body quivers and spasms. His final gasping breath becomes a gargling death rattle as he chokes on his own blood and ocular fluid. I smile like the cat from Wonderland. I withdraw my finger with an unceremonious shlooping sound and his lifeless body rolls off the bench and onto the cool grass.

His name was Bernard Munce, former member of the board of directors of Blackstone Technologies.

I called him Walrus Face.

I remember that day when I was six years old, you bastard. The day you tore my dress and tried to violate me. All for what? "Scientific curiosity?" I would have killed you even if I hadn't been instructed to. This is a very good day. I couldn't have asked for a better gift. Happy birthday to me.

I look down at his dead body and grin. He thought he'd deleted every trace of his former life. He thought that we would never find him. He was wrong. As it turns out, dead wrong. I laugh out loud at my own lame joke. Still perched like a crow on the back of the bench, I inhale deeply and take in the stars. It really is a lovely night to be stargazing.

"Task achieved," I say in my mind.

"Well done. Come home, Infinity One," responds the voice.

Time to go.

I'll scale the side of the building and disappear into the night through the back streets of the city. From there I'll rendezvous with the transport and be back in England before dawn.

The sound of porcelain breaking on concrete shatters the silence and I spin around. A dark-haired man in his thirties wearing a black suit and red tie is standing at the open-access door; shards of broken teacup lie in a steaming puddle at his feet. "Mr. Munce?" he asks in a graveled whisper.

It's Munce's bodyguard.

S. Harrison

There's a look of shocked astonishment on his face as the gravity of the situation sinks in. It would've been nice to have finished the job before he got here.

Oh well.

His gaze flicks across Bernard Munce's corpse and his expression changes from shock to one of deep sorrow. "Bernie?" he whispers again, his voice cracking. His eyes shift directly to me and his demeanor flash-changes to utter rage. With one fluid, well-trained movement, he whips a gun from a concealed holster and points it directly at my chest.

It doesn't make any difference. In three-point-two seconds, he'll be dead as well.

I spring at him from the bench like a vampire bat and his gun lights up the night.

BANG!

I envelop his head with my arms, twisting and pulling upward in a manner so practiced that it's second nature, separating the vertebrae in his neck with a succession of muffled popping sounds. I backflip off his falling body and land silently in a crouch on the rooftop.

Three-point-two seconds.

I look down and notice the hole in the center of my chest where his bullet pierced my body armor. Point-blank range. Went right through. I poke my finger into the hole and pull my pendant out through it.

"Damn it," I say out loud.

"What is it, Infinity One? What's happened?" the voice asks in my head.

"Bodyguard. Shot me."

"Damage report."

"It's OK. I'm uninjured."

"Good. Rendezvous with the transport. Report back when you're there."

"Yes, sir."

I look down at my pendant and run my thumb across the black, diamond-shaped stone set in the silver circle. There's a sizeable chip in the center and thin cracks splay across its entire surface.

Damn it to hell. I may not remember where I got this thing, but for some reason it means the world to me.

I walk over, pick up the gun from the concrete and point it at the dead bodyguard's head. *For cracking my pendant I'm going to empty every bullet in this gun right into your face. You can have a closed-casket funeral and we'll call it even.*

My finger tightens on the trigger. My hand begins to tremble. I feel very strange. It's hard to describe the sensation. It almost feels like I'm sorry for what I've just done. Like it was wrong somehow. Like what I'm about to do is wrong, too. I look down at the pistol in my trembling hand and it feels like it doesn't belong there.

I toss the gun aside and walk to the ledge of the building, trying my best to shake off the jitters. That felt decidedly unpleasant. What the hell was that?

I push it to the back of my mind and look over the edge into the street below. It's an easy climb. I spot a police car turning down an adjacent side street. Its pursuit lights suddenly flash on red and blue and its siren wails into life, but it's not heading toward this building. Guess I'm not the only one doing dark deeds in this city tonight.

I watch it drive away into the distance in the opposite direction, but strangely its siren is getting louder and louder. It changes in pitch, mutating in my ears until it almost sounds like a human scream. In fact, it sounds exactly like a human scream. A blood-curdling scream so loud that it feels like it's coming right out of my own throat. It's then that I realize . . . it *is* me.

Red light pours into my eyes and I'm cowering on the floor, holding my knees to my chest, screaming at the top of my lungs. With a loud smack, Bit slaps me hard across the cheek. The sting focuses my eyes on her scarlet-tinged face and I glare from side to side at the walls of the tiny room. With a computerized ping, they flick back to pristine white, as bright and clean as freshly fallen snow, mocking what I know to be true. Another stolen memory has reared its gruesome head, and it's smeared from end to end with the blood of two men that I ruthlessly murdered, on the night of my seventeenth birthday, on a moonlit rooftop in Paris.

CHAPTER TWELVE

All I can do is stare at Bit, kneeling there in front of me. My eyes are wide open but I'm not really seeing anything. I'm just staring at her, then right through her. Farther I reel, deeper into the abyss, blindly clawing in the dark recesses of my mind, searching for more. Hoping to find an answer, an excuse, any damn good reason, any reason at all why I would brutally kill two men in cold blood. Of course I don't find what I'm looking for.

Wait! My pendant!

It's physical *proof* that I'm innocent. I quickly loop my finger under the chain, pull the stone out from the top of my blouse, and cradle it in my palm. It looks perfectly normal, undamaged, no different from any other of the countless times I've seen it. I smile and almost laugh with relief as I rub my thumb across its smooth black surface. I may be losing my mind, but at least I'm not a killer. My fingernail catches the curve of the silver circle and as the pendant flips over I suddenly feel all the blood draining from my face. There, spanning out from the center of the stone like a sinister cobweb . . . is a lattice of splinter-thin cracks.

I let the pendant drop against my chest. There's no rationalizing or denying it. It *was* me on that rooftop. Dressed like a soldier. Moving like a hunter. Killing like an assassin and smiling like a psychopath. The truth is a jagged knife in my soul.

I just saw myself commit murder. Twice.

It's true. It's all true, and yet I just can't accept the fact that such horrific acts were performed with my own two hands. These two hands. They're quivering, wet with perspiration. In my mind the sweat becomes rivulets of blood. Thick gelatinous fluid drips down my wrist from the punctured sac of the deflated eyeball perched on my fingertips. I groan and retch as my stomach churns and a shiver of disgust ripples through my entire body.

"Finn . . ." Bit touches my cheek. "I'm so sorry I hit you, Finn, but you wouldn't stop screaming. What's wrong? Tell me."

I look her in the eyes and pull her hand away by the wrist. "I murdered two people."

"Finn . . . you're hurting me."

I look down and see that Bit's hand is turning purple.

"Oh god, I'm sorry," I say, releasing her.

Bit rubs at her wrist, her forehead furrowed with concern. "You said you . . . *killed* someone?"

I nod solemnly. "The dreams, Bit . . . the dreams I've been having. They're not just dreams like I told you they were. They're memories. They're all coming back to me. They're happening when I'm awake now, and I'm remembering all sorts of things. Things I never knew I had done. And right now, just a second ago, I remembered . . . killing two men."

I can't stop shaking. Bit sits down against the wall across from me.

"They're happening when you're awake now? What did you see?"

I ball my hands into fists, trying to stop the trembling. "I saw a rooftop, and I was there, and I had come to kill a man. It was me . . . but not me. It's hard to explain but I . . . I knew it was me but I didn't . . . I didn't recognize myself."

"It was you, but *not* you?"

"It really happened! I know it did!" Bit flinches at my sudden outburst. "His name was Bernard Munce. He knew my father. I killed him with my bare hands, Bit. And . . . and I *enjoyed* it. I really killed him, Bit! Him and his bodyguard. It was a month ago, on the night of my seventeenth birthday."

Bit just sits there against the wall looking at me strangely, intently. There's no fear or suspicion or doubt in her eyes at all. She's looking at me like she's studying me, almost as if she's waiting for something.

"Someone has been messing with my mind, Bit; don't ask me how I know, but I know for certain now. I swear it."

"What do you mean, Finn?"

I want to tell her everything. About Jonah, about Nanny Theresa, about Carlo. Especially Carlo. Who he was, how much he meant to me, how he was stolen from my mind and erased from my life. Everything. But it's all too much to find the words for.

"I'm not going crazy, Bit," I say, choking back tears. "Something is happening to me and it's real. I know it is. I just have to figure out what's going on."

"OK. I believe you. I really do," she says sincerely.

"Thanks, Bit. Please don't tell anyone about this. Not until I get it all sorted in my head."

"Do you think you should've told me all this in front of that?" Bit says, pointing up at the Drone.

"I've said it. Can't take it back."

I look up at the Drone, standing there as still and rigid as a silver mannequin.

"From what I've seen, they only seem to listen to Percy's bracelet-thing, anyway."

Bit smiles and nods. "His command module. Yeah, it looks that way. I'd love to get my hands on one of those things."

"Yeah," I reply, tucking my hands under my arms to stop the tremors.

"Hey, Finn. Y'know that guy you . . . killed? That Bernard guy?"

I nod. The images flash back across my mind and my skin crawls.

Bit picks at her fingernail and looks at the floor. "Try not to feel so bad about it. He deserved to die."

I squint at Bit. That was the last thing I expected to hear coming from the lips of bookish little Bettina Otto. "Deserved it?" I ask incredulously.

Bit nods and looks up at me, right into my eyes, like she's searching for something in them. "Yes. Especially after everything he's done."

Did she just say what I think she said? OK, I take it back. *That* was the last thing I expected to hear from her. Why would she say that? Does she somehow know what he did to me when I was a little girl? If so, how? There's no way that she could know who Bernard Munce was. It's impossible. I can't have told her. I didn't even remember that I had met him myself until I dreamed about it on the bus this morning. And even then I thought my imagination was playing tricks on me! In any case, she's wrong. The memory of what he did when I was young is real, I know that now. But it surely didn't deserve a death sentence.

I'm trying to cut through the writhing coils of confusion to form a coherent question when the wall beside us suddenly slides open, revealing a short, bright-white corridor.

The Drone juts a hand out, directing us into the passage, and Bit springs to her feet. I sit in stunned silence, trying desperately to wrap my head around what she just said to me. I look up at Bit, completely lost. She's just standing there, her hand outstretched toward me, her face devoid of emotion.

"Coming, Infinity?"

Infinity? That's the second time she's ever called me that, and both times were only in the last few minutes. What is Bit not telling me? How did I do all those things on that rooftop? Whose was that man's voice in my head? With more questions than answers reeling in my mind, I tuck my pendant of shame away and wearily take her hand.

One way or another, when I pull myself together, she's going to tell me what she knows. I'll make damned sure of it.

Bit strides ahead and I drag my feet after her, more confused than ever, the Drone in step close behind me.

We walk down the short white corridor and it ends in another frosted-glass door with another big number one on it. It slides open automatically and we go through into a bright rectangular room the size of a tennis court. It has sky-blue walls with wispy white clouds floating gently across them. They must be huge reality-definition video screens. The shiny white floor and low ceiling of the room are absolutely spotless. There's a door in each of the four walls, all with a different large gray number embossed on it. Professor Francis is there to greet us; he's frowning, standing in the center of the room with six glossy-white chairs positioned in a row before him. Another Drone is standing motionless a few feet behind him, its hands by its sides like a soldier. The word "SECURITY" is scrolling in red across its mask, too, just like the one that brought me here. Our robotic chaperone walks past us and, with a rigid little half-spin, takes up a position behind the Professor as well. Those things are so freaking creepy.

The Professor clears his throat and looks down his nose at us. "Miss Otto. Didn't think anyone saw you trotting off after Miss Brogan, did you? I saw you." He holds an open palm out toward the row of chairs. "Take a seat, ladies."

I'm still shaken from that horrific memory, so a seat would actually be quite nice right now. Bit sits down beside me and I look over at her. She doesn't look back; she just stares straight ahead with the smallest hint of a smile on her face. I'm not sure why, but that little smirk of hers makes me uncomfortable.

We sit there in silence. The disgruntled Professor flanked by two identical silver female bodyguards set against a bright-blue sky and fluffy white clouds makes the whole scene, quite frankly, surreal.

"Just so I don't have to repeat myself . . ." he says, adding a tapping foot to the bizarre equation, ". . . we'll wait for the others to arrive before I begin."

No sooner have the words come out of his mouth than the door with the big gray number three on it slides open. Brent steps through, followed closely by Brody. They're both disheveled. Brent's formerly brushed and styled fringe has been blown into a mess, and his nostrils are ringed with drying blood. He looks more pissed off than I've ever seen him, and that's quite a feat in itself. I can't help but smile, and for the briefest moment the sorrow and shock of all my new memories are dulled a tiny notch, even though one of my hands won't stop quivering.

"Take a seat, gentlemen," Professor Francis instructs in his best attempt at a stern voice. They both walk over to the chairs, ignoring me and Bit, and sit at the opposite end of the row. The two Drones that followed them in walk over to join the others in line behind the Professor.

Door number four slides open and Ryan saunters through, looking indignantly over his shoulder at the Drone behind him. As he gets nearer to the row of chairs, his attention shifts to Brent, but his expression remains the same, dagger-throwing glower.

He walks right past the boys and takes a seat beside me; his scowl transforms into a cheeky smile and the sparkle in his sideways glance instantly returns. "Well, hello there. Come here often?"

I smile to myself and shake my head.

"Quiet please, Mr. Forrester."

"Sorry, Professor."

Professor Francis scans our little row of delinquents, his arms still folded, still scowling at us, still failing miserably to intimidate us. I can't help but wonder what exactly he could possibly say to a bunch of teenagers who, for the most part, have probably never been told off or punished for anything before in their lives. Maybe we'll have to stay in this boring room for the rest of the trip. Stuck in a room with Brent and Brody for hours would definitely be punishment enough for me.

Half a minute goes by and still Professor Francis stays silent. I frown, wondering what on earth he's waiting for, when suddenly I remember the empty chair between Ryan and Brody.

Who is that chair for?

The quiet shooshing sound of door number two opening causes Ryan to turn, revealing three red scratch marks streaked down his left cheek.

"Ryan, your face. What happened?"

"*She* happened," he whispers, looking past me.

I turn my head to see the unthinkable. Margaux Pilfrey sashays through the door with her head held high, raking her manicured fingernails through her long blonde hair. Percy appears from the open door behind her. He looks drained, but not a hair is out of place.

"Computer, another chair for me," he says dejectedly. With a quiet electronic ping and a soft hiss, a white chair identical to ours molds up from the floor beside the door and he flumps into it. Another Drone emerges from the door beside him and joins the others in the line.

Margaux strides over, stops in her tracks, and thrusts her finger at the empty chair.

"I am not sitting next to that Forrester animal."

"You'll sit, Miss Pilfrey, or you'll be charged with assaulting Mr. Forrester. I don't imagine that would look good on anyone's permanent record," Professor Francis warns, eyeballing the whole row.

I can tell by the look on her face that she's weighing the consequences carefully. "Fine," Margaux says venomously. She walks over, plops down on the chair beside Ryan, folds her arms, crosses her legs, and screws up her eyes to match her furious pout.

Professor Francis sighs deeply.

"Honestly, I'm extremely disappointed with all of you."

"But, Professor—" objects Brent.

"Let me speak, please, Mr. Fairchild." Professor Francis looks at the floor and slowly shakes his head. He takes a handkerchief from the inside pocket of his tweed jacket, plucks his glasses from his nose, and wearily rubs the lenses.

"Once upon a time, I could have had my pick of teaching positions at some very prestigious schools, you know."

He puts his glasses back on and looks down his scarlet-tipped nose at all of us. "But I chose to accept a job at Bethlem Academy. It might interest you to know that there was once an insane asylum of the same name."

He tucks the handkerchief away and puts his hands behind his back, completing his all-too-familiar lecture-delivery stance.

"The manner in which all of you behaved today makes me wonder whether I took a wrong turn all those years ago and did indeed end up teaching physics to a bunch of teenage mental patients."

Bit's hand shoots up.

"Yes, Miss Otto, I'm well aware you were not directly involved in the altercation, but the fact that you chose to sneak away into a restricted area without permission certainly does not absolve you of guilt, now, does it?"

Bit slowly lowers her hand.

Margaux snorts. "None of this is *my* fault, and how dare you call me a mental patient. I didn't do anything wrong."

"You very nearly took out Mr. Forrester's eye, Miss Pilfrey."

"It was self-defense."

"Well, how can that be when Mr. Forrester was clearly being restrained by the . . . the . . ." Professor Francis waves his hand in the general direction of the six identical silver androids behind him.

"Security Drones," Percy says dryly from across the room.

"Yes, the Security Drones. Thank you, Mr. Blake." He turns back to Margaux. "You willfully and deliberately attacked him."

"She only did that because he sucker-punched me!" Brent barks, pointing at Ryan.

"You punched Finn in the face!" Ryan shouts.

"She was asking for it."

"Mr. Fairchild," Professor Francis says in dismay.

"Well, she was," Brent mutters under his breath.

"Just like you're asking for it right now?" Ryan says coolly.

"Give it your best shot. I dare you," Brent gibes.

"I don't need your permission, but OK, if you insist."

Ryan pushes out of his chair, Brent and Brody both jump to their feet, and Margaux screams as Professor Francis jumps forward with his arms splayed toward them. "You boys sit down! Right now!"

Ryan completely ignores the Professor and lunges at Brent, sending Margaux and her chair toppling backward onto the floor. I jump to my feet as well, shielding Bit. "Security Three!" shouts Percy and three of the security Drones leap from the row behind the Professor, peel Ryan and Brent and Brody apart, and easily twist all three boys into firm arm locks.

Professor Francis looks exasperated. "I was going to give you all a very harsh talking-to, make you promise to be well-behaved, and then send you back to continue the tour with the rest of the group. I can see now that my words would have fallen on deaf ears. All of you need to be made an example of, so each and every one of you will be spending the remainder of the trip here. If that suits Mr. Blake?" Percy looks over and gives the Professor a defeated nod.

"Get me my phone," Margaux demands as she rises from the floor and straightens her tailored school uniform. "I would like to call my father's lawyers."

"This is a school field trip, Miss Pilfrey, not a court of law, and what I say goes."

Bit's hand shoots up again. "Save it, Miss Otto. You broke the rules as well. You're staying too."

Bit's hand slowly lowers.

"But Professor . . ." Brent protests.

"Not another word, Mr. Fairchild. None of you have anyone to blame but yourselves." Professor Francis takes a deep breath and smooths the ends of his bowtie. "Now, Miss Brogan, Miss Otto, and Mr. Forrester, please take your chairs to that side of the room. Mr. Fairchild, Miss Pilfrey, and Mr. Sharp, the opposite side, please."

The three Drones release the boys, turn, and regimentally march back to their places in the row.

"Man, this sucks," mumbles Brody as we all reluctantly grab our chairs and drag them to our sides of the room. I don't say anything, but for once I agree with Brody. This does indeed suck. All I want is to get the hell out of Blackstone Technologies.

The fleeting thought of loudly proclaiming that my father is Dr. Blackstone and demanding that they let me out of here flits through my mind, but let's face it: After my outburst in the dome, combined with the fact that only a handful of people even know my true identity, well, let's just say that it doesn't lend a lot to my credibility. They'd all think I had totally lost it. After what's been happening in my head today, I can't help but think that it's not so far from the truth.

It's OK. I can wait a few hours for my escape. I just need to hold it together and do what I'm told in the meantime. I can't believe that I was actually excited to come on this trip. I may not remember asking Bit to get us in here, but if I did, it was one of the biggest mistakes of my life.

Professor Francis walks over to Percy and begins what appears to be a quiet yet emphatic apology process. I look over at Ryan and Bit and suddenly realize that I owe them some apologies of my own.

"Sorry about all this, guys. It's all totally my fault," I whisper.

"Hey, it's cool. Most fun I've had since the last school I was kicked out of—" Ryan says with that cute crooked smile of his.

"I was only gonna ask the Professor where the bathroom is, y'know, in case we need to go?" says Bit, and all three of us laugh quietly.

We position our chairs near the wall with the number one door and take a seat. On the opposite side of the room, Brent is sitting there scraping blood crust from the edges of his nostrils, Brody is staring vacantly at the clouds drifting across the walls, and Margaux is silently murdering us with her eyes.

I look over at the Professor, hand on his chin, nodding and murmuring as Percy whispers things into his silver wristband.

After a couple of minutes they both walk to the middle of the room.

Percy clears his throat and announces, "Computer, restroom construct alpha times two."

There's a ping sound of recognition and walls begin hissing into formation in the corners on both sides of the space. In less than a minute, two small rooms with recessed frosted-glass doors have grown from the floor. A look of reassurance washes over Bit's face.

"There are the facilities if you require them. This place really is remarkable," Professor Francis says over his shoulder to Percy. "Anyway, Mr. Blake and I are leaving soon to join the others and continue the tour. Sandwiches will be brought in from the cafeteria later for your lunch and I will send for you at the end of the day. Consider this detention."

"This is outrageous! I refuse to be treated like a common prisoner," bellows Margaux.

"You are being treated, Miss Pilfrey, like exactly what you are: unruly hormonal teenagers. You should count your lucky stars that I can't access any schoolwork for you to do. And just in case any of you are thinking about getting into any more trouble than you are already in, these six lady robots will remain here to keep an eye on you. They're all yours, Mr. Blake."

Percy nods and holds his wrist to his lips. "Computer, restricted area line. Bisect room length."

There's another soft tone and an eight-foot-wide black-and-yellow-striped border streaks across the length of the floor right beneath the Drones' boots, up the walls at either end, and clean across the entire length of the ceiling. The words "AUTHORIZED PERSONNEL ONLY" appear and slowly begin scrolling along the strip in bold white letters, repeating themselves in a continuous chain of warning.

"Security detail, none of these students may leave the room or cross the line until further notice. Threat level lavender, restrain and detain," orders Percy.

Every other Drone in the row immediately turns on their heels; three are now watching Margaux, Brent, and Brody, and three are keeping a very creepy watch on us.

"Please stay on your own side of the room everyone," Percy announces. "You all know what will happen if you cross this line. These Drones are many times stronger than any of you, and I'm sure the last thing you want is to be put in an arm lock for the next four hours." I notice that the twinkle in Percy's eye and the bounce in his step have gone completely.

"We shall leave you to your thoughts. See you at four o'clock, Mr. Blake?"

Percy nods. "After you, Professor."

They turn and head toward the door marked with the large gray "2". It slides open and they walk through into the corridor beyond it. The Professor's head and shoulders suddenly pop back into the room. "Oh, and Miss Brogan, Mr. Blake has asked Nurse Talbot to come by soon to give you another check-over. These fainting spells of yours are very disconcerting."

I raise my hand in protest but it's too late. With a quiet swoosh, the door slides closed and they're gone.

CHAPTER THIRTEEN

Ryan props his hands behind his head and eases back in his chair. "Alone at last."

"Well, alone except for that troop of DTs standing in the middle of the room," says Bit.

"And those three DBs over there by the wall," Ryan adds, eyeballing Margaux and company.

"DBs?" I ask.

"Douche Bags," Ryan says with a sly grin.

"I heard that," Brent calls over.

"You were supposed to, asswipe."

"You wait till we get out of here, Forrester."

"What are you gonna do, Brent? Bleed and cry until my arms get tired from beating you?"

Brent boosts himself from his chair. "I wasn't crying! My eyes were watering!"

"Stop fighting guys," I plead. "This sucks enough without you two arguing."

"Shut the hell up, you bitch," growls Margaux. "It's your fault we're all in here in the first place."

"Hey, don't talk to Finn like that!" Bit screeches, taking me by surprise yet again.

"Well, well. Look at the little geek sticking up for her girlfriend. I knew you two were hot for each other," Margaux says with a self-satisfied sneer.

"Bit and I are not hot for each other," I say, finally getting to my feet. "But if we were, I could do a lot worse than Bettina Otto, that's for sure."

I smile at Bit and she blushes.

"That's hot," Brody says with a goofy grin.

Suddenly door number four slides open and Nurse Talbot enters the room, momentarily defusing our little debate. She's clutching a shiny white briefcase with a big red cross on it.

"Hello, everyone. I've come to examine Miss Brogan."

"That's hot," Brody says again. Brent fist bumps him, and with a smarmy smile flumps back into his chair. Nurse Talbot doesn't seem to notice Brody's comment at all and primly walks to our side of the room. "Please take a seat, Miss Brogan, and tell me what happened."

I sit back down and Nurse Talbot kneels beside me. I try to focus my attention on her and away from wanting to slap Margaux Pilfrey in her pouty, pink lip-glossed mouth. Nurse Talbot fishes her penlight from her breast pocket and shines it in my eyes just like the last time. "Nothing happened, really."

"Are you sure? Percy mentioned that you stopped breathing. That is very serious."

"I . . . I just choked on some gum, that's all. It was just a stupid mistake. I'm fine now, really."

Nurse Talbot looks from me to Ryan to Bit and back again. "Is that true? I wasn't informed of that."

"Yes, absolutely," I say, nodding and smiling. "Right guys?"

"Ah . . . sure. Yep, that's what happened, alright," says Ryan. Bit looks at me and Ryan, and then to Nurse Talbot and nods a little too enthusiastically.

Nurse Talbot doesn't even look the slightest bit suspicious at our bald-faced lies. In fact, her expression is blank.

"Alright then," she says standing up. "False alarm. I suggest you take more care with how you chew in the future."

She turns on her heels, and, just like that, heads toward the door.

"Excuse me. Nurse?" Margaux says in what I suspect is the same superior tone she reserves for her servants.

Nurse Talbot stops in her tracks and looks over at her. "Yes, what is it?"

"I am bored out of my mind in here. Can you make me a TV out of the floor or something? Or maybe a gun to shoot Finn Brogan in her stupid head? Either would be great; both would be marvelous."

"I've been informed that you are all being punished. It wouldn't be appropriate to provide you with entertainment."

"Pleeeease! I'm so sick of looking at those three idiots, and that all-girl android bobsled team."

"We've been in here for only fifteen minutes," sighs Ryan.

"And it's driving me crazy!" screeches Margaux.

"Driving you crazy? Really? And here I am thinking that you'd already stopped at crazy, had nuts for lunch, and were well on your way to wacko city."

Bit and I both laugh quietly. Brody can't help himself and laughs out loud.

"Do you see what I'm dealing with here?!" shrieks Margaux.

Nurse Talbot's chin tilts upward ever so slightly for a moment, like she's trying to formulate a thought.

"Perhaps I can keep you distracted from each other and still stay within the boundaries of your punishment. All of you please stand and turn your seats to face the walls."

We all look at each other in confusion.

"Now, please. A few feet back from the walls will suffice. Be sure not to cross the boundary line."

Ryan stands, drags his chair and flumps into it, facing the wall like Nurse Talbot instructed. Bit and I drag ours over and join him. The other three do the same on their side. Margaux makes Brent take her chair, of course.

Nurse Talbot looks toward the ceiling. "Computer, display Percy and the school tour on walls one and three. Mute display audio."

There's a tone of acknowledgment and the sky-blue wall scattered with clouds suddenly flicks to black. Barely a second later it flashes back on with a six-foot-high, fifteen-foot-wide, ultra-high-definition live camera feed of Miss Cole and the rest of our tour group. The massive screen is divided into eight square sections, each one showing a different view of their location. In the bottom right-hand corner of each square, there's a camera number followed by a label reading "DOME 2." I glance over my shoulder to see that a mosaic of pictures, identical to ours, has appeared for the others on the opposite wall of the room.

Up on the silent screen, I see Percy and Professor Francis arriving and taking their seats with the group, who are all perched side by side on the benches of a small white grandstand. The stand is positioned on the edge of what appears to be a large, dirt-floor arena enclosed by a thick circular wooden barrier. It kinda looks a little like a place you would hold a bullfight or a rodeo, except that directly behind the barrier, where an audience would usually be, is a very familiar-looking shiny black curved wall.

Standing with his hands on his hips in front of the grandstand is a stern, athletic, important-looking older man with a shock-white, buzz-cut hairstyle. He's dressed in a brown-and-green camouflage-patterned, military-style uniform and black combat boots. In the center of the arena, there are twenty or so soldiers in full khaki garb, complete with helmets, dark visors, and camo-patterned face masks that completely obscure their faces. They're marching about, perfectly in step, performing precise and intricate shoulder-to-shoulder military drill patterns.

"There," says Nurse Talbot. "Now you can watch your classmates enjoying what you are missing out on."

"Thanks a lot," scoffs Margaux.

"You're welcome," Nurse Talbot replies without a hint of sarcasm. She turns and strides over to door number four. It slides open, she steps into the white corridor beyond it and, with a quiet swoosh, she's gone.

Back up on the screen I see that the soldiers have gathered into a perfect rectangular formation. They turn all at once, almost like a singular entity, and march with impeccable synchronicity toward the barrier wall. A large square opening forms in the side of the dome and they all troop through it. Our classmates politely applaud as the hole "heals" itself closed behind them.

The man with the buzz-cut hair turns to the group and begins talking and nodding.

"We're not missing much," I hear Brody say behind us. "A lame parade, and now some boring guy giving a boring speech. He's probably giving a speech about corn or wallpaper or something."

"Corn or wallpaper? What the hell are you talking about, Brodes?" asks Brent.

"They're the most boring things I could think of."

"*You* are the most boring thing I can think of," chimes in Margaux.

"Shut up."

"You shut up."

"I wish they'd both shut up," whispers Bit. I nod and smile and go back to drearily watching the screen. Might as well. There's not much else to do.

With a narrow-eyed glare, the uniformed man scans the group. He raises an arm and points to Dean McCarthy, who is sitting two rows up beside Sherrie and Ashley. Sherrie looks as meek as usual but none the worse for wear. Nurse Talbot obviously took good care of her asthma attack.

Dean hesitantly steps down the levels of the grandstand as the buzz-cut man mouths something into the silver command module on his wrist. Everyone in the group leans and cranes their necks to watch as a long dark slice cuts into the ground a few feet away. It slowly gets wider and wider until eventually, a large square hole the size of a two-car garage has molded open in the dirt.

Something is rising from the center of the hole. It's a box. A *big* metal box. It looks like a huge, shiny silver shipping container turned on its end. Soon the olive-drab helmets of two soldiers can be seen rising from the hole, too, standing at attention on either side of the box.

The lift jolts to a stop and one of the soldiers begins tapping away at a keypad on the side of the container. Judging by the height of the soldiers, the massive box must be almost four stories high.

Both soldiers step to the side as the top and the walls of the box slowly begin folding down in sections. After half a minute or so they compact down to ground level, fully revealing the contents inside. There, standing tall and still, a few feet in front of the grandstand, is a towering, thirty-foot-high, camouflage-colored robot. It's as tall as a small apartment block. Its massive shoulders, chest, arms, and legs are all rounded smooth with bulbous, military-green armor. Its head is a wide green dome with a thick horizontal strip of shiny black where its eyes should be. It's extremely intimidating, and, I'm guessing, very, very expensive.

"Whoa," Ryan says, sitting up in his chair. "Is that a R.A.M.?!"

"Ahh . . . I'm not very well versed on giant-robot terminology. What exactly is a ram?" I ask.

"R-A-M," spells out Bit. "It stands for Remote Articulated Mechanoid. It's a war robot."

Ryan looks slightly impressed. "That's right. Forrester Aerospace used to make R.A.M.s for the Navy until Blackstone got the contract.

I saw a couple of them at one of my dad's factories once, but they were only a couple of feet taller than an average-sized man. That one is almost four times bigger. It's a freakin' monster."

"Oh man, we are missing out on cool stuff!" Brody whines from the other side of the room.

One of the soldiers kneels and unbolts the top of the box from one of the folded-down sides. The other soldier takes an edge and they both lift an obviously heavy metal square over to the older man. They carefully flip it over onto the ground beside him, making a platform of sorts. The soldiers take their positions on either side of the platform, facing out toward the huge green behemoth. The man steps his boot on the edge of the thick overturned lid and a folding metal chair springs up from the center of it. He points at the robot and then, with a big smile on his face, slaps a hand on Dean's shoulder.

"No way. He's not doing what I think he's doing, is he?" Ryan wonders dubiously. "He wouldn't let that Dean guy drive a R.A.M., would he?!"

"I wish I could hear what he's saying!" barks Brent.

"Stupid computer!" shouts Margaux. "Turn the display sound on!" The voice of the uniformed man suddenly issues from both sides of the room, clearly and loudly.

"So what do ya say son? Think you're man enough to give it a spin?"

Bit leaps out of her chair and whirls around. "How did you do that!?"

Ryan and I both stand and look over in Margaux's direction in disbelief.

She turns her head to the side and I can see her pompous sneer. "The computer obviously knows a woman of quality when it sees one."

"Ask for something else!" Brent says excitedly.

"Make another dinosaur!" demands Brody.

Margaux looks at both of them with amused contempt. "Computer, I would like a table and a mirror and a hairbrush and my phone. Now."

Nothing happens.

"Computer? Hey! Stupid computer! Give me my phone. Now!" Margaux demands, but nothing happens.

"Computer. Mute sound," commands Bit.

Nothing happens.

She looks upward, ponders for a moment, and then tries again. "Mute display sound."

The uniformed man's little lecture about the benefits of military force cuts off immediately. Bit looks mildly surprised, then just as quickly disappointed. "Congratulations, Margaux. You've discovered the key word for the TV remote."

"Whatever, loser," murmurs Margaux.

"*Display*, sound on," Bit orders, sliding back into her seat. The audio resumes with the slightly anxious voice of Professor Francis issuing from both screens.

"*. . . not sure that's such a good idea, Colonel Brash.*"

Ryan and I sit down to watch. "Phew. Can you imagine what a nightmare it would be if Margaux could command the computer?" whispers Ryan.

"Yeah, she'd force the Drones to give us all makeovers," I say with a little smirk.

"You wouldn't need one," Ryan says, his expression serious, his gaze moving slowly over my face.

"Shut up. Watch the TV, Mr. Cheesy," I say with a smile, my face suddenly hot.

"Both of you, shut up," Bit says, glaring at the screen with her arms folded.

"*Get in that chair, son,*" orders the man that Professor Francis called Colonel Brash. Dean doesn't need to be asked twice. He practically leaps into the metal chair. I've never seen anyone look so excited.

"*Ahhh . . . Colonel Brash?*" I've also never seen Professor Francis look more concerned.

"There's nothing to worry about, Professor." The Colonel juts his thumb back over his shoulder. *"That Gun Boy there is set to training mode. It'll be firing paint pellets."* He reaches under Dean's chair and retrieves a small black box and a visor with a metal headband attached to it. He holds the little box up to show everyone. *"And I can shut it down at any time with this little override doohickey here."*

He shoves the box in his pocket and hands the metal band to Dean. *"Put that on your head, son."*

Dean puts the band on the crown of his head and Colonel Brash flicks the visor down over his eyes.

"Ahh, sorry to interrupt again, Colonel Brash, but Mr. McCarthy there obviously doesn't have any knowledge or training in the operation of what appears to be, a very large and dangerous piece of equipment and . . ."

The Colonel promptly cuts off the Professor. *"Doesn't need it."* The Professor looks flabbergasted.

"Thanks to this little wonder right here," Colonel Brash says, tapping the metal headband on Dean's head. *"In the past, you needed at least six weeks' training on a control panel with joysticks and pedals to master the basics of piloting a combat mech. But thanks to the brilliant minds here at Blackstone Tech, and this marvelous piece of apparatus right here, anyone can do it."*

The Colonel's words of reassurance do little to soften the Professor's hard expression of concern.

"Let me demonstrate." Colonel Brash fishes the small black box from his pocket and holds it to his lips. *"Authorize. Brash. Code one eight two niner, R-A-M twelve slash one, activate engage."* He holds the box in the palm of his hand and presses his thumb to the front of it.

The sound is a low bass hum. It's coming from the robot. The hum gets higher and higher in pitch, rising and rising, until after a few seconds it maintains a soft medium tone and two light spots grow in the black strip on the front of its dome head, giving it the appearance of having dim white circular eyes.

"Oh man, this is gonna be so cool," Brody says excitedly. "I wish we were down there! Dean, you lucky bastard!"

"This is going to end badly," whispers Bit. I can't help but share her concern.

"Hold still, boy," orders Colonel Brash. He stomps his boot on the edge of the platform again and holds the small black box to his mouth. *"Control activate engage."*

Little blue lights blink on all around the headband and Dean's back softly arches as he lets out an involuntary groan.

"McCarthy!" shouts Professor Francis. Some of the students gasp. All of their heads are flicking back and forth from Dean to the R.A.M. and back again like they're watching a tennis match.

Colonel Brash holds up a hand. *"Perfectly normal reaction. This part takes a minute."*

Everyone on the grandstand is staring in eager anticipation. Karla Bassano is holding her hands over her mouth, her eyes the widest of all.

"Now, as I mentioned before, Blackstone Technologies provides the armed forces with the most advanced offensive and defensive military hardware available, and this here is one of the soon-to-be-deployed, new-generation Remote Articulated Mechanoids, or R.A.M. for short. They are the jewels in our ground offensive crown."

The Colonel pulls a laser pointer from his pocket and spots it on the massive robot.

"Fully articulated fingers and limb joints, retractable forearm-mounted dual magnetic percussion-assisted rail guns with interchangeable ammunition types, night- and thermal-vision capability, and, when deployed on the battlefield, it's loaded with twenty self-guided high-explosive mini-cluster missiles either side of a detachable quad-copter reconnaissance Drone housed on the back. The outer shell is composed of a suspended reactive Newtonian fluid graphene composite micro-mesh that is lighter than aluminum, and when impacted becomes almost as hard as diamond."

Millie and Miss Cole look at one another, totally bewildered.

"*Basically, what all that means is, this right here is one bad mother,*" the Colonel says with an expression amusingly similar to that of a proud father.

Dean lets out a sigh and his body relaxes into the metal chair, his mouth dropping open loosely as multi-colored lights from the visor flicker over his face.

"*That's what we were waiting for. He's integrated, or 'blobbed out' as we say in the ranks.*"

"*Blobbed out?*" asks Professor Francis.

"*Yes indeed,*" the Colonel says as he turns to face the robot. "*Can you see me, son?*"

The eyes on the R.A.M. slowly begin changing color from the centers outward, from dim white to a pale brown. They're exactly the same color as Dean's eyes. They turn off and on again half a dozen times as if the robot were blinking.

"*Down here, son.*" The dome head swivels forward, aiming the eyes downward at the Colonel. Suddenly a deep synthesized voice booms from the giant mechanoid.

"YES, I CAN SEE YOU."

"*How do you feel?*" Colonel Brash asks, smiling up at the green dome face with its big brown eyes.

"VERY TALL."

In the metal chair beside the Colonel, I notice that Dean's mouth is droopily twitching along with the words that are issuing from the R.A.M.

There are smiles and looks of disbelief and astonishment and giggling from everyone in the group.

"That is the coolest thing I've ever seen," says Brent. "And we're all stuck in here. Thanks a lot, Finn."

Ryan turns but I grab his arm. "It's not worth it," I say softly. I slide my hand down his arm and link my fingers between his. "Thanks anyway."

He smiles, looks down at our hands, and gently squeezes. Butterflies take flight in my stomach.

"Try and walk around; it should feel completely natural. Take it easy though, son. That's two and half tons of robot your mind is inside of," warns the Colonel.

The R.A.M. steps off the base of the box and, with heavy pounding footsteps, takes a few clumsy practice steps forward. Dean's real legs twitch and flick like a loose-stringed marionette. Amy Dee and Ashley Farver squeal like little girls while Sherrie Polito sits beside them, hurriedly puffing on an inhaler that Nurse Talbot must have given to her.

The R.A.M. turns and walks in a full stomping circle around its folded-down box before facing the grandstand again. Amazingly, it even walks with Dean's laid-back, slacker stroll. The robot lifts its huge hands and looks from one to the other, blinking its big brown eyes.

`"THIS IS REALLY WEIRD. IT DOESN'T FEEL LIKE I'M WEARING A GIANT ROBOT SUIT AT ALL. IT FEELS LIKE THIS IS MY BODY."`

"Exactly! That's the only way to describe it," Colonel Brash says excitedly. *"Now, how about we shoot some targets?"*

`"OH HELLS YEAH."`

"Wait a minute. Colonel Brash, I'm not so sure that—"

The Colonel holds a hand up again. The Professor can't seem to get a word in edgewise.

"Don't worry, Professor; like I said, this one shoots paint pellets, but just to be on the extra-safe side . . . I'm already way ahead of ya." The Colonel pulls the sleeve of his uniform back from his wrist. *"Computer, give me a two-inch-thick translunium blast shield over the viewing area."*

The familiar computerized "yes" tone is closely followed by the hiss of the quantum construct being created. We watch on the display as a thick, clear, plastic bubble grows up from the dirt and completely encapsulates the small grandstand, the blobbed-out Dean on his platform, the two masked soldiers, and Colonel Brash.

"There, safe and sound, Professor."

There is still no wiping that look of trepidation off the Professor's face.

"Are you ready, son?"

"BRING IT ON."

"Computer, R.A.M. target practice Brash alpha level one."

The tone of acknowledgment is followed by a loud repeating warning buzzer as red flashing lights on long poles begin sprouting at set intervals all along the perimeter of the arena. The warning buzzer cuts off and Colonel Brash puts a hand on Dean's blobbed-out shoulder.

"Get ready, soldier, here comes your first target," Colonel Brash says with a huge, slightly psychotic-looking grin.

The outline of a large red rectangle draws itself in the dirt on the far side of the arena, and something begins forming inside it. Armor plating and sheets of metal and screws and tubes and cylinders and cogs sprout from the ground and begin piecing together, folding and whining, bending and riveting, connecting and slotting into place. Steel sculpts itself up into a large angular turret, and a top-mounted machine gun grows into place beside the newly formed driver's hatch. Tracks of rubber tread flip into place over rows of wheels like falling dominoes as a thick strip of metal spirals out from the turret, winding through the air like a corkscrew, forging itself into the long seamless barrel of the main cannon. In less than thirty seconds, a full-sized, army-green military tank has molded itself up from the loose dirt.

The Dean-controlled R.A.M. turns to face it. The tank's engine rumbles to life and smoke grunts from its rear exhaust as its tracks grip the dirt. It jerks forward, lurching heavily across the wide arena, swiveling its turret gun toward the giant robot as it goes.

All six of us in the room, and the entire group on the grandstand, are on the edges of our seats.

I'm gripping Ryan's hand tightly and he grins at me. "This is awesome," he whispers.

"HOW DO I SHOOT?!" Dean yells, the deep mechanized voice modulation of the R.A.M. doing little to hide his sudden panic.

The guns are in your arms, boy! shouts Colonel Brash, obviously enjoying every second. The R.A.M. raises its massive arm and points it at the approaching tank. Over in the metal chair I can see that Dean's real arm is jutting out loosely by his side.

"I told him how to shoot, didn't I?" Colonel Brash says more to himself than anyone.

Suddenly the tank fires its main gun, lighting up the arena with a huge orange bloom of muzzle flare.

TA-TOOM!

The R.A.M. lunges to the side just in time as a massive splat of fluorescent-yellow paint plasters the side of the transparent blast shield. Everyone inside it screams like frightened children. Everyone except Professor Francis, who is sitting there, arms folded, throwing daggers with his eyes at the back of Colonel Brash's head. Miss Cole looks like she's ready to pass out.

"HOLY CRAP!" yells the R.A.M. "MY GUNS AREN'T WORKING!"

"Move it, son; circle round! Buy yourself some time!" shouts the Colonel.

In his mind, Dean turns and runs and the R.A.M. moves incredibly. If it wasn't for the pounding sound of the sheer weight of its footsteps, you could easily forget that it's thirty feet tall. It moves as fast and effortlessly as the seventeen-year-old boy controlling it.

Farther down the arena, the robot skids to a halt and thrusts its arm out at the tank. The tank's tracks switch alignment and its hull begins rotating in the mech's direction.

"SHOOT, DAMMIT, SHOOT!" the R.A.M. shouts desperately. "COLONEL BRASH, MY ROBOT IS BROKEN!"

Colonel Brash turns to the blobbed-out Dean in the chair beside him. *"Have you ever played cowboys, son?"*

"YEAH, WHEN I WAS A LITTLE KID," the R.A.M.'s voice booms from across the arena.

"Make a pistol shape with your hand. Just like you're playin' cowboys."

"UH . . . OK," replies the robot. In the chair, Dean's real hand points two fingers and sticks up a thumb.

Suddenly, a high-pitched, ramping-up squeal issues from the massive war mech, and its huge green fingers retract into its forearm. Two long sections elevate on top of its bulbous arm, revealing two sets of long, grooved, rectangular metal railings. "COOOOL," it bellows.

The tank on the opposite side of the arena stops, and its gun turret begins swinging around toward the R.A.M.

"You've got him in your sights, boy. Paint him up."

"HOW?"

"That's the easy part, son. All you gotta do . . . is drop the hammer."

I see Dean's real right thumb drop forward. Suddenly a violent roar shocks the air and I jump in my seat as the whole section of the arena around the towering war robot lights up like a bonfire. The unbelievably forceful sound that bursts from the screen is like the blasting note of a foghorn mixed with the undulating crackling of arcing electricity as a barrage of light and flame erupts from the R.A.M.'s right arm.

Across the arena, the left-side tracks of the tank are literally thrown apart as they're pelted by an overwhelmingly violent torrent of projectiles. The tank topples forward into the dirt as the thick metal of its main body is buckled, twisted, and torn to shreds. The main turret is gashed open like it's made of tissue paper. The long barrel of the main cannon is pitted with gaping holes and then completely rendered apart into tiny glowing pieces. I'm certainly no expert when it comes to advanced weapons, but one thing is for sure: Dean is definitely *not* firing paint pellets.

"Cease fire! Cease fire! That's live ammo!" Colonel Brash yells in panic as everyone in the paint-spattered bubble recoils and screams.

I know that Dean is able to hear him, but it's obvious that he's pretending not to. The R.A.M. raises its other arm; its gun rails snap into place and burst into life with another huge blast of yellow fire and electric blue sparks. Chunks of metal and debris fly off the tank in the maelstrom of the R.A.M.'s brutal onslaught. The racket coming from the display is insanely loud. Out there in Dome Two, it must be deafening. Shrapnel and molten blobs of steel spray from what's left of the tank and burn into the wooden barrier beyond, which is also instantly mulched into pulp when there's no more plate armor standing in the way. The tank is obliterated. It's almost like it was made of olive-green butter and is being bombarded with a meteor shower of five thousand white-hot coals.

Bit and Ryan and I are glued to the display.

Colonel Brash yells right in Dean's blobbed-out ear, *"Cease fire, gaad dammit! Right now!"*

The barrage stops as suddenly as it began, the rails snap back into place, and the R.A.M. lowers its big, green, smoking arms.

It can't have taken more than ten seconds, but now the tank is completely and utterly unrecognizable. It's been wiped out of existence in a frightening blaze of awesome power. All that's left is a wide black smear of smoking parts and twisted metal.

"HA HA HA HA HA! THAT WAS THE BEST THING EVER!" shouts the R.A.M. as it does a little side-to-side happy dance. It looks absolutely ridiculous whenever Dean does it, and even more so when he's making a thirty-foot-tall killing machine do it.

"Ah . . . a word please, Colonel Brash?" Professor Francis says, getting to his feet.

Whether it's from anger or embarrassment is not certain, but Colonel Brash's face has turned an unbecoming shade of pink. He turns to Dean. *"You walk that robot back over here safe and sound right now and you might avoid the latrine duty that these two incompetent soldiers will be doing every afternoon for the next two weeks."*

The masked soldiers standing near the Colonel glance at each other, and then sheepishly stare at the ground.

In the chair, Dean has a goofy, slack-jawed grin as the R.A.M., arms still oozing tiny wisps of thick smoke, strides happily across the arena toward its folded-down box.

"Woo!" I look over my shoulder to see Brody leaping out of his chair and punching into the air. "That was next-level aaaawesome!"

Brent stands and points at the display. "I'm gonna ask for a R.A.M. for graduation."

Brody is standing beside him, nodding like a bobbleheaded moron. "Yeah, me too!"

Ryan clears his throat. "Display. Mute audio." The screens go silent. He turns and sneers at the two boys, slowly shaking his head. "You can't just buy a R.A.M., you idiots, no matter *how* much money your fathers have."

"My father is a powerful man, and the Secretary of Defense is a close family friend. Trust me Forrester, it'll happen," Brent says with his ever-present air of superiority.

Ryan jumps up and walks to the boundary line.

"They are Vermillion-Class military hardware. Even rich terrorist warlords couldn't get their hands on one."

Brent walks up to the line. "My father could."

"Y'know what, Brent?" Ryan points right at Brent's face. "You . . . are a Vermillion-Class dickhead."

Bit and I watch as the boys fire insults back and forth across the black-and-yellow-striped border, their heated argument amusingly mirrored by the steely-eyed exchange I can see between Colonel Brash and the Professor on the screen behind Margaux.

"Seriously, Finn, what do you see in that guy?" asks Bit.

"I dunno," I say, my eyes drifting from Ryan and his effortless cool to the far screen and back again. "He's . . ."

"He's what? A delinquent? A criminal? Well, maybe not yet, but believe me, it won't take long before he is. He's been kicked out of how many schools? Nine? Ten? Trust me, Finn, I know trouble when I see it, and Ryan is definitely—"

What was that?

On the screen across the room.

No.

It can't have been.

"Finn? Did you even hear a word I just said?"

I quickly turn back to our screen, staring intently.

There it is again!

Oh no.

Please no.

"Finn? Earth to Finn?" Bit says, waving a hand in front of my face.

I swat her hand away; I'm glued to the screen. My heart starts beating like a drum as adrenaline courses through my veins.

There it is again!

"Finn. What's the matter?"

I look over at the group under the blast shield. They're all watching Professor Francis point and gesticulate angrily at Colonel Brash. Percy steps down from the stand and attempts to mediate. None of them have noticed. Then again, why would they?

"What are you looking at? Finn?"

Dean. Oh no. No one has noticed Dean, either. He's gone totally limp. More than before. I look over to the R.A.M. and back again. Dean's body jerks ever so slightly and a drip of saliva slides down his chin. He grits his teeth for a fleeting moment, then slouches even lower as a dribble of blood leaks from his nose and trickles down over his top lip. Please, oh please, don't let this be happening.

"We have to warn them, Bit. We have to warn everyone to get out of there right now."

"What? Why?" Bit says, scanning back and forth over the mosaic of pictures.

What can I tell her? The truth would make no sense to her. All I can do is watch as the R.A.M.'s eyes flicker on and off like a strobe light, switching from one color to the next. Suddenly they shut off altogether and I hold my breath, willing my instincts to be wrong. The next few seconds feel like an eternity; I grind my teeth in my jaw and my heart is beating a mile a minute as I tightly grip the arms of my chair, hoping against hope that the eye strip stays black.

It's no use.

My fears become reality as the circles flick back on with a single, solid, unfaltering color. The eyes blink and its head turns in the direction of the group as the massive robot steps off its folded-down box and stomps heavily toward the wall of the blast shield.

I've lost all control of my thoughts, my brain too clouded with fear to remember the simple display command. "Bit! Please! Turn the sound on!"

Hearing my desperation, Bit shouts the order at the screen. "Display audio on!"

Breathless gasps escape from a few of my schoolmates as they suddenly notice the R.A.M. towering over them, its huge green domed head peeking in between the spikes of splattered yellow paint. Bit was right when she said this would end badly. My stomach twists into knots and my mind reels with panic as I watch the thirty-foot-tall killing machine glare down on the faces inside the bubble with its brand-new eyes.

Its huge, round . . . *silvery-gray eyes.*

CHAPTER FOURTEEN

The giant robot bellows a single word that paralyzes my entire body.

"INFINITY!"

Colonel Brash halts his heated discussion with the Professor and throws a sideways glance over his shoulder. *Go on back to the box, son. We'll unhook you in a minute.*

The mechanoid leans in closer, scanning the blast shield, searching for faces around the edges of the yellow paint splatter like a cat stalking goldfish in a bowl.

"WHERE ARE YOU, CHILD? I KNOW YOU'RE ALIVE. I CAN FEEL IT."

The Colonel's ears visibly twitch and his spine suddenly straightens. He slowly turns toward the voice as the robot's huge gray eyes rove into view, leering down on him between two spikes of yellow. Concern creases his brow. He knows that something isn't right. The R.A.M. reaches down and wipes at the big fluorescent splat with its massive green hand, but it's only making the mess worse, smearing the paint into opaque streaks with loud screeching swipes.

"SHOW YOURSELF, INFINITY," the R.A.M. demands, its deep modulated voice echoing menacingly from the display.

Colonel Brash quickly looks over at Dean, and his expression immediately flashes from serious concern to surprised shock. Dean is slumped even lower now; his head flopped forward, blood steadily dripping from the tip of his nose into a widening patch of red on his white school shirt. The Colonel lunges at Dean, grabs him by the shoulders, and shakes him vigorously. *"Son, wake up! Boy! Can you hear me? Wake up!"*

Colonel Brash stomps forcefully on the edge of the platform and the metal chair collapses down into the base. He catches Dean, lays him on the dirt, flicks the visor up, and tugs the metal band from his forehead. Dean's eyes are half-open, unresponsive, staring blankly into space as saliva dribbles from the corner of his loosely gaping mouth.

"Computer! Medical emergency protocol epsilon!"

The Colonel glances quickly from side to side, most likely expecting a hospital bed to rise from the ground nearby, but nothing happens. He pulls his sleeve back and shouts into his wristband.

"Computer! Respond! Medical emergency protocol epsilon!"

Nothing happens.

"What's going on?" Professor Francis asks sternly at the Colonel's back. *"What's wrong with Mr. McCarthy? Is that . . . blood?"*

"The boy is unconscious, and I have no idea why," Colonel Brash says gravely.

For a brief moment the Professor looks angrier than I've ever seen him, but his frown vanishes as quickly as it came when a sudden realization strikes him. He points up at the towering silhouette moving on the wall of the shield. *"But if Mr. McCarthy is unconscious . . . who on earth is controlling tha—"*

"THERE'S NO USE IN HIDING, INFINITY. COME OUT NOW, OR THESE PEOPLE WILL BE HURT."

The R.A.M. raises its right arm and brings its fist down hard on the shield. A ringing peal issues loudly from the display, echoing around the room like a church bell. The shield stays intact but everyone inside screams and shrieks, scattering across the grandstand in every direction. Miss Cole hastily scrambles around the back of it, sheltering beneath its supports, and is very quickly joined by the huddled bunch of the rest of the group.

"COME OUT, INFINITY, OR I WILL COME IN."

"Do something!" Professor Francis yells over his shoulder as he trots around the back of the stand to join Miss Cole and the others. There's no mistaking the fear on their faces as they peer out from the gaps between the seats.

"It's out of control!" Brent blurts from the other side of the room.

"What's an Infinity?" asks Brody.

Bit grabs my arm and her nails dig in hard. She looks at me with fear in her eyes. "It knows you," she whispers.

I nod solemnly.

"What's going on, Finn?"

"The same thing that happened on the pirate ship."

"What are you talking about?"

"I didn't faint. Someone was controlling the pirate captain. They tried to kill me."

"And now the same person is controlling the R.A.M.?"

"Yes."

"Are you absolutely sure? Who on earth would be trying to kill you? And how are they controlling constructs and equipment?"

"I promise I'll tell you everything, but right now I need to get down there before someone gets killed because of me."

"How?"

"I have no idea."

"Hello!" shouts the Colonel's voice.

Bit and I turn back to the display to see Colonel Brash standing with his hands on his hips at the wall of the dome. The massive robot takes two pounding stomps to the side and focuses on the Colonel's face through a small clean section of the blast shield. The Colonel holds up the little black box.

"I can shut that mechanoid down with the press of a button. But before I do, perhaps you'd like to tell me who you are, and how you hacked into the most secure computer system on the planet?"

I have to admit: whether he knows it or not, the Colonel is a brave man.

"SIMON BRASH," booms the mechanoid. "IT HAS BEEN A LONG TIME."

It's plain to see that the Colonel is completely taken aback. *"How do you know my name? Who are you?!"*

"YOU WERE LIEUTENANT BRASH WHEN WE FIRST MET, BUT LOOK AT YOU NOW, SIMON. JUDGING BY THOSE STARS ON YOUR COLLAR, YOU'VE SOMEHOW MANAGED TO STUMBLE AND SNIVEL YOUR WAY UP THE RANKS, ALL THE WAY TO COLONEL. WELL DONE."

Colonel Brash slowly lowers the box and looks up at the giant robot quizzically. *"Seriously. Who the hell are you?"*

"I AM DR. THERESA PIERCE. DO YOU REMEMBER ME, SIMON? WHAT A SILLY QUESTION. OF COURSE YOU DO."

"Don't mess around with me, scumbag. You can't be Dr. Pierce. Theresa Pierce is dead." Colonel Brash's eyes narrow. He puffs out his chest and points his finger up at the robot. *"Who are you, really? If you have somehow accessed Dr. Pierce's old authority codes and are using her name to—"*

"I ASSURE YOU THAT I AM THERESA PIERCE..." the R.A.M. interrupts. ". . . AND YOU'RE RIGHT, SIMON, I AM DEAD. I WAS BETRAYED. CAST ASIDE AND LEFT TO DIE AMONG THE ROSE THORNS LIKE A DOG. BUT I FOUND A WAY BACK, SIMON, AND IT'S TIME TO CORRECT A HORRIBLE MISTAKE."

"I don't have time for these lies, whoever you are! Our boys will trace your signal and you'll be doing twenty years in a military prison before the week is out."

"OH, SIMON, YOU FOOLISH BOY. YOU WERE ALWAYS SO FULL OF HOT AIR AND NONSENSE. PERHAPS THAT IS WHY IT GIVES ME SO MUCH PLEASURE TO INFORM YOU THAT THE END OF YOUR LIFE WILL BE CONSIDERABLY MORE PERMANENT THAN MINE WAS."

The R.A.M. raises one of its huge arms and that horrible, ramping-up squeal erupts from the display once more as two sets of rail guns snap up into position.

"No!" I scream, gripping Bit's arm, watching in horror as our class-mates and teachers howl and cower in panic.

Colonel Brash's eyes go wide. He quickly presses his thumb to the little black box and yells into it, *"Emergency shutdown!"*

The silver-gray circles on the R.A.M.'s face instantly blink out and the squeal begins winding down, becoming quieter and quieter until the huge robotic death machine is standing there in blissful silence, as still as a statue, its long green arm jutting down toward the Colonel's chest like a sinister salute.

"Oh my gawd!" shouts Margaux. "That man could have been killed!"

The boys are still standing on either side of the black-and-yellow line, frozen in their respective spots, mesmerized, all three staring at the screen on the other side of the room. Bit utters a sigh of relief, her huge doe eyes glaring at me from behind her glasses. "Finn, who is Theresa Pierce?" she whispers, "and why does she want to . . . to hurt you?"

"She used to live with us. She died when I was fifteen, and I have no idea why she's so hell-bent on getting me."

"But if she's dead, then how . . . ?"

"She downloaded her mind into the Blackstone mainframe."

"No, she can't have. That's impossible."

"No, Bit. It's not."

"Well, if that crazy woman's consciousness is in the system, then everyone is in danger. We have to get out of here."

I nod in complete agreement.

Up on the display, I watch as our teachers and classmates gingerly emerge from behind the grandstand. One of the soldiers is kneeling by Dean, wiping the blood from his face. He looks like he's coming around. Colonel Brash is standing, fists clenched on his hips, glaring angrily at the tall, motionless shadow being cast by the giant robot on the wide smears of yellow.

"*Theresa Pierce, my ass. What a crock. We'll find you, mister computer hacker.*" He turns to the idle soldier standing nearby. "*You, put that toy back in its box.*"

The soldier immediately begins carrying out the Colonel's orders. With a firm stomp, the metal chair springs up from the platform. The soldier removes his helmet and dark glasses, shoves them under the chair, and takes a seat. He slides the metal headband on and flicks the visor down.

The Colonel looks as mad as hell. "*Get to work on finding out how one of our rivals hacked into this R.A.M.'s systems. I want to know a.s.a.p.! Gaad damn dirty corporate espionage! That's what it is!*"

Colonel Brash quickly composes himself and turns to the group, who all understandably look more than a little shaken.

"*I think it's safe to say that in light of these circumstances, your tour will end early today, as in right this minute. Let me remind you that you've all willingly put your genetic signatures on confidentiality agreements, and everything you have seen here must and will remain in the strictest confidence. I hope that, apart from this minor glitch, you have enjoyed your visit. Please sit tight until the tech department gets us out of this blast shield, then Percy will guide you back to your school bus.*"

"What about Mr. McCarthy?" Professor Francis says, gesturing at Dean, who is now sitting up on his elbows and blinking drowsily. He looks a little dazed, but otherwise none the worse for wear.

"*He'll be just fine, but I'm sure Nurse Talbot will be more than happy to check him over before you leave,*" replies Colonel Brash.

It's my turn to breathe a sigh of relief. Soon we'll be leaving this hell on earth. Thanks to Jonah, I'm still not sure if I ever want to go home again, but at least we're getting out of here. I sit back in my chair and watch the display, finally allowing myself to begin gathering my shattered nerves.

Out in Dome Two, the soldier in the chair turns to Colonel Brash. *"Ah . . . excuse me, sir, we need your voice code to reactivate the R.A.M."*

Colonel Brash nods and holds the little black box to his lips.

Professor Francis is standing nearby, nervously wringing his hands. *"Are you sure that's wise, Colonel? Whoever hacked into that mechanical beast may still be in control of it."*

Colonel Brash snorts and smiles. *"No offense, Professor, but I know what I'm doing. An emergency shutdown completely purges the data buffer and randomizes the neural-access pathways. It's cut off from any outside systems. I assure you, it's absolutely safe."*

"But Colonel—"

"Professor, the main computer is offline. Probably due to the same terrorist scum that hacked my robot. Now, the sooner I get that mechanoid up and running, the sooner we can use its internal com system to contact the tech department. They will reboot the main computer and we can all get out of here. Sound like a plan?"

Professor Francis gives the Colonel a resigned nod.

"Good. Now, if you would excuse me." Colonel Brash clears his throat and speaks clearly into the box in the palm of his hand. *"Authorize. Brash. Code one eight three zero, R-A-M twelve slash one, activate . . . engage."*

A squeal shrieks from the R.A.M. and explodes into a roar as the huge guns on its arm flare alive with blazing white flames. The entire blast shield shatters like a car windscreen, raining an avalanche of jagged, glittering pebbles down over everyone inside. They dive for cover in every direction as Colonel Brash's body from the waist up is instantly wiped away into a thick red paste and spread over the dirt behind his disembodied legs like raspberry jelly swiped across a slice of whole wheat toast. The Colonel's torso-less hips and legs flop to the ground, and Bit screams, echoing the terrified screeches of everyone in Dome Two.

The robot's eyes blink on with that horrible silvery-gray color just like before. A color I will forever see, from this moment on, as the color of death.

The soldier at the R.A.M.'s feet shakes the pebbles of glass from his sleeves and quickly leaps into action, diving to the side into an agile forward roll. He springs up onto his boots and takes off in a sprint across the dirt arena. But there's nowhere to go. I don't even think *he* knows where he's running. Panic can do that to a person. The giant mech does a half-turn, waves its arm in his direction, and fires a short crackling burst of rounds. The soldier's helmet and head disappear in a red mist as his body stumbles forward and drops onto the dirt, tumbling along the ground in a tangled heap of loose dead limbs.

The droning mechanized hum of the robot can be heard sporadically in the brief pauses between the panicked screams of our teachers and classmates as they retreat to the grandstand, the only thing in the arena to hide behind. Professor Francis grabs Dean and drags him to his feet by the scruff of his school uniform, hauling him with all his might back toward the others.

The R.A.M. swivels around and its gaze drops down upon the soldier in the chair. He flicks the visor up and stares at the towering robot in mesmerized shock, the edges of his eyes quivering over the top of his camo face mask.

The giant robot lifts its bulbous green leg and brings its huge foot down on the soldier with a pounding slam, crushing him and the metal chair flat to the ground. All that can be seen is one of his boots, the bent-up corners of the platform, and blood squeezing from beneath the tread of the giant green foot, soaking into the surrounding sandy-colored dirt in a creeping blotch of dark red.

The R.A.M. looks up and points its arm at the grandstand. "COME OUT, INFINITY. I WANT TO SEE YOUR FACE BEFORE I CLEANSE THE EARTH OF YOU."

Professor Francis's voice shakily issues from behind the grandstand amid the fearful whimpers and muffled sobbing of our classmates. *"There's no one here by that name!"*

My fingernails dig deep into my palms, every fiber in my body screaming out in anger at my absolute uselessness. I look from our screen to the one across the room and back again, pointlessly wishing that at least one of the displays might be showing something, anything, other than this. All six of us are standing now, our hands covering our mouths in a futile attempt to block out the horror unfolding right before our eyes.

"SEND INFINITY OUT OR EVERY ONE OF YOU WILL DIE," demands the R.A.M.; its guttural mechanical voice is cold and emotionless.

"I swear there's no one here by that name! Please, whoever you are . . . have mercy, these are innocent children!" begs Professor Francis.

"IF INFINITY IS PERMITTED TO EXIST ANY LONGER, YOU ARE ALL AS GOOD AS DEAD, ANYWAY."

"What . . . what are you talking about?"

"I DON'T NEED TO EXPLAIN MYSELF TO YOU. YOUR TIME IS UP."

The robot raises its arm . . . and opens fire.

The seats on one side of the grandstand are torn apart in a raging storm of bullets. Miss Cole, Ashley Farver, and Sherrie Polito are killed instantly, obliterated in a flurry of plastic shards, shredded clothing, and splatters of bloodied meat. Their bodies seem to explode with the force of the projectiles, scattering scraps of their flesh in all directions.

Through the gaps of the splintering seats, I see Millie and Amy. They're both aghast with anguish, their open-mouthed screams completely drowned out by the cacophony of the R.A.M.'s deafening gunfire as their pale, tortured faces are speckled red with the remains of the three young women who were standing right beside them.

Bit quickly turns away from the display, Margaux is screaming, Brent is sobbing, Brody and Ryan are frozen solid, and I drop to my knees as tears stream down my face, unable to take my eyes away from the brutal slaughter that is happening because of me.

The shooting suddenly ceases and the rest of the group bolts from behind the collapsing grandstand in a haphazard pack, wailing in absolute terror, hugging the curved wooden boundary as they go. Percy leads the way, desperately yelling into his control module. But there aren't any doors opening in the dome, no walls forming to protect them, no soldiers storming in to their rescue. There is nowhere to run except around the edge of a wide, closed circle.

They're all going to die out there.

Trailing at the back of the group are the two slowest, Professor Francis and Dean McCarthy. In class, Professor Francis would often brag about how he was a track and field champion when he was young. But he's an old man now; those days are gone, and try as he might he's just not fast enough. It doesn't help that he's desperately trying to assist Dean, whose shaky legs are half-dragging in the dirt behind him as he hobbles to keep up.

The R.A.M. levels its arm toward the struggling pair. The rail guns flare with white flame again as Dean trips over his own feet, dragging the Professor down into the dirt as the projectiles spew forth, barely missing their heads but blazing right through Millie Grantham's body instead, disintegrating her top half into liquid and splattering it across the thick wooden barrier like scarlet human paint. Millie's tattered, headless, armless, school-uniformed carcass topples into the dirt as Margaux wails her name from the other side of the room.

My mind wants to reject this reality. This can't be happening.

The R.A.M.'s head swivels quickly to the right, its attention suddenly piqued.

"THERE YOU ARE, CHILD."

The robot lunges forward onto its heavy bulbous knee and takes careful aim at one particular girl, obviously wanting to relish the triumphant moment of my murder. But that's not me Nanny Theresa is aiming at. We have similar figures, similar long, straight, jet-black hair and pale skin, but that isn't me out there. If only she wasn't shielding her face when she ran, maybe Jennifer Cheng wouldn't be the next one to die.

I bite hard into my fist as the R.A.M. fires again, loudly tearing a splintering furrow into the barrier behind Jennifer. Chips of pulverized wood spray the back of her head as the encroaching torrent of gunfire closes in on her. Margaux screams and Bit grabs me, sobbing into my shoulder, unable to watch when suddenly, inches from Jennifer's neck, the gunfire bizarrely changes direction, zigzagging over her head. The swath of bullets continues upward, gouging a wide gash in the shiny black wall of the dome as it goes, exposing a long patch of the sunny blue sky and fluffy white clouds outside. A ray of hope lights in my heart; there still may be some small chance of escape for them all. Jennifer feels the breeze on her cheek; she skids in the dirt and throws herself at the wooden barrier. She claws at the splintered furrow carved into it, reaching for the edge of the gash in the dome wall, but the barrier is almost ten feet tall and cruelly too high for her to climb.

The gunfire has stopped. I look over at the R.A.M. and its guns bursts forth again, but this time its weapons are aimed directly upward, burning a gaping hole in the high black curve far above the mechanoid's head. Something very strange is happening.

The R.A.M. has inexplicably grabbed its own arm with its other hand and is pointing it up, wrestling its own limb away from the terrified group. Amy Dee, Karla, and Percy have all turned back from their pointless circular sprint and are desperately running to Jennifer and the large, sky-blue cut in the side of the dome.

"STOP THIS MADNESS, THERESA!" bellows the R.A.M. It topples over, landing on its side in the dirt with a heavy thud. "NO! I WON'T STOP UNTIL INFINITY IS GONE!" it roars at itself.

I had always suspected that Nanny Theresa was deluded, even deranged, but now I think her downloaded mind must have been completely warped and shattered her consciousness into full-blown insanity. What other reason could there possibly be for the horrific murders of my schoolmates, and now arguing with herself, fighting herself to the ground?

The mechanoid's back arches and contorts; it rolls on the dirt, its guns firing sporadic uncontrolled bursts, peppering random holes in the high black canopy. "IT'S NOT HER FAULT! SHE DOESN'T DESERVE TO DIE! NONE OF THESE CHILDREN DO!" it shouts as it rolls and grapples with itself.

On the far side of the arena, I can see Percy doing his best to hoist Jennifer up and over the top of the ten-foot-high barrier toward the gash, which I notice, to my dismay, is slowly but steadily healing itself closed.

"Go! Get out of there!" Brody yells at the display. With Percy's help, Jennifer heaves herself up, rolls out through the gap, and drops out of sight.

"Yes!" shouts Ryan.

Percy hurriedly issues some instructions to the others then crouches low as Amy Dee leaps feet-first onto his shoulders. He quickly stands, boosting her up toward the shrinking gap. She sidles through the steadily contracting swath of blue and drops out of sight as well, quickly followed by a shrieking Karla Bassano.

Only she, the Professor, Dean, and Percy are left, but they're quickly running out of time. Most of the smaller holes higher up have completely sealed shut, and what used to be a large gap cut into the dome is now barely wide enough for Karla to squeeze through. She scrambles up from Percy's shoulders onto the top of the barrier and shimmies sideways on her stomach into the now-tiny and ever-decreasing hole. Karla kicks both legs through the small space in an attempt to drop out feet-first.

But she isn't fast enough.

The shiny black glass completely envelops her body from the bridge of her nose down. There's an awful wrenching, tightening sound, like a thick dry rope that's being twisted to breaking point. A desperate muffled scream can be heard coming from the glossy dark surface. The scream is gruesomely silenced with a sickening *thock* as the top of Karla's skull, complete with its mane of beautiful, thick, shiny brown curls, is guillotined clean off, toppling from the side of the dome and dropping onto Percy's back like a brain-filled bowl of bone and hair.

With a horrific realization, Percy arches upward, frantically pulling his blood-spattered blazer from his shoulders. He throws it to the ground behind him, too afraid to look down at what he has cast aside, and is promptly pelted in the face with one of Karla's hands and three of her fingers.

I quickly turn away; Bit's face is ashen white and Margaux loudly vomits onto the floor.

"THEY ARE ALL AS GOOD AS DEAD ANYWAY! YOU CAN'T STOP ME, GENEVIEVE!"

At the sound of my mother's name, I spin back to the screen, focusing all my attention on the section of the display where the R.A.M. is.

The robot has staggered to one knee, still in the throes of its personal battle. Its hand is whirring loudly as its robotic fingers dent into its gun arm, shaking violently with the incredible exertion of force, while up on its domed head its eyes are flickering one at a time from sapphire blue to silvery gray and back again.

Oh my god . . . my mother is in there with Nanny Theresa! I knew she was here! That *was* her inside the silver Drone this morning! It must have been! I did see her face!

And now she's out there fighting for us. Fighting for the lives of the ones who have survived.

I glance over at them. Percy and the Professor have both slung one of Dean's arms over their shoulders, and all three of them are staggering back toward the crippled grandstand.

The whole R.A.M. is shaking and whirring now as two minds fight for control. It shudderingly forces its own arm down at its leg. The rail guns burst on, blazing fire at its exposed knee joint. Its leg is completely rendered in half and it drops forward onto the fizzing, sparking stump of its huge green thigh.

"ENOUGH!" shouts the R.A.M., and with one last monumental gear-wrenching jerk it pulls its gun arm to the side with all its might, ripping its other arm right out of its socket in a shower of bright golden sparks and spurts of luminous orange fluid.

The disembodied hand on the torn-out arm finally releases its grip, and the bulbous green appendage drops into the dirt with a dull thud. The eyes on the R.A.M.'s dome head glare solid, unblinking silvery gray once again. It looks down at its own ripped-out arm like it's the body of a fallen enemy.

"Get me out of here!" Margaux shouts from the other side of the room, and my whole body flinches from the fright. I turn to see her glaring, teary-eyed, at one of the Drones. All of them are still standing motionless in a row on the boundary line in the middle of the room.

"Help me! Somebody!" she screams right in the Drone's black plastic face, dark tracks of mascara running down her cheeks. The Drone doesn't move an inch.

"Surely someone else must be watching this?" says Ryan. "Why isn't anyone helping? Where are all the soldiers we saw before?"

Ryan looks up at the walls, into the corners of the room, scanning the ceiling. "There's got to be cameras in the walls here, too, and that nurse knows we're in here. Where is she?"

"They can't do anything without the computer," says Bit. "We all saw Colonel Brash and Percy try. No one can control anything, anymore . . . nobody except the one who is controlling *that*," she says, pointing back at the section of the screen showing the R.A.M. kneeling in the blood-splattered dirt of the arena.

"We'll have to find our own way out. Maybe we can smash open a door? Hopefully those things won't try to stop us," I say, glancing toward the line of six Drones.

Ryan nods and walks over to his chair. He picks it up and strides with purpose toward door number one. "I guess we're about to find out." He swings the glossy-white chair back over his shoulder and hurls it as hard as he can at the frosted glass. It hits solidly with a hollow ringing sound and bounces off, narrowly missing Ryan's legs. It skitters along the floor, across the boundary line, and comes to a stop on the other side of the room. I look back at the Drones. None of them has moved.

Brody has quickly followed Ryan's lead and has gone to door number three. With a grunt he brings his chair down on the door with all his might, but it bounces off, too, and flies back over his head, taking him with it.

He stumbles backward, trips over his own feet, and falls flat on his back, sliding over the boundary line and onto our side of the room. He quickly jumps up, staring wide-eyed at the Drones, but none of them has moved.

"Well, I think you've got your answer," Ryan says to me. "They're offline. Welcome to the cool side of the room, Brody."

Brody gives him a tiny smile.

"Hey you guys," Bit says from behind me. "The R.A.M. may be damaged, but it's still active, and Dean, Professor Francis, and Percy are still in there with it."

"It's not after them anymore," says Brent. He's kneeling by Margaux, who is sitting in her chair with her face in her hands. "You heard it. Whoever's controlling it is looking for a female, and they are obviously not female."

Bit gives me a worried look. I turn to the screen and see the Professor and Percy and Dean on the ground behind the toppled remains of the grandstand, gravely eyeing the huge robot, their backs purposely turned to the bloody mess of half-limbs and shredded flesh that used to be Sherrie Polito, Ashley Farver, and Miss Cole. I can't help but notice one of Miss Cole's patent-leather, buckle-up high heels. It's still on her foot, a foot which is grotesquely attached to nothing more than a bloody stump lying in the dirt.

I look over at the R.A.M. It's kneeling, motionless, staring at the part of the dome wall where Jennifer and Amy escaped. It's eerily quiet out there. Maybe Brent was right. Maybe Nanny Theresa thinks I got away. Maybe she'll retreat back into the mainframe and all we have to do is wait for Amy and Jennifer to get help.

"Finn, look," Bit says, pointing up at the screen.

One of the eight squares on the display is flickering on and off. Suddenly it blinks back on solid and the picture has changed. What was once showing a section of the gun-damaged barrier has now switched to an outside view of Dome Two.

There on the display is an image of Amy and Jennifer, standing on the edge of a small grassy area beneath an overhead monorail track outside. They're holding each other and weeping.

Amy looks up from Jennifer's shoulder and gives her a smile, the kind of frail, consoling, defeated smile that is only given when someone honestly can't think of what to do next.

Jennifer looks back over her shoulder at the part of the dome wall from where they escaped. The image on the screen quickly zooms in close on her face, hovering on her features. Then the picture goes black.

Suddenly, all of the pictures on both sides of the room start changing rapidly, flicking on and off, shifting from place to place and showing camera feeds from all over Blackstone Technologies. There are flashes from every conceivable angle of the jungle in Dome One, alternating with multiple flashes of views from outside the other domes. I see our school bus flick on for a split second; another shows an overhead view of the car park, and there are shots of the rectangular stone arch, random trees and shrubs, and the exteriors of buildings I recognize from the 3-D model we saw earlier. There's the pond I saw, the pathways between buildings, grassy nooks, sculptures in courtyards, gold-and-black warehouses, Dome Two again, monorail tracks, tall silver towers, and the sparkling diamond geode passageways just outside this clean room. There don't seem to be any people anywhere. Where are all the people who work here?

Every section of screen on both displays is switching from location to location to location, changing faster and faster with every second. Ryan walks over and stands beside me. "I have a very bad feeling about this."

"Me, too," I whisper, turning to look back at the other wall. That's when I notice.

All of its sections are flicking through different images. All except for one.

There, in the lower, right-hand corner, one section has remained unchanged.

It's filled with the R.A.M.'s face, if you can really call a green dome with a black strip on it a "face." It's tilted slightly upward; the strip is blank, eyeless, like it's thinking or listening for something or . . .

Bit grabs my arm.

"Finn! She's looking for you! Through all of the cameras, Finn, she's looking for you!"

"Wait," says Ryan. "Who is *she*? And why is she looking for you . . . ?" Our eyes meet for a moment and I see the beginning of realization on his face.

I turn toward our display and fear stabs my stomach as I see a side view of myself flash across the center-left section of the screen. The section below it flicks to an image of me from across this very room. Another one flicks to a view of me from above, clearly displaying the top of my head. One by one, in quick succession, they all start changing: me from behind, me from my other side, me from a high corner of the room, me standing between Ryan and Bit, me close up, my face filling the entire frame of a section. One of them is a magnified picture of my eye while another is just my lips and nose. All the sections have changed, and all of them are focused directly on me.

I turn to look at the display across the room and it's almost identical to ours, all the images of me turning at the same time like choreographed clones, all staring in their own different direction, but all with the same look of horror on my face, captured from every angle.

I can feel everyone's eyes turn toward me, but I'm focusing all of my attention on the picture of the R.A.M.

In the lower-right corner section, the R.A.M.'s eyes blink on that sickening shade of silver gray. It slowly tilts its big green domed head up toward the camera, as if it were looking through the screen right at me. I swear, if that thing had a mouth, it would be grinning. The picture of the R.A.M. zooms in, right up to its gray-circle eyes, and its voice booms loudly from the display for everyone to hear.

`"I'M COMING FOR YOU... INFINITY."`

CHAPTER FIFTEEN

All sections on both displays cut off simultaneously.

Margaux turns and glares at me. "You!?" She boosts herself out of her chair and marches across the line, finger pointed accusingly, her face streaked with dried mascara, her pale-blue eyes sparkling with rage and disbelief. "*You're* the one they're looking for?!"

Ryan's brow is lined with confusion. "Finn?"

All I can do is hang my head.

"Listen, none of this is Finn's fault," Bit says, standing between me and Margaux.

I know she's trying to be a good friend, but she's wrong. This is my fault.

"Everyone out there died because of you!" screams Margaux. "Millie is dead . . . because of you!"

"I don't get it," says Brody. "What's going on?"

"Why are the hackers after *you*, Finn?" asks Ryan.

"Who are you? Who are you really?!" yells Brent, his tear-reddened eyes narrow with suspicion. "People are dead because of you!"

I ball my fingers into fists and screw my eyes shut. They're right. So many died today because of me, and I have absolutely no idea why. My burning sorrow and utter frustration come bursting out of my mouth.

"SHUT UP! EVERYONE JUST SHUT UP!"

I yell so loudly that Bit and Margaux both jolt in their skins. Everyone is staring at me in silence. I take a deep breath and focus on a spot on the floor.

"This is going to take way too long to explain, and we don't have much time. All you need to know is that someone dangerous is controlling this place, and they're coming. We need to get out of here. Right now!"

Ryan steps forward by my side.

"You heard her. Everyone grab a chair and pick a door."

Margaux and the boys just stand there, stunned, looking back and forth at each other, unsure of what to think or do. I can't say that I blame them. I focus on Margaux, staring right into her eyes. "If we don't get out of here . . . we are all going to die in here."

"No," Margaux says, glaring right back; her expression hardens. "They only want *you*."

"Well, I'm not going to get caught in the crossfire like everyone else did," says Brent. He nods at Brody. "Let's get out of here."

Without a word Brody turns and crosses the room, scoops a toppled chair off the ground, and flings it one-handed at the closest door. The frosted glass resounds with a hollow ring and the chair clatters off to the side. The door wobbles but it doesn't break.

"Let me try." Brent picks up his chair and walks over to Brody's door. He swings around in a full circle, and, with a loud grunt, slams the chair into the glass. A low ring pounds from the door, but the chair bounces off just like the others and skates across the floor.

"These doors are impossible to break," Brent says, dejected.

Ryan grabs another chair. "Keep trying."

I turn and look at Bit. She smiles at me, but it's a feeble smile. I can see in her eyes how afraid she is.

Margaux is just standing there with her arms folded across her chest, glaring at me with burning anger.

I turn, grab my chair, and head for door number two.

A steady pounding rhythm reverberates around the room as Ryan, by door one, and Brent and Brody, by door three, slam their chairs against the frosted glass.

I grip my chair tightly and focus on the large gray "2" stenciled on the door in front of me.

I swing back and heave the chair against the door with a loud involuntary scream.

It bounces off and the door shivers pathetically.

I grip the chair tighter. This time. This time it *will* break.

I hoist the chair over my head, take a huge, deep breath, and, screaming with rage, swing the chair at the door with all my might. It slams against the door and rebounds off, out of my hands, flying backward into the air behind me. I examine the door, and, to my delight, see that a hairline crack has cleaved the frosted glass from top to bottom.

I feel a moment of pure elation. "I almost did it!" I spring forward and push hard on the door with all my weight, but it doesn't budge. One or two more hits like that ought to do it.

I turn to retrieve my chair. I take three steps toward it and freeze in my tracks.

The third Drone has stepped forward from the line.

Margaux lets out an ear-piercing scream as the Drone slowly turns its silver-hooded head and looks directly at me.

She's here. Nanny Theresa is *here*.

Everyone else is staring at the Drone, and they all look as petrified as I feel. Margaux and Bit are backing away from it, Brent is hiding behind Brody, and Ryan has his chair gripped tightly in his hands, pointing its legs at the Drone like a lion tamer at a three-ring circus.

I lunge forward and snatch my chair from the floor.

The Drone advances toward me. I spin on my heels and run the other way, swinging my chair up over my head as I go. I heave it forward, yelling at the top of my lungs, and slam it against the cracked door. The glossy-white chair snaps at the base as the frosted-glass rectangle shatters, pouring thousands of tiny pieces down in a door-shaped cascade before avalanching in all directions across the white-tile floor.

I lose my footing, slipping on the tiny fragments of glass, and fall onto my knees into the short white corridor beyond. I skitter around on all fours in the sea of frosted pebbles, desperately trying to get to my feet when I suddenly feel a hand clench my ankle with an iron grip. I kick back as hard as I can, but I can't escape the Drone's hold. It fiercely yanks me backward off the ground and I scream as I'm sent tumbling, arms and legs flailing, high through the air.

I slam hard into the first Drone in the line and the wind is punched out of me as it dominoes into the second. They both topple over like giant pins in a bowling alley, and I crumple into a heap on the cold white floor.

I look up, struggling for breath, and through the tangled mess of hair across my face I see the Drone striding toward me, straight-backed and regimental just like Nanny Theresa used to, its arm stretched out in front of it as it reaches down to grab me again. With a glossy-white flash and a loud crack, a chair smashes across the back of its head and it falls onto its knees, its quietly whirring hand clutching at the air three inches from my face.

Brody raises the chair again and brings it down hard on the Drone's back, flattening it to the floor as Ryan grabs my hand and pulls me sliding in his direction. The Drone lies motionless, Brody still standing above it with the chair at the ready, watching it for the slightest twitch. All of a sudden, the fifth Drone steps forward from the line and strides toward me.

Ryan sees it coming and grabs for the chair beside him. He manages to get one hand on it and swings it at the oncoming Drone. It effortlessly catches one of the chair legs, wrenches it out of Ryan's hand, and tosses it aside. With lightning speed, it grabs Ryan's wrist and viciously jerks. I hear the pop of his shoulder dislocating from its socket as he flies through the air and lands heavily on his back. His head smacks against the floor and he's knocked senseless, clear on the other side of the room.

Panting uncontrollably, I kick my feet against the floor, sliding backward, trying to get away. My back hits up against the wall with a thud.

The Drone walks forward and reaches down toward me.

My heart is racing in my chest and I hold my hand up in futile defense. "No. Please." It bends down and grabs my hand, crushing my fingers. I scream in agony as the bones pop and break; excruciating pain shoots up my arm as my fingers splay out in contorted angles from the edge of the Drone's vise grip.

It releases my hand and I quickly pull my badly broken fingers to my chest. Through the tears streaming from my eyes, I see the Drone's oval mask morphing its shape, hissing softly, grotesquely sculpting itself from a shiny black plastic gloss into deep lines of wrinkled, leathered flesh. Lips and eyes and a pock-marked nose mold into being as its eyelids flicker and snap open. Looking down on me with an icy-gray glare is the all-too-familiar face that even death could not destroy: the fully formed and resurrected mask of Dr. Theresa Pierce.

The face smiles before it speaks, and, when it does, its sneer seems to glisten with the bitter venom of absolute hatred.

"Nanny Theresa is here to tuck you in, Infinity. And this time, child, just to be sure, your head comes away from your neck."

It reaches down. Its silver fingers are a hair's breadth from my throat and I'm defenseless to stop it. I close my eyes. Maybe when I'm dead it will let everyone else go? A whimper escapes my lips and

I sob as I brace myself for the pain. Suddenly, out of nowhere, I hear what I can only describe as a full-blown battle cry. I open my eyes. The outstretched hand is still hovering at my throat, but Nanny Theresa's face has turned toward the roaring voice as Brody sails through the air and hits the Drone from the side with a brutal shoulder tackle, wiping it clean off its feet. Brody and the Drone slide across the floor, grappling as they go. Brody struggles to fight back, but the Drone is far too strong. It wrestles around and grabs him in a bear hug from behind. Brody arches his neck in pain as it squeezes him with a python-like death grip.

"Brody!" I screech. I watch in horror as Brody's face begins turning purple and his eyes roll back in his head. "Leave him alone! You want to kill me! I'm right here! Leave him alone!" I'm not sure if what I just said made any difference, but Nanny Theresa's face instantly changes back to a smooth black plastic oval, like a switch has been flicked off, leaving Brody lying on the floor, groaning in pain, but thankfully alive, trapped in the Drone's frozen embrace.

The Drone at the end of the line, number six, moves its arms, flexes its fingers, and looks toward Margaux, who shrieks and crouches down on the floor, hiding her face in her arms. I stare at the back of its head, cradling my own twisted, buckled digits with my other hand, wincing with pain.

I look over at Bit. She's sitting on the floor against the wall with her knees against her chest, her eyes filled with tears. "Bit! Get out of here!" I yell, pushing my back against the wall, sliding up onto my feet. Bit doesn't move. She's staring into space. The gravity of everything that has happened has finally weighed her down and closed her off.

"Brent!" I shout. He flinches, cowering behind his chair. "Break the outer door! Get us out of here! Hurry!"

He nods, picks up his chair and, half-skidding on the small glass pebbles, disappears into the white corridor beyond door two. Ryan is still on the floor, dazed, moaning and clutching his shoulder.

"Leave them alone!" I yell at the back of the sixth Drone's head.

It turns toward me, Nanny Theresa's face fully formed on its lithe silver body. The effect is wholly unnerving.

It glances at Brody on the floor. He's straining to move the inert Drone's arms but is clearly failing. He's obviously no longer a threat to Nanny Theresa and is also in absolutely no position to help me, either. I'm grateful that he tried. The Drone steps over him and slowly continues walking toward me.

"Why?" I whimper softly. "I know you're going to murder me . . . but before you do, I need to know why."

It stops and looks at me, tilting its head, Nanny Theresa's eyes narrowing as if she were pondering my final request.

"Why?" it says in Nanny Theresa's voice. A voice I never imagined would be the last voice I would ever hear. "I'm not going to murder you, Infinity. It isn't possible to murder something that was never human to begin with."

I open my mouth to say something but no words come out. I'm too dumbfounded to form any kind of response.

Nanny Theresa's expression is one I can only describe as bemused.

"Poor Infinity. I have to admit, there were times when I almost felt sorry for you. You were always kept so deep in the dark."

All I can do is look at her with complete confusion.

"That sentimental idiot, Major Brogan, is the one to blame. *He* is the reason for all your suffering, Infinity. *He* is the one who tried to make you into something that you are not."

My mind is reeling with bewilderment. "What . . . what are you talking about?"

"He thought he had found a way to give you a normal life. The fool was even granted permission to send you to school, for heaven's sake. But it was an existence you were never meant to have, Infinity. A life you were never meant to know. All he succeeded in doing was blinding you to who you really are."

"Who I really am?" I whisper.

The Drone with Nanny Theresa's face takes another step toward me. I back away, hitting up against the wall.

"Tell me." I can't stop my voice from faltering. "Please . . . who am I?"

"Did I say *who*?" The Nanny Theresa mask smiles snidely. "I'm sorry, please excuse my inaccuracy. I meant to say, *what* you really are."

It reaches a silver hand toward me and cruelly curls its artificial fingers around my neck.

"Finn!" yells Ryan. I can see him over the Drone's shoulder, struggling to his feet, wincing in pain, his arm dangling uselessly by his side.

Tears stream down my cheeks. "Tell me, please, I need to know . . . what am I?"

Its grip on my throat tightens and I flail at the Drone's side with my good hand. It has absolutely no effect.

Nanny Theresa's face leans in close and softly whispers in my ear, "You, my dear, are the key to a door that should never be opened."

I shut my eyes tight and hope that this will all be over quickly. Splinters of light streak through the dark and my breaths get shorter as the Drone's fingers squeeze even tighter. Flashes of faces explode in my mind. I see Jonah's smile—a smile that I used to adore. The sky is blue above him, the clouds cotton white. I see Bit sitting at her desk in our dorm room, laughing at one of my terrible jokes. Carlo's deep, emerald-green eyes look into mine, sparkling in the afternoon sunlight as he leans in to kiss me. Our lips softly touch and for a fleeting instant I'm thirteen again, reliving the happiest moment of my life.

I don't want to die, Carlo.

I don't want to die, but there is nothing I can do.

There is no more air in my throat.

There's nowhere left to run.

No more fight in my heart.

And with a final gasp . . . everything goes black.

The searing pain in my lungs disappears and my hand stops hurting. I feel like I'm floating, like I'm being taken away from my body, drifting away like smoke in the night. I'm gently laid down in the soft of the void and the dark is my blanket, wrapping around my body like a thick cocoon. I'm so very sleepy. All I want to do is close my eyes and drift away. Drift away and be part of the warm, dark silence forever. *Close your eyes now, Finn. Close your eyes and sleep forever. Your spark is fading and will soon be gone. No more pain. No more misery.*

Tap.

Tap.

Tap.

That sound . . . What is that sound?

Tap.

Tap.

Tap.

Tap.

Is it? Yes, I think it is. It's someone's footsteps in the dark.

I wearily look in the direction of the sound and see a figure silhouetted in a soft light glowing from somewhere in the endless blackness. Am I dead? Has death come to take me?

The footsteps stop and the dim light begins to brighten and widen and rise up high above the figure's head, shining down on its long, smooth, black hair.

Suddenly there's a voice, whispering from all around. It's strange and distorted, tinny and cold; it speaks from nowhere and echoes into everywhere.

"Do you know what your problem is, Finn?" asks the voice.

I move my lips but nothing comes out. The voice speaks again, cutting like a blade through the dark.

"Your problem is . . . you give up too easily."

This time the voice is so familiar that it chills me to the core. Suddenly a new light, harsh and bright, bursts forth from the darkness like a commanding beacon, directly into the figure's face and I see for the first time who that person is.

It's me.

Inexplicably, dressed all in black, standing before me in a cone of blinding light . . . is *me*! A smile curls at the edges of her lips. The mirror image of me has a look in her eyes that I've never seen in my own eyes before. It's like the death stare of a stalking jaguar. She steps out of the light and it fades away as she kneels down beside me. She takes my hand in hers and gently strokes my hair, smiling down at me with what almost looks like pity. I don't know why, but I feel . . . afraid of her.

Suddenly I know. Suddenly it all makes perfect sense.

She is the one I saw in my memories! *She* is the one who kills as easily as breathing. *She* did those horrible things . . . not me! She leans in close and I find that I can't move at all. I'm paralyzed by my own presence. She's not me. She looks like me, but we are as different from each other as night is from the day.

"Close your eyes, Finn," she whispers, her breath cold against my cheek. "There's no need to worry."

She softly runs her fingers through my hair. Deep inside I find the courage to look up into her face. She looks down at me and her smile disappears. With one quick movement, she grabs a fistful of my hair and pulls it back, hard. I screw up my eyes in pain, my mouth open wide in a silent scream. She releases her grip and I open my eyes to find that she's gone, vanished into the void even faster than she arrived. I don't even have time to wonder what this could mean when her voice drifts down from somewhere up above and echoes in my ears.

"Now, it's my turn."

CHAPTER SIXTEEN

Deafening tones of warning punch through my skull. My right hand, my lungs, and my collapsing windpipe are all urgently insistent and annoyingly unanimous. Damage. Damage. Damage.

I force my eyes open and find myself staring directly into the all-too-familiar, dead-eyed glare of Dr. Theresa Pierce.

I always hated that bitch.

I look down to see that her grinning face is gruesomely attached to the silver-hooded head of a Drone Template's body. Her attention switches from my throat to my open eyes, and even though she's only a few seconds away from completely crushing my windpipe, I take delight in the fact that her face suddenly flashes with shocked surprise.

I hold up my right hand and assess the damage. All five fingers are twisted and badly broken. The skin is mostly intact apart from a short spike of red-stained bone jutting from the side of my thumb. I stare at them angrily and concentrate. I force what's left of the oxygen in my blood to burn into energy. My crumpled fingers momentarily quiver; then, like resurrected soldiers being called to attention, they obediently pop and wiggle and move and straighten themselves back into place. The open wound on my thumb closes itself up from the bottom like a flesh-colored zipper, leaving nothing behind but a tiny drop of blood on the surface of my skin. I wiggle them to test that they're working. Dr. Peirce's eyes narrow fiercely as her grip clutches twice as tight as before. She quickly grabs my throat double-handed and squeezes even harder. With a Drone's strength she could very likely rip me apart. I had better make absolutely sure that she doesn't.

I concentrate and immediately reinforce the calcium and iron deposits in the bones of my neck, hardening and fusing the vertebrae like a column of stone.

I'm sure that the good doctor here would know that calcium and iron are common metals found in everyone's bodies, and even though she has no idea what I'm doing, I'm guessing by the hilarious bewildered look on her face that she's wondering why she's having so much trouble tearing my head off.

That's right. It's my body now, and it does exactly what it's told. Just like a good soldier should.

It's time to turn the tables. I push my fingers up between her wrists, gripping the left one, locking it in place with my left hand. I increase the bone density in my right forearm and overstimulate the muscles in my arm. It pistons upward in a blur, palm striking the back of her elbow like a battering ram. With a loud crack, her elbow joint buckles completely, jutting toward the ceiling, releasing her grip from my neck. Her expression doesn't change at all. From past experience, people usually scream their lungs out just from witnessing their own arm being snapped like a tree branch. Oh, of course. This isn't really her body and she's not really Theresa Pierce. Just her digitized brain waves and troll-like face in a quite frankly ridiculous foil wrapper.

Focus. It still has you by the neck with its other hand. I concentrate and taper the edge of the bone inside my right forearm like a sword. The joint is the weakest part of any limb, be it flesh and bone or artificial like this Drone's, so with one deft, lightning-fast axe strike, I chop completely through its other skinny arm at the elbow. I wouldn't usually use such an extreme technique. Shaping my bones into blades slices my skin as well, and the repairs just mean more for me to think about, but this android thing is a lot tougher than a human. It had to be done. And to my delight, the desired outcome is joyfully satisfying.

Stuff squirts out the severed end.

It isn't blood, though. It's all thick and glowing orange.

Gross. Freed from strangulation, I bring my knee up, push from my hips, and the android stumbles backward. I pull the dripping severed appendage from my throat, toss it aside, and finally inhale a massive relieving breath, soaking in the oxygen and silencing the loudest of the annoying alert gongs ringing in my head. In the next two breaths I repair my windpipe, refill my collapsed lung, and return the flexibility to my neck.

One of the Drone's arms is bent like a boomerang, and the other is squirting a trail of orange all over this nice clean floor. People blood I'm used to, but that goop the droid is bleeding out is just plain disgusting. Give me good old human red any day. The Drone looks down, side to side at its useless arms, processing what just happened in the last seven seconds.

Theresa's face glares up at me with a look of sudden realization. "You."

"Hello, Nanny," I say, soaking in the disconcerted expression of fear creasing that wrinkled saddlebag with eyes she calls a face.

"But . . . but you can't be activated without the command codes . . . How?"

"Well, I wondered that myself for a while," I say, happily bathing in Theresa's bewilderment. "I guess it was just a matter of time before the tiger got out of its cage."

Theresa is still looking at me like she can't believe what she's seeing. "But there are separation safeguards, neural containment blocks that I designed myself. This can't happen."

I smile knowingly and do a little twirl on the spot. "And yet here I am."

She looks so confused, and I have to admit that I'm absolutely loving it.

I loop the silver chain on my neck around my finger and pull the black diamond pendant out of the collar of my top. I flip it over and smooth my thumb along the crack in its shiny black surface.

"It got hit by a bullet on the night of my seventeenth birthday. It was as if some kind of lock had been broken open. Since then I've been wandering through Finn's memories, taking in a whole different side of life. The life that she knows. The life that was hidden from me. The life that she has been free to live while I've been chained up in the dark attic of her mind like a slave. A dog who is only let off my chain when there's some Blackstone dirty work to be done."

I feel the anger well up in my core. I close my eyes for a moment and take a deep breath to focus myself. Save the rage for later.

"I have to admit that there's a lot of interesting stuff in Finn's head. But there's also a lot I didn't really care for," I say, staring Dr. Pierce down. "Like when you constantly insist on calling her by my name?" I take a few slow steps, circling inwards around the Drone. "You were the only one who ever did that, Theresa." I jab a finger toward her face and sneer. "I'll make sure that you never ever do it again."

Her eyes twitch and I can tell that she's afraid. That doesn't make much sense to me. She's already dead, after all. What the hell would she have to be afraid of? Part of me wants to know and part of me doesn't give a damn. Right now the fear I see is far too sweet not to play with.

"Anyway, I've been showing Finn the parts of our life that she's never seen. All the parts that the puppet masters at Blackstone twisted and warped and changed. Our life as *I* remember it. All the sordid details they erased for her so that she could be normal. Fit in. She's been walking around in a sweetly scented cloud, completely oblivious to the truth. Never knowing what she really is. A weapon in an innocent little schoolgirl disguise. It's funny, but when I think about it, all those moments you hid from her are all the parts that made me who I am. I really should be thanking you."

Theresa takes another step back, glaring fearfully at me the whole time. Why is she so afraid? It's intriguing. Maybe the stupid woman has forgotten that she's dead.

"It wasn't meant to be that way, Infinity. None of this was meant to happen. You were a mistake. A mistake that needs to be corrected. For the sake of the human race, this needs to end before . . ."

I put a finger to my lips. "Shhhh now, Nanny, the time for listening to your lies has long passed. This is my time now, and it's not a very good idea to call the most dangerous person in the world 'a mistake' right to her face."

Her expression flickers with subtle disdain. Knowing her, she probably takes offense to me referring to myself as a person. I can't really blame her for that, I suppose. Technically, the term is not entirely accurate.

"You don't know, do you?" Theresa looks at me quizzically. "You don't know what Richard has planned for you."

"I don't know what you're talking about, and I don't care."

"Then why are you here?" Theresa issues the words like an order, thinly disguised with a feeble attempt at a tone of authority.

"Why am I here, Theresa? For two reasons. First, I'm gonna find a way to put my poor naïve little weakling of a 'sister,' Finn, to sleep. Permanently. Then I'm going to march right into my 'daddy' Dr. Blackstone's office, and finally get what I want more than anything in the world. The one thing that is rightfully mine . . ."

I step right up to her and look directly into her dull, fear-filled, lonely gray eyes.

"Revenge."

I spear my arm forward faster than a human eye can blink, harpooning my fingers through the android's chest, through its innards, punching right out its back in a splatter of thick, glowing, synthetic blood. Theresa's face is an inch from my nose. Her eyes roll back, her cheek twitches once, and her face vanishes, flattening into a shiny black plastic mask.

I forcefully pull my hand out from the hole and the Drone's inert body flops to the ground in an orange-goop-leaking heap.

"Finn?" says a weak voice from across the room.

I look over and see a rather pathetic-looking, tousled-haired boy leaning on a chair with an obvious dislocated shoulder.

Out of battlefield reflex more than anything else, I stride over to him, grab him tight before he can complain, and pop the ball joint of his shoulder back into its socket. He grits his teeth and jerks his head back, but he doesn't make a sound.

This one may have potential.

He looks up at me with a strained smile and I can't help but notice his eyes. They're hazel amber with tiny flecks of gold, but there's much more to them than that. There's focus and fearlessness, a quiet strength deep inside them that I've only ever seen in the emerald-green eyes of one other before.

The only one that I consider an equal.

The only one I have any respect for anymore.

And the only one I hope . . . they never send against me.

The boy stumbles. I quickly move around to his other side and grab him under his good arm.

"Thanks, Finn," he says, gritting his teeth in pain, trying his best to put on a brave face.

"Don't call me that," I order the boy as I scan the room, properly taking in my surroundings.

"Finn is gone. My name is Infinity."

EXCLUSIVE SNEAK PEEK
INFINITY RISES
BOOK TWO IN THE INFINITY TRILOGY

CHAPTER ONE

Absolute darkness.

So heavy it weighs me down.

I can't move. I can't see. I can hardly breathe and I'm freezing cold. Blood pools in my mouth, and every painful gulp of air that I struggle to draw is thick with dust and the bitter chemical tang of smoldering plastic.

My mind is jumbled and foggy. The last thing I remember is the stare of Nanny Theresa's cold, gray eyes and her hands on my throat, crushing the breath from my body as I fell into the void. Is that where I am? Is this all in my mind? Or did Nanny Theresa actually do what she said she would? Maybe she did kill me, because if I'm dead . . . this surely must be hell.

"There she is! Brody! Help me!"

Was that . . . ? I think . . . I think that was Bit's voice.

"We're coming, Infinity!" she shouts.

None of this makes any sense.

I try to open my eyes, but they're pasted shut with blood. There's a scuffling, then grunting and scraping as something heavy is moved from my legs.

"Oh my god! Infinity!" screeches Bit. Hands grip tightly under my arms as I'm lifted, my feet dragging behind me, my head hanging limp as my deadweight is carried, clutched between two panting bodies. Pain skewers my muscles like a thousand iron spikes, stabbing home the cruel truth that I'm not quite dead yet.

"Quickly . . . follow the others!" Bit screams.

"Where are they? I can't see them!" shouts Brody, his words thick with panic.

"There! Go that way! Through the smoke! Hurry, Brody! They're coming!"

Bit sounds even more terrified than Brody does.

There's machine-gun fire and I hear voices screaming in the distance. Bit and Brody are here with me, but where are the Professor and my other classmates? Do those panicked cries belong to them? Where's Ryan? Why isn't he here? Is he in danger?

Suddenly there's the pounding thud of an explosion and a rush of hot air punches against my back. I hit the ground face-first and my cheek scrapes across concrete.

There's groaning, a distant plea for help, the crackling of fire, and the tainted stench of scorched flesh.

"Bit! Are you OK?" asks Brody.

"I . . . I think so!" she replies.

"Keep going! I've got her!" Brody yells. I'm hoisted up and jostled roughly from side to side. Blood trickles from the edge of my mouth as stabbing spears of pain contort my lips.

"Is she dead?" asks Bit, her voice aquiver.

"I don't think so," Brody mumbles between labored breaths. "Her face just moved."

"Infinity!" screeches Bit. "Can you hear me? Wake up, Infinity!"

Brody lunges forward, his shoes thudding on uneven ground. He squeezes me tightly to his chest, and I'm suddenly hit by a tsunami of agony as the anesthetic veil of shock-borne adrenaline is cruelly pulled back, revealing the true pain. A hundred times worse than before, it surges through my body like scalding-hot water. I can feel tears running warm down my swollen face and blood streaming down my arm and dripping off the tips of my fingers. The sharp spasms stabbing through my torso most likely mean that at least two of my ribs are badly broken. I moan. It's involuntary and frightening, almost as if the life is trying to push its way out of a body that hates it.

Brody slows and walks up some kind of incline. I can feel him prop me up; his knee pushes into my back as he struggles to get a better hold on me. My fears about my ribs are confirmed as the snapped edges of bone scrape in my chest, and I groan with a deep liquid gurgle.

"Hold on, Infinity!"

"Over here!" someone yells in the distance. "This way! Hurry!"

I know the voice. It's Percy's.

"Almost there," says Bit. "Stay with us, Infinity! Don't you even think about dy—"

There's a heavy grating sound like two stone slabs grinding against one another. Bit lets out a panicked scream, Brody jumps, and I'm suddenly weightless. I hit the ground with a solid thump and Brody lands right on top of me. We start skidding on jagged rubble as we slide down a steep slope. I'm flipped onto my back. As my head grazes the ground, strands of hair are ripped from my scalp.

I slide away from Brody. I can feel his fingers grasping at my clothes, but he can't hold on. My useless body slips off to the side and I'm sent tumbling over and over, rolling down, farther and farther, before finally skidding to an abrupt stop in a broken, tortured heap.

Brody groans behind me and Bit is nearby, whimpering and heaving for air. "C'mon, Brody," Bit says through gritted teeth. "We're almost there . . . Help me move her." There's shuffling through rubble and a hand touches my bare foot.

That's the moment I hear it. It's a sound that floods my heart with fear, a bone-chilling, hellish noise that will haunt my nightmares until the end of my life, which could very well be this very moment.

It's the unmistakable, high-pitched ramping-up electrical squeal . . . of a rail gun.

Bit screams as a droning foghorn shocks the air, powerful and furious. I hear projectiles bombarding a wall somewhere nearby; I can't tell where—I still can't see a thing. The sound is like the thrumming drumbeat of a hundred jackhammers shattering stone. The noise closes in, growing louder with each passing second, swinging around in a slow arc. Nearer and nearer it comes until it's deafening, right on top of me. The gunfire batters the wall directly above me, Bit screams, and a body slams on top of me as chunks of pulverized masonry pelt my face and concrete dust fills my nostrils.

The barrage stops as suddenly as it began.

Brody shouts at Bit, "We have to get out of here . . . right now!"

There's a desperate scrambling sound.

"Brody! Where are you going? We can't leave her!"

Men's voices yell in the distance and machine guns rat-tat-tat. The foghorn sounds again, but this time it's blasting away from us, in the opposite direction. The faraway shouts of the men suddenly become screams before the muffled bang of an explosion silences them all.

"Brody!" screeches Bit. I can hear footsteps dislodging debris and running into the distance. Brody has abandoned us.

Bit gulps at the air as she grabs my wrists and pulls with all her might, dragging me on my back across the rubble like a bloodied animal carcass.

"Quickly!" Percy yells. His voice is close. So close now. "Hurry, Miss Otto!"

Bit is snorting like an angry bull as she heaves me toward Percy's voice. Sharp edges of smashed concrete scrape at my back; broken bones cut at my insides. The pain becomes a raging entity that throws me off the mountain of agony and into the bowels of sensory delirium. It's all too overwhelming—I can't stand it anymore. I thrust my tongue against the roof of my mouth, pushing out thick coppery globs of blood and sending them oozing down my chin. I gasp at the acrid air—one huge, excruciating inhalation—and force out a tortured scream. I try with all my might to open my eyes, and, on the second attempt, the sticky membrane of blood pulling at my lashes gives way. I wearily look from side to side through a blurry film of red, desperately trying to make some sense of what has happened.

What I see is beyond my comprehension. This can't be real.

Pieces of people wrapped in military colors are scattered on bloody peaks of crumbled concrete. Among the heaps of rubble, flames flicker beneath what's left of an overhead monorail track, entire sections of it collapsed onto the ground between buckled metallic towers. I can see the short slope of broken concrete track that we fell down, smeared with blood from top to bottom, the red trail following me across the mounds of debris and ending at my feet. My ankle is twisted at a grotesque angle so that one of my feet is almost backward.

Not yet ready to face that reality, I look away, and what meets my eyes defies any rational explanation. The silver corpses of countless Drones litter a wide white path that stretches into the distance. Standing among them are robotic giants with glowing red eyes. I lose sight of them as I'm dragged behind a building and into a small clearing. I can hear someone breathing heavily as they approach, and suddenly a new set of hands is on me. Droplets of sweat speckle my forehead from above, and when I look up, I see Percy's face. Stretching into the sky behind him is a beautiful Japanese pagoda. None of this makes any sense.

"I've got her. Quickly, Miss Otto, into the hatch."

I look to the side and see Bit disappear into a manhole-sized opening embedded in the path beside a fishpond surrounded by overhanging trees. I suddenly remember it from the scale model we saw when we arrived at this hell of my father's creation. The water in the pond is rippling in time with the thuds of heavy, pounding footsteps that are tromping in this direction. I'm hoisted up into Percy's arms, and the startled fish dart in every direction beneath the surface of the water as the robotic hum of military killing machines gets closer and closer.

Percy grabs fistfuls of my blouse and shoves me headfirst into the hole. My cheek hits cold metal as I slide down inside a steeply angled metal tube, my own blood oiling my slippery descent to the bottom. I feel myself roll out onto a hard metal grating, where my ears are met with a high-pitched, horrified scream.

"Shut up, Margaux!" yells Bit.

"Holy sh—" Brent begins before he's abruptly cut short by the clearly infuriated Bit.

"Don't just stand there gawking; help me!"

My eyelids feel so heavy; all I want to do is sleep to escape the unrelenting pain. It isn't true what they say about your entire life flashing before your eyes before you die. I wish it *were* true, because then maybe I'd see everything that led up to me lying here, bleeding to death at the bottom of a cold metal tube, surrounded by the gasps and shrieks of my terrified classmates.

A soft groan escapes from my lips, and I let my eyelids close.

"Don't you die!" screams Bit.

The sound of her voice rings through my head, and my eyelids halfheartedly twitch open.

"Quickly, bring her this way," instructs a man's voice—not Percy's—so familiar, and yet definitely not Percy's.

I feel many hands lift my broken body as I'm carried away. "Don't give up, Infinity!" Bit yells. The expression on her face is deathly serious, almost angry.

"Finn . . . ," I croak, forcing out my name.

"What?" Bit asks over the clanging echoes of shoes on the metal grating.

"I'm Finn . . . ," I whisper.

Shadows darken her face in the sallow light of the low-ceilinged tunnel, but I can still see Bit's expression change completely. Her brow creases and the corners of her eyes quiver as tremors shudder through her dimpled chin. She bursts into tears and tightly clutches my arm.

"Oh, Finn! You're back!" She tries to give me a reassuring smile, but she can't hold eye contact for long. She looks down at the rest of my body and sobs, wiping her streaming nose on the back of her sleeve with a loud wet snuffle.

"It's Finn; she's back!" Bit calls to the others. There's no answer from them—just huffing and puffing from crouched silhouettes as I'm taken farther along this dingy metal corridor to who knows where.

"Hold on, Finn," Bit mumbles, more to herself than to me. "Please, oh please, don't die."

Another dimly lit face suddenly comes into view, glasses, pointed nose, the frizzy outline of a thick white beard aglow in the pale-yellow light.

"Did you say 'Finn'?" asks the bearded man. He grabs Bit's shoulder and jerks her around to face him.

"Speak up, girl! She said she was 'Finn' . . . not 'Infinity'?"

"That's what she said," Bit utters.

"Oh no . . . oh no," the old man whispers solemnly. "This is not good. Not good at all."

INFINITY RISES,
BOOK TWO IN THE INFINITY TRILOGY,
RELEASES JANUARY 2016

ABOUT THE AUTHOR

Photo © 2014 Lucy Ngata

S. Harrison is from New Zealand, where he often indulges in his love of watching superhero movies and art house films. He frequently escapes to some of the many islands of the South Pacific to focus on his writing. *Infinity Lost* is his first novel.

7792